"Promise me one th

Taylor asked, her eyes huge and vulnerable.

Ryan moistened his lips. "What?"

"Be honest with me. I can't deal with games. Not from you."

Oh, hell. Ryan swallowed hard, coming close to hating himself. Why hadn't he just told her the truth from the beginning? When had deception and subterfuge become such a part of his life that he hadn't even considered honesty an option? Could Taylor accept that he'd been forced to live that way? Could she understand the bitterness in his past, the frightening blanks in his memory?

"Ryan?" She sounded wary, disturbed by his silence.

He had to make her his, no matter what it took. He tugged her down for a long, tender kiss. "I won't hurt you, Taylor," he promised.

And he told himself he wasn't lying....

Dear Reader,

Welcome to Silhouette **Special Edition** . . . welcome to romance. We've got lots of excitement in store for you this April—and, no fooling, it's all about love!

Annette Broadrick, the author of over thirty-five novels for Silhouette Books, is making her debut in the Special Edition line with a book in our THAT SPECIAL WOMAN! promotion. *Mystery Wife* is a tantalizing, compelling tale about a woman who wakes up with a new lease on life—and a handsome, charismatic husband she doesn't remember marrying. . . .

And that's not all! *Shadows and Light,* the first book in the MEN OF COURAGE series by Lindsay McKenna, is due out this month. It takes a special breed of men to defy death and fight for right! Salute their bravery while sharing their lives and loves!

Loving and Giving by Gina Ferris, the new addition to Gina's enormously popular FAMILY FOUND series, is due out this month, as well as work by other favorite authors Nikki Benjamin, Natalie Bishop and Ruth Wind. April is a month not to be missed!

Sincerely,

Tara Gavin
Senior Editor

Please address questions and book requests to:
Reader Service
U.S.: P.O. Box 1325, Buffalo, NY 14269
Canadian: P.O. Box 1050, Niagara Falls, Ont. L2E 7G7

GINA
FERRIS

LOVING AND GIVING

Silhouette®

SPECIAL ▼ EDITION®

Published by Silhouette Books

America's Publisher of Contemporary Romance

For Mary Clare Kersten, Lucia Macro and Tara Gavin of Silhouette Books, for working with me on this series that has been so special to me. Thanks for being such supportive editors!

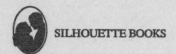 SILHOUETTE BOOKS

ISBN 0-373-09879-0

LOVING AND GIVING

Books by Gina Ferris

Silhouette Special Edition

Healing Sympathy #496
Lady Beware #549
In from The Rain #677
Prodigal Father #711
Full of Grace #793
Hardworking Man #806
Fair and Wise #819
Far To Go #862
Loving and Giving #879

*Family Found

GINA FERRIS

Married and the mother of three, Gina Ferris chose to write romances because she believes in happy beginnings—and a wedding, she says, is only the beginning of a lifelong commitment. When she isn't shopping, she enjoys reading, traveling, and attending plays and concerts. She collects porcelain brides and music boxes, loves music of almost all kinds, but hates doing laundry and mopping floors. She especially enjoys meeting and hearing from her readers, who continually give her inspiration for her stories. She also writes as Gina Wilkins.

Monday's child is fair of face.
Tuesday's child is full of grace.
Wednesday's child is full of woe.
Thursday's child has far to go.
Friday's child is loving and giving.
Saturday's child has to work hard for its living.
But the child that is born on the Sabbath Day
is fair and wise and good and gay.

—Anon.

Chapter One

Ryan had been sitting in his rented car outside the massive gates of the Dallas estate for nearly half an hour, sipping a lukewarm soft drink and studying the place. Just to satisfy his curiosity, of course.

The house was more elegant than he'd expected, a Tudor-style mansion set on several acres of beautifully landscaped grounds. He wondered if he'd ever have the nerve—or the real desire—to walk up those sweeping marble steps and ring the doorbell.

His eyes narrowed with interest when two women came out the front door, apparently laughing at something one of them had said. They were a striking pair, close to the same age—he'd guess late twenties—and almost the same height—five-six? five-seven? Both lovely.

One was slender, almost fragile looking, her gleaming brown hair loose to her shoulders, her face a pretty, delicate oval. She wore a stylish, casual outfit, a short-sleeve plaid jacket over a T-shirt and matching plaid walking shorts. The very image of an affluent young matron on a warm weekday afternoon. Ryan stared at her for several long, unmoving moments, instinctively certain this was the woman who had unknowingly brought him to Dallas. Michelle Walker Trent D'Alessandro.

His fingers tightened around the aluminum can hard enough to buckle the sides. He set it in the drink holder built into the console, his movements automatic, his attention still focused on the woman.

He hadn't realized his first glimpse of her would affect him this way. His hand wasn't quite steady when he shoved it through his hair. *Shelley*.

Slowly, almost reluctantly, he turned his attention to the other woman, who seemed to be leaving the estate, though taking her time about it.

Her hair was almost black, and much shorter than he usually liked, baring her nape and ears in a cut that would have looked boyish on most women. But not this one. She was stunning.

Though he sat yards away, too far to be sure, he thought her eyes were almost as dark as her hair, and exotically slanted. She had a figure that could stop traffic—full-busted, slim-hipped, long-legged. The snug Western-cut shirt she wore with tight jeans and slant-heeled boots displayed all her assets to their best advantage. She was, quite simply, gorgeous. And Ryan couldn't stop staring at her.

Who was she? A friend of Michelle's, perhaps? An in-law? The two women parted at the bottom of the stairs, Michelle waving farewell as the dark-haired one climbed behind the wheel of a black sports car. From long years of habit, Ryan ducked out of sight when she drove through the gates and down the street past him. Aware of an inexplicable impulse to follow her, he shook his head and straightened, glancing toward the house.

Standing in the same spot where her companion had left her, Michelle was looking very hard at Ryan's nondescript rental sedan. Immediately, he made a show of spreading a map across the steering wheel, tilting the soda can to his lips again as he made a pretense of studying the map. A few moments later, he slowly, casually folded the map, tossed it into the back seat and slid the car into gear. When he looked through the side window again, as if to check for traffic before pulling into the street, he saw that Michelle was gone.

He drove away, wishing he could come to a decision about whether to approach Michelle, let her know who he was and why he was here—or whether he should quietly leave Dallas now that he'd satisfied his curiosity by seeing her. But even as that thought crossed his mind, he knew he hadn't really satisfied his curiosity at all, only bolstered it. Now that he'd seen Michelle, he wasn't sure he would be able to resist meeting her.

And the other woman—what was it about *her* that had affected him so oddly? He'd found himself staring at her as though . . . well, as though he should know her—even though he would have bet money that he'd never laid eyes on her.

Joe had been right, Ryan thought with a rueful grimace. He shouldn't have come. This trip could turn out to be even more complicated than he'd imagined.

Later that afternoon, Ryan sat at a window table in a busy snack shop, sipping coffee from a plain white mug. The snack shop was located in a large corporate complex. Across the hallway, clearly visible through the window beside Ryan, was a smoked glass door leading into

the offices of D'Alessandro Investigations. He kept his
gaze focused on that door as he drank his coffee. No one
had gone in or out during the fifteen minutes Ryan had
been watching—slow afternoon, apparently.

He was rewarded for his patience a few minutes later,
when the door opened and someone stepped out. He was
startled to recognize the same dark-haired woman he'd
seen leaving Michelle's house only an hour or so earlier.
A tall, lean man with wavy dark hair and clean-cut features accompanied her out of the offices. They looked
very cozy as they stopped to chat in the hallway, their
dark heads close together, smiles warm and intimate.

"Want me to warm that coffee up for you?"

Ryan glanced around in response to the question,
finding his waitress standing beside him, a coffee carafe
in one hand. He gave her an absent smile, automatically
noting the name stitched above her right uniform pocket.
"Yes, thank you, Wanda."

She'd seemed the friendly, talkative sort when she'd
seated him and taken his order. He tested that impression now, motioning toward the couple on the other side
of the snack shop window. "That guy looks familiar to
me. Do you know him, by any chance?"

His cup refilled, she obligingly glanced through the
window. "Oh, sure. That's Mr. D'Alessandro. He comes
in all the time. He's a private investigator," she added,
obviously impressed by the dashing career.

"And the woman?"

"Never seen her. Not his wife, though. *She* comes in a
lot, too." Wanda frowned with a trace of disapproval as
she and Ryan watched the dark-haired woman rise on
tiptoes to kiss D'Alessandro's cheek, then turn and walk
away, leaving the investigator smiling after her.

"Humph," the waitress muttered with a shake of her gray head, as D'Alessandro went into his offices, apparently unaware that he'd been watched from the snack shop. "Those guys are just as bad as they show 'em on TV. When they ain't chasing crooks, they're chasing women. Never seen Mr. D'Alessandro with another woman since he got married, but it don't surprise me much, good-looking, smooth-talking man like that."

Ryan sensed that Wanda would love an excuse to share some juicy gossip with him. He wasn't disappointed when an impatient customer summoned her away. He'd already gotten the information he wanted.

So that was Michelle's husband, the investigator who'd been looking for Ryan for over a year—and who'd come closer than anyone had before to finding him. And the woman? Could be a relative. D'Alessandro's sister, perhaps, though she didn't look much like him. Maybe a friend of the family, whose visit with D'Alessandro had been perfectly innocent.

But Ryan hadn't had a great deal of experience with innocence, or with families, for that matter. He tended to view the world with a cynical amusement meant to conceal a touch of old, painful anger. He'd long since learned that very few situations were quite as they appeared to be—but if something looked suspect, it usually was.

He couldn't have explained the impulse that made him suddenly stand, toss a couple of bills onto the table and hurry out of the snack shop. Out in the parking lot, the dark-haired woman was just sliding into the black sports car he recognized from earlier. When she drove out of the parking lot, he was right behind her in his unobtrusive rental car.

Long accustomed to acting on impulse, Ryan didn't even pause to analyze his motivation; he simply slipped on his sunglasses and followed her, using the professional skills he'd honed during the past seven years to make sure she never knew she was being tailed. And when she pulled into the parking lot of a large discount store, he turned in, as well.

After all, he reasoned, he was out of toothpaste. Now seemed as good a time as any to pick some up.

Taylor Simmons didn't bother with a shopping cart when she entered the discount store. Smiling at the silver-haired woman who greeted her at the door, she headed straight for the paper goods. After leaving Tony's office, she'd remembered that she was almost out of facial tissues, and she was coming down with a summer cold. She intended to make her purchase quickly and then head home, to spend the remainder of the rare weekday afternoon away from the office drinking hot tea with honey and lemon, to ward off her cold, and going over some paperwork.

It didn't take her long to find the brand of tissues she usually favored. Holding a box in each hand, she turned toward the cash registers. And then she spotted the man standing at the end of the aisle, looking at her.

Released from her suddenly limp fingers, the tissue boxes tumbled to the floor, as did her purse, which spilled its contents at her feet. Taylor's mouth opened, but no sound emerged. Her breath had lodged somewhere in the middle of her painfully tight throat.

The man looked at her quizzically from behind the aviator sunglasses he wore. She knew she must have paled, knew she must look as though she'd suddenly lost her mind. She couldn't stop staring at him. No wonder he tilted his golden-brown head in question and asked, "Are you all right?"

Oh, God, even the voice was the same! Deep, warm, slightly gravelly. "It—it can't be you!" she whispered, the words barely audible, even to her. "You—you—" Her voice died.

Obviously concerned now, the man removed his dark glasses and came a step closer. "I'm sorry, but I'm afraid you have me at a loss. Have we met?" he asked, searching her stricken face rather warily.

She took a deep breath, trying to get a grip on her emotions, aware of the curious looks she was getting from other shoppers passing by. It wasn't like her to lose her composure this way—she'd never made a scene in a public place! But she'd been so shaken by seeing him standing there....

She was finally brought to her senses when her stricken gaze met his puzzled eyes. His eyes were a pale, almost icy blue, so light they made a startling contrast to his dark eyelashes and tanned skin.

Dylan's eyes had been green. Deep, emerald green. And his hair had been almost as dark as her own, whereas this man's lighter brown hair was richly streaked with gold, as though from long hours spent in the sun. A thin white scar bisected his left eyebrow and marked his forehead; Dylan had had no visible scars. But most telling of all was the utter lack of recognition on this man's attractive face—a face so like Dylan's she found it impossible to tear her gaze away.

"I'm sorry," she murmured, hating the shakiness of her voice. "You remind me of someone—"

When she paused, when it became apparent that she didn't know what else to say, the man gave her a warm smile of understanding. "You look as though you've seen a ghost," he said, his sunglasses dangling from one large, capable-looking hand.

"I thought I had," she answered, unable to smile in return.

His own faded. "Oh. Then I'm sorry I startled you."

She shook her head and ran a hand through her short hair, ruffling it in spikes around her face, a habitual nervous gesture. "It isn't your fault. It's just—you look so amazingly like someone I used to know. I'm sorry I acted like such an idiot."

"Let me help you with your things," he offered, kneeling in front of her.

She looked at the items she'd dropped, and her throat tightened again. This was the way she'd met Dylan, she found herself thinking dazedly. She'd dropped her packages and he'd helped her pick them up.

She could still remember how the crowds, the noise and the bustle of the Caribbean marketplace had seemed to fade to insignificance when her eyes had first locked with his. How Dylan's slow, wicked smile had made her heart stop and then kick into overtime. How it had felt to lie in his arms, their pulses pounding in unison, damp skin fused, vows of love and commitment still echoing in the intimate silence around them.

"Here you are. Is there anything else?"

Taylor blinked herself back to the present, trying to concentrate on the man in front of her rather than the one who haunted her memories. "I, um, what did you say?"

Though his brow creased with a faint frown, he obligingly nodded toward the things she was now holding. "Is that all you dropped? Did you have anything else?"

She looked blankly at her purse and the two boxes of tissues. *Had* she been holding anything else? "No, this is all. Thank you."

"Are you sure you're all right?" the man asked again, his crystalline blue eyes searching her face intently.

She took a deep breath and shook off her lingering paralysis. *Honestly, Simmons, you're acting like an idiot! Get a grip, will you?*

Her mental scolding helped. She managed a smile and took a step away from him. "I'm fine, really. Just embarrassed that I caused such a scene. I'll let you get back to your own shopping now."

He seemed reluctant to leave her. "Would you like me to get a shopping cart for you?"

"No, I have all I need," she refused politely.

She was suddenly in a desperate hurry to get away from him, to get out of this store before she made an even bigger fool of herself. She couldn't bear the thought of standing in line at the cash registers. She abruptly shoved the boxes on a nearby shelf, turned and headed toward the exit, as quickly as she could without breaking into a run.

She'd get tissues later, she told herself. Tomorrow, maybe. Right now she just had to get away.

She was relieved that he didn't follow, though she felt his eyes on her back as she all but bolted away.

It's finally happened, Simmons, she told herself in self-disgust as she fell into the driver's seat of her car and shoved the key into the ignition. *You've finally gone over the edge.*

Maybe he wouldn't have followed her again if it hadn't been for the way she'd acted when she'd seen him. He knew he had to be especially careful about her spotting him now. If she were to see him again, obviously following her home, she'd head straight for the nearest police department and report him as a crazy stalker.

Which, he thought with a trace of discomfort, was exactly the way he was starting to feel as he kept her dark sports car in sight on the busy Dallas streets. What the hell was he doing? Why hadn't he just let her drive away after that weird confrontation in the discount store?

But he knew the strange episode was exactly why he hadn't let her get away that easily. What in the hell had that been about? Why had she looked at him as though— well, as though she'd seen a ghost? He wondered, remembering his own words to her as well as her grim reaction to them.

Something had drawn him to her from the moment he'd seen her, even from the distance that had separated them when he'd spotted her leaving Michelle's house. At first he'd written it off as attraction—which, in itself, had been a pleasant surprise. For the past couple of years, his marked decline of interest in women—a dramatic contrast to the ten years prior to that—had worried him. He'd begun to wonder if something was wrong with him, though he'd hidden his concerns from everyone else, even his brother, with whom he shared almost everything.

But it had been more than attraction that had made him trail her to that store after seeing her with D'Alessandro. Just as it was a lot more than that making him follow her now.

Who *was* she? Why had the sight of him driven all the color from her face, left her shaken and trembling? And why did he have this strange, nagging feeling that he should know her, despite his near certainty that he'd never laid eyes on her before?

What the hell was going on here? he asked himself as he watched her car turn into the lot of an apartment complex in an upscale Dallas neighborhood.

From an inconspicuous parking place, he watched her climb out of her car and hurry toward one of the apartments on the lower level. Only after she'd opened her door and closed herself inside did he look at the open wallet in his hand.

Taylor Anne Simmons, the driver's license said. Twenty-seven years old. Five feet six inches. One hundred and twenty pounds. He found a business card stuck into a slot behind several credit cards and an insurance card. He read the address carefully, a plan already forming in his mind.

He was curious. And, despite his brother's frequent warnings about the dangers of avid curiosity, Ryan knew he wouldn't rest until he'd found some answers to his many questions.

The dream was so real. Taylor could almost smell the vivid tropical flowers, could almost touch the man walking beside her through the streets of the crowded Caribbean marketplace. She knew she was dreaming, but she wanted so badly for it to be real. She wished time could freeze and leave her here on this warm, fragrant, perfect late afternoon.

She looked longingly at the man beside her. *Dylan.*

He was smiling at her—that charming, heartbreaking smile that had captivated her from the moment she'd first seen it, when they'd awkwardly collided in this same marketplace three weeks earlier. Several inches over six feet, he towered above her, but she'd never felt threatened by his size, nor by the innate strength and authority that seemed to radiate from him.

Ten minutes after they'd met, he'd offered to buy her a drink at a nearby outdoor café. She'd accepted. By the time her glass was empty, she'd fallen in love. That quickly. That simply. That devastatingly.

He'd told her during the three weeks since that he'd never been in love before. That he'd never known anyone like her. That she was beautiful.

She'd found herself believing every word—maybe because she wanted so badly to believe him.

Matching his steps to hers, Dylan reached out and took her hand. It frustrated her greatly that she could almost—but not quite—feel his skin against hers. A dream, she thought sadly. It was only a dream.

"We need to talk, Taylor," he said, as he had on that day two years ago. "There are some things I must tell you."

She frowned at the gravity of his voice, so different from his usual teasing, lighthearted manner. "What is it? What's wrong?"

His fingers tightened around hers. "Nothing serious," he assured her. "I just want to talk to you, tell you some things about me you need to know before we go any further with our relationship. Things I should have already told you, I suppose."

Her frown deepened, though she tried to speak lightly. "If you tell me you've got a wife and six kids back in the States, I swear I'll strangle you."

He laughed. "No wife. No kids."

"Several outstanding warrants? A criminal record?"

"No and no. I told you, sugar, it's not serious. It's just . . . a little awkward."

"Is it going to change anything between us?" she asked quietly, unable to smile because his answer was so desperately important.

"I hope not," he answered, just as seriously. "I love you, Taylor. I want to spend the rest of my life with you, wherever that may be, whatever we may be doing. Nothing can change the way I feel."

She gave him a bright smile of relief. "Then whatever it is, I can handle it," she promised. "All I need to know is that you love me."

"I love you more than I ever thought it possible to love anyone." His deep voice throbbed with a sincerity she couldn't have mistaken. Beneath the boyish tumble of near-black hair on his forehead, his emerald-green eyes glowed with his love for her.

Taylor had never been happier in her life. "Where would you like to go to talk?" she asked huskily, thinking of her hotel room or his, where they'd already spent so many deliriously pleasurable hours.

"Let's go to the Vagabond for dinner. We'll talk there."

She hid a tiny ripple of disappointment and nodded, telling herself that whatever he wanted to talk about couldn't be all that bad if he was willing to discuss it in a public place. "All right."

The Vagabond was several blocks from the marketplace. They walked slowly, enjoying the lovely weather and each other. Paying no attention to anyone around them, they chattered happily as they navigated the crowded sidewalks and crossed busy streets, dodging speeding cab drivers whom Dylan laughingly declared were all in training for a demolition derby. The restaurant was in sight when Taylor's happiness was abruptly, horribly shattered.

They stepped into the street. There'd been no cars in sight, so they weren't as careful as they should have been, being so deeply absorbed with each other. Dylan said something amusing, and Taylor looked up to respond....

The car seemed to come out of nowhere. With quiet, deadly speed, it headed right toward them. Almost before she'd realized she was in danger, Taylor felt herself being shoved hard, flying through the air to land in a graceless heap on the sidewalk. Her bare knees stung from numerous painful scrapes, and her palms burned from the sudden, violent contact with the rough concrete.

It took her a moment to catch her breath, to confirm that she was still in one piece and capable of movement. The previously quiet afternoon was suddenly filled with noise—shouts, screams, the high-pitched squeal of tires racing into the distance. Blinking the spinning world into focus, Taylor eased herself upright and turned to look for Dylan.

He was lying in the street, his body crumpled like a rag doll carelessly tossed aside by a bored child. There was blood on his face, on his shirt, on the street beneath him, around him. His eyes were open. Fixed. Staring.

"Dylan," she whispered, horrified.

She reached out to him, her dream movements playing in slow motion. "Dylan?" she said, a little louder.

And then she screamed. *"Dylan!"*

The sound of her echoing cry woke her. Taylor sat bolt upright in her bed. She was trembling, gasping for breath, hot tears streaming down her cheeks. And then she buried her face in her hands and wept, the grief as fresh, as sharp as it had been two years earlier, on the day she'd lost Dylan forever.

Everything that could go wrong the next morning had, and Taylor was already in an irritable mood when she

reached her office. On top of everything else, her cold
was growing worse, leaving her with a nagging headache
and an uncomfortably stuffy nose. Knowing her partners and co-workers at the ad agency didn't deserve for
her to take her problems out on them, she managed to be
pleasant enough—until Jay Stern stopped by her office
late that morning to ask if she had a quarter he could
borrow for the coffee machine downstairs.

"You know how lousy that vending machine coffee is.
Why are you wasting your, er, my money on it?" she
asked, digging in her purse for her wallet.

Jay grimaced. "Until we get our office coffeemaker
fixed or come up with a replacement, the lobby vending
machine will have to do. Can't go without my coffee—
even bad coffee."

She listened to him with half her attention as she continued to dig in her purse. Her brows furrowed. "I've *got*
to clean this thing out," she muttered, finally upending
the deep leather bag and dumping its jumbled contents on
her desk. "Can't find anything."

Jay made some teasing remarks about the wild assort-
ment of items Taylor carried around with her, but she
ignored him, still searching through the pile for her wallet. "It's not here," she said finally, looking up with a
frown. "My wallet—it's not here."

Jay cocked his curly head, peering at her through his
thick glasses. "Where did you last see it?"

"I can't remember. I haven't needed it this morning,
so I— Oh, damn."

"What?"

She'd suddenly remembered the episode in the discount store yesterday afternoon—her purse and its contents scattered at her feet, a disturbing stranger crouching
to retrieve everything for her. Had the wallet been over-

looked, slipped beneath a shelf or something? Or had he stolen it?

Either way, there was only one conclusion. She groaned. "It's gone."

"Do you remember where you might have lost it?"

She told Jay about the incident in the store.

"You could call the store, ask if anyone turned it in," he suggested.

"Yeah, right," she muttered, knowing how slim the odds were. Still, she might as well give it a try before she started calling to report her missing credit cards. "Damn. This is all I need to make today a complete washout. And it isn't even noon yet."

"Want to talk about it?" her partner asked sympathetically. Jay was a good listener and a good friend. Unfortunately, there was nothing he could do to help her today.

"Thanks, but I guess I'd better start making phone calls," she replied, giving him a weak attempt at a smile. "I'm just in a lousy mood today. Didn't sleep well last night."

"Let me know if there's anything I can do. I'm going to hit Maxie up for a quarter now."

"Good luck." She picked up the phone.

She talked to a customer service representative at the discount store and was assured that her wallet had not been turned in. Disappointed but not at all surprised, she'd just hung up when Erika, the agency secretary and receptionist, stuck her head in Taylor's office doorway. "Taylor? There's a man here to see you."

Erika was a nice young woman, eager to learn and willing to work for very little pay—which was the primary reason she'd been hired in the first place—but she had a tendency to be annoyingly vague when delivering messages or making announcements. Like now. "Who is it, Erika?" Taylor asked, trying to be patient. "I'm pretty busy right now."

"He said his name is Ryan Kent. And he says he has something that belongs to you. He wants to return it personally."

Something that belonged to *her?* Taylor knew of only one thing she was missing. "Send him in."

For some reason she wasn't particularly surprised when the blue-eyed, golden-brown-haired stranger from the discount store strolled into her office. The same man who'd startled her so badly the day before, who looked so much like Dylan her heart clenched again at the sight of him, who had probably triggered the recurring nightmare she'd hoped to never have again. She stood silently behind her desk trying to think of something to say, the contents of her purse still scattered in front of her.

He smiled, and her hand tightened on the back of her chair. God, he was so much like . . .

But, no. Enough, already. She could go crazy this way. "Hello," she said, pleased that her voice was relatively calm. "This is a surprise."

He held her wallet up with his right hand. "I see you've been ransacking your purse. Were you looking for this?"

"As a matter of fact, I was."

He handed it to her. "I spotted it sticking out from beneath a shelf just after you walked away yesterday. I tried to catch you to return it, but you left too quickly."

She suppressed a grimace as she remembered the way she'd all but bolted from the store. He must have thought she was a lunatic.

"Anyway," he continued, unaware of her self-recriminations, "I found your business card inside and thought I'd drop this by. I'm sure you must have been worried about your credit cards."

"I was just about to report them missing," she admitted.

"Then I'm glad I caught you in time. Your cash is still there, but feel free to check."

She set the wallet on her desk, unopened. "I doubt that you'd have gone to the trouble to return it if you'd taken the money out first," she pointed out, and then forced a smile. "I haven't even thanked you yet, Mr.—"

"Just call me Ryan," he said, extending his right hand. "And you're Taylor Simmons, according to your business card."

"Yes." She slipped her hand into his, intending to give him a brief, impersonal, polite shake. Instead, she found her hand caught and held in his firm, warm grip as she stood staring into his smiling eyes.

"Will you have lunch with me?"

Startled by the unexpected question, she blinked. "Um—today?"

"If you have no other plans," he amended. "I realize you don't even know me, but I'd like to change that. If it will make you feel more comfortable, we can ask some of your co-workers to join us."

She was tempted—*very* tempted—but she couldn't get over his similarities to Dylan. It was all just a little too strange. Almost eerie.

"I'm afraid I haven't much time today," she began, intending to let him down easily. After all, he *had* very nicely returned her wallet.

"We'll eat quickly," he bargained. "Somewhere close—the cafeteria downstairs, perhaps. Say yes."

"But I—"

"I'm being pushy, I know. It's a weakness of mine—one of only a few, of course," he added with a cocky, teasing grin. "I just hate to take no for an answer—especially when it's this important to me."

"Why is it so important to you?" Taylor asked, intrigued despite her better judgment.

"I like your eyes," he replied.

The memory flashed through her mind before she could stop it. *"I love your eyes. So dark and smoky. So beautiful."* Taylor could almost hear Dylan saying the words. If she closed her eyes, she could almost convince herself that Ryan's voice was exactly the same as Dylan's had been.

She shook her head, forcing herself back to the present. This, of course, was exactly why she should avoid this man.

"I have to be frank with you," she said, suddenly aware that he was still holding her hand. Cheeks warming, she quickly snatched it back. "I'm sure you're a nice man, pushiness notwithstanding, but I can't have lunch with you. Or anything else."

He cocked his head, looking more curious than offended. "Is it something I've done?"

She was quite sure he didn't often meet such resistance from women. An attractive man like Ryan, with his sexy physique and killer smile, would have no trouble finding luncheon dates. And yet...

"I just can't," she said, a bit desperately. "It's nothing you've done. Really. I just... can't."

He hesitated for a long, silent moment, as though he wanted very much to insist that she give him a reason for her rebuff. And then he gave a small sigh, a rueful smile and a slight shrug. "Then I won't keep you any longer from your work. Goodbye, Taylor Simmons. It was very nice to meet you."

"Goodbye. And thank you again for returning my wallet."

He sketched a salute and sauntered out of the office without looking back. She watched him until he was out of sight.

At least he didn't walk like Dylan, she thought with a touch of gratitude for small mercies. Dylan's steps had been quick, springy, almost humorous in their barely restrained energy. She'd chided him often for making it so hard for her shorter legs to keep up. Ryan strolled with a lazy roll of his hips, a sexy cowboy walk that only added to his attraction.

She found herself wishing there'd been other, more significant differences. Maybe then she could have accepted his invitation without feeling as though she'd be dining with a memory. Or a ghost.

Chapter Two

Ryan Kent was barely out of sight when Taylor's doorway was suddenly filled with curious faces. Her partners, Jay Stern and Maxie O'Brien, scrabbled in the doorway as each tried to enter her office first. Maxie stumbled in ahead—whether because Jay had politely yielded or because Maxie had been most persistent, Taylor couldn't tell, though she would have bet on the latter. Persistence should have been Maxie O'Brien's middle name.

"Okay, who was he?" Maxie demanded, dropping into one of the two chairs in front of Taylor's desk. "Is he single? Where'd you meet him? When are you going out with him? How soon until you dump him so I can take a shot at him?"

Shaking her head in mild exasperation, Taylor sank into her chair, realizing that she had been standing fro-

zen in the spot where Ryan had left her. "Don't be an idiot, Max."

"She can't help it," Jay drawled, taking the chair beside Maxie. "It's those crazy Irish genes of hers. They
tend to go periodically berserk. We should be patient with
her, sympathetic to her weaknesses, as difficult as it may
be for us at times."

"I hate it when you start talking like your rabbi,"
Maxie grumbled with only a fleeting glance at him.
"Well?" she prodded Taylor. "Who *was* he?"

Taylor sighed. "His name is Ryan Kent. He's a nice
stranger who found my wallet in a store yesterday and
thoughtfully returned it to me today. End of story."

"Did he ask you out?"

"He offered to take me to lunch."

"And?"

"I declined."

Maxie growled her frustration and threw up her hands.
"You turned him *down?* Have you lost your mind?"

"I just wasn't interested, okay?"

"How come?" Jay rather surprised her by asking.
Unlike Maxie, Jay didn't usually pry into his friends'
personal business. Still, Taylor knew Jay worried about
her—just as he fretted over Maxie's recklessly impulsive
nature, always glumly certain it would lead to disaster if
he didn't keep close watch.

Of the three partners in the ad agency, dark-haired,
dark-eyed, thirty-two-year-old Jay was the worrier, the
one who paid most attention to expenses and deadlines
and other portentous details, the one who always managed to find a dark lining to every silver cloud. He was
also generous, dry-witted, kindhearted and brilliant.
Taylor was very fond of him.

Maxie was three inches taller than Jay's compact five feet six inches, her hair a glorious, if artificial, red, her expressive face displaying her every thought and emotion. Thirty-six years old, several years divorced and the mother of two, she was incapable of subtlety, sadly lacking in tact, outspoken, opinionated and imaginative. She was fiercely loyal, cheerfully optimistic, avidly inquisitive, deliberately eccentric. Despite her frequent exasperation with her, Taylor was crazy about Maxie. As were most people who knew her.

It had been Maxie who'd convinced Taylor to give up her career as a much-sought-after fashion photographer nine months ago and take a chance on becoming a partner in a fledgling ad agency, now named O'Brien, Stern and Simmons. Maxie, of course, had demanded top billing. It had, after all, been her concept, she'd often reminded her partners.

Taylor had always wondered if Maxie's timing was purely coincidental, or if she'd sensed that Taylor was close to burnout in her photography career, ready for a drastic change in her life. Whatever the motivation, it hadn't taken her long to talk Taylor into taking the risk of joining her and Jay in their newly formed operation. And the risk was paying off, the agency becoming profitable in a remarkably short time, their client list growing longer and more impressive.

The odds had been against them—Dallas was, after all, already glutted with advertising agencies—but O'Brien's creativity, Stern's acumen and Taylor's artistic eye had impressed several big businessmen who'd grown weary of the usual marketing fare.

"Why did you turn down Kent's invitation?" Jay repeated. "Was there something about him that concerned you? Should we worry that he had access to your wallet and your home address?''

So Jay wasn't being nosy, but typically concerned about her welfare. Taylor smiled reassuringly at him. "He seemed very nice, Jay. He went out of his way to return my wallet, and he didn't even attempt to contact me at home, but waited to reach me here at the office. He even suggested I bring someone from the office with me to lunch with him, in case I felt uncomfortable dining with a stranger.''

Jay looked only partially mollified. "You should still be careful," he insisted. "Keep your doors locked at home and don't open them unless you know who's on the other side.''

"Yes, Papa," Taylor answered with indulgent teasing.

He gave her a particularly sweet smile in response.

"If he's such a nice guy, then why'd you turn him down?" Maxie asked, still visibly dismayed. "Taylor, the man was gorgeous. I thought I was going to swallow my tongue when he smiled at me out in the lobby. If I hadn't thought you'd already staked a claim, I'd have thrown myself at his feet right then and there and begged him to take me. And *you* wouldn't even have lunch with him.''

Taylor couldn't help chuckling at Maxie's exaggerated distress. "It's no big deal, Max. I just wasn't interested.''

Maxie threw up her hands. "I give up. You're impossible.''

Taylor's smile faded. Unable to prevaricate any longer with her friends, she finally spoke honestly. "He looked like Dylan, okay? So much like Dylan that I thought I'd lost my mind when I first saw him yesterday. So much like him that I couldn't stand the thought of sitting across a table from him, remembering and wishing—'' She stopped abruptly, embarrassed that she'd said so much.

Both Maxie and Jay had gone silent, their expressions somber. Taylor had told them about Dylan six months ago, one night when they'd had a little too much to drink in celebration of signing a profitable new client. They'd started swapping personal stories—Maxie's divorce, Jay's broken engagement to a woman who'd run off with another man—and Taylor had told them about Dylan. Not everything, of course. Just enough to let them know that she had once loved very deeply and had still not recovered from the loss of that love.

"Oh, Taylor, I'm sorry," Maxie apologized with a sincerity that was as genuine and as characteristic as her aggressive curiosity had been. "I didn't know."

"Of course you didn't. But, well—now you do."

"Are you all right, Taylor?" Jay asked.

"I'm fine. Really," she assured them both when they continued to look at her with pitying eyes. "I'm fine. It just shook me up a little."

"More than a little, I think," Jay said.

"Maybe," Taylor admitted. "But I'll get over it. I just didn't think it would be a good idea to spend much time with him."

"You're probably right," Maxie conceded. "If he's that much like your Dylan, you could find yourself getting involved with him for all the wrong reasons. And that would only lead to someone getting hurt—probably you. You should definitely stay away from him."

Smiling again at Maxie's direct turnaround, Taylor said, "Don't let this stop you from going after him yourself. If you run, you might catch him out on the street."

"Too much trouble," Maxie answered with a lazy stretch that pulled the fabric of her white blouse taut across her full breasts. "Besides, he was too young for me, anyway."

"Much too young," Jay agreed, studying Maxie's chest with apparently detached appreciation.

She lowered her arms to take a sideways swing at him, just brushing his shoulder with her fist. "Jerk. I don't know why I tolerate you."

"Because your investment money is firmly tied up with mine," he reminded her. "And because you love me."

"I love chocolate mousse, too, but too much of it makes me sick," she retorted, pushing herself out of the chair. "And don't you have a meeting with Bob Killibrew this morning?"

"A lunch meeting," Jay confirmed, glancing at his practical watch. "I suppose I should be leaving."

"Why don't you do that?" Maxie suggested, motioning toward the door. "How about it, Taylor—want to grab a sandwich with me? We'll stuff our faces while I tell you all about the little cheerleader hussy who's been making a play for my sweet, innocent young son."

"Your son is sixteen," Taylor reminded her. "And he is sweet, but I'm not so sure about innocent. Something about those devilish blue eyes of his . . ."

"My son, the future priest?" Maxie demanded in mock outrage. "How could you say such a thing?"

Since Taylor knew Josh O'Brien had no such career plans, she laughed, as Maxie had obviously intended her to do. "All right, you can tell me all about it over lunch," she said. "But don't get mad if I start taking up for the cheerleader."

* * *

At the counter of the fast-food restaurant only a few blocks from Taylor's office, Ryan ordered a grilled chicken sandwich, a small side salad and a large soft drink. He carried the tray to a table by the window, where he began to eat without a great deal of enthusiasm. His attention wasn't on the rather bland food, but on the woman who'd behaved so strangely with him.

Taylor. What was it about her that drew him? And what was it about *him* that seemed to shake her so badly?

He didn't believe she was the meek, timid sort who shied at her shadow. Everything he'd noted about her— her trendy haircut, her striking clothing, her flashy little sports car, her job as art director of a small advertising agency—all contributed to the picture of a woman who was confident, capable, self-assured. Yet with him, she seemed almost...dazed, he decided. She'd looked at him as though she hadn't seen him at all, but someone else entirely. Who did he remind her of? And why did that resemblance upset her so much?

It briefly occurred to him that she might have turned down his luncheon invitation because she simply hadn't been attracted, hadn't been interested in getting to know him better, and not for another, more significant reason. He brushed the possibility aside with an arrogance he was honest enough to acknowledge, confident enough to accept. That hadn't been her reason.

Nor did he believe a commitment to another man lay behind her refusal. Again, his usually reliable instincts told him there was no other man—not a serious relationship, anyway. She just hadn't had that...well, that committed look to her, he thought, taking a bite out of his sandwich and chewing thoughtfully.

He nearly choked when he heard her voice behind him. He looked quickly over his shoulder to find her settling at the next table with a taller, somewhat older, brilliant-haired woman. He remembered seeing the redhead at the ad agency, remembered smiling at her as he'd passed through the reception area and receiving a bright, flirtatious smile in return. One of Taylor's co-workers, obviously. A partner, perhaps. O'Brien? She didn't look like a Stern.

He almost shook his head at the irony of ending up in the same restaurant for lunch after Taylor had turned down his invitation. He really hadn't planned this one, but he fully intended to take advantage of the coincidence.

He coughed.

Automatically, Taylor lifted her eyes in the direction of the sound. Her smile froze almost comically on her face.

The redhead turned in her seat, apparently to find out what her friend was staring at. Her eyes widened when she saw Ryan. "Oh. Hello."

"Hello. What a nice surprise."

"Mr. Kent, are you following me?" Taylor demanded, suddenly aggressive as she hadn't been before.

He lifted a questioning brow and gestured with his half-eaten sandwich. "As you can see, I've been here for a while. You, on the other hand, have only just arrived. Perhaps we should turn the question around."

Her tanned cheeks pinkened at his matter-of-fact response. "Sorry," she muttered, so quietly he barely heard her.

The redhead, who was sitting with her back to Ryan, turned in her seat and offered him a hand. "I'm Maxie O'Brien," she said.

"Ryan Kent," he replied, taking the proffered hand for a brief, polite shake. "Nice to meet you."

"Would you like to join us?" she surprised him by asking.

Taylor choked. "Maxie," she hissed.

"I'd love to," Ryan answered blandly, turning to gather his lunch.

Behind his back, he heard Maxie whisper, "Well, it would have been rude not to ask him."

He stifled a grin as he moved to an empty seat at their table.

Ryan quickly discovered that Maxie was an almost nonstop chatterer—which was a good thing, since Taylor hardly said a word for the first fifteen minutes or so. During that time, Ryan learned quite a bit about Maxie— and almost nothing about Taylor. And then Maxie turned the conversation to him, obviously trying to be subtle about her questioning, though he could tell that subtlety wasn't one of her talents.

"What do you do, Ryan?" she asked, studying him through bright, speculative hazel eyes.

"I'm in sales," he lied easily—after all, he'd been lying about his career for years. "Commercial security equipment." That was a bit closer to the truth.

"Really? Do you live here in Dallas?"

"No. I'm based in Colorado. I'm just passing through Dallas," he said, sticking to the full truth this time.

"And do you have a family back in Colorado?" Maxie asked blandly.

He smothered a grin. "I have a brother, but he's in Mexico right now. On his honeymoon."

"Your brother just got married? How nice. And what about you, Ryan? Ever been married yourself?"

This time he did smile. "No," he assured her. "I'm single, always have been."

Maxie leaned a bit closer over the table, forgetting her lunch for the moment in her avid curiosity about Ryan. "How come?"

"Maxie," Taylor protested thinly. "Really, that's none of our business."

Maxie looked vaguely surprised. "Oh, I wasn't trying to pry. I just wondered how such a good-looking, charming man has escaped matrimony for so long."

Ryan chuckled. "Thank you. And I don't look at it as escaping matrimony, but rather missing out on the opportunity," he replied. "I'd love to find someone who makes me as happy as my brother's new bride makes him. It just hasn't happened yet."

He glanced at Taylor as he spoke, and found that she was looking at him with an expression that wrung his heart. Her eyes were so sorrowful—so *lost*. What had he said to make her so sad?

What was it about this woman that so intrigued and bemused him?

"That's very nice," Maxie said approvingly, regaining his partial attention. "Most handsome young bachelors wouldn't admit for the world that they aren't deliriously happy with their single lives."

"I recently turned thirty," Ryan informed her. "Not so young."

She grimaced comically. "Six years younger than me," she said with an exaggerated sigh. "Too bad."

He smiled, sensing she was only teasing and not seriously flirting. "I wouldn't let a little thing like that stop me—if you didn't remind me so much of my second-grade teacher," he added. "Mrs. McNulty. She was a red-haired beauty, like you, but with the soul of a Spanish inquisitor. I still have nightmares about her.''

Obviously flattered by his physical description, Maxie returned his smile. ''I can certainly understand why you wouldn't want to get involved with someone who stirs such painful memories.''

Taylor spilled her soft drink. With a sound of disgust, she made a hasty grab for the napkins as the puddle spread toward the edge of the table. Ryan and Maxie came swiftly to her rescue, contributing their own paper napkins to the cause and mopping the mess up before any damage was done.

''Sorry,'' Taylor said, looking embarrassed and annoyed with herself. ''I don't know what's gotten into me lately.''

Ryan would have liked the answer to that himself. She didn't appear to be the naturally clumsy type. So why was she always dropping and spilling things around him?

Maxie glanced at her watch and groaned. ''We've got a client meeting in an hour and a half and I'm not even close to being prepared for it. Guess I'd better get to the office and start looking over my notes. You walking back with me, Taylor?''

''Of course. I have a lot to do myself.'' Taylor stood with an eagerness that was only too obvious to Ryan.

He rose with them. ''It was nice meeting you, Maxie.''

''You, too, Ryan. Enjoy your stay in Dallas.''

''I hope to.'' He caught Taylor's arm when she would have followed Maxie. She paused at the feel of his hand on her arm, looking up at him with a wariness that exasperated him. Just what did she think he was going to do to her?

He was probably being a masochist, but he felt compelled to ask, anyway, ''Would you like to have dinner

with me this evening? Maybe take in a movie or something? I'd really like to see you again."

"Thank you, but no," she answered without even
hesitating. "I have a really miserable cold coming on. I
think I'm going to leave work early and spend the weekend in bed with a book."

This was definitely getting frustrating. Oh, he could tell
she really had a cold—the tip of her nose was a bit reddened, her voice growing huskier, her dark eyes slightly
puffy and heavy-lidded. But something told him her cold
was mostly a convenient excuse; if she wasn't sick, she'd
have come up with another.

He really couldn't understand why she kept rejecting
him—or why he kept asking, for that matter.

He could see that it would do no good to argue with
her now. Sometimes there was nothing to do but step
back, let the other person make the next move, if another move was to be made. "If you change your mind,
I'll be staying at the West Side Inn for the next couple of
days. I'd still like to have dinner with you while I'm in
town."

She didn't respond, except to say, "Goodbye, Ryan. It
was . . . very nice meeting you." She stumbled a bit over
the formality. And then she pulled her arm from beneath his hand, turned and left without looking back.

Ryan watched her join Maxie, saw Maxie ask something to which Taylor shook her head, and then the
women were gone. He glanced at the table to find that
Taylor had forgotten to clear away her tray. He took care
of it for her, thinking of the challenge that Taylor Simmons's continued resistance presented him. He hadn't yet
accepted defeat. He suspected he'd be seeing her again,
particularly if he finally found the nerve to make contact with Michelle D'Alessandro.

Ryan had known when he'd come to Dallas that the trip would be complicated, probably stressful. He just hadn't realized quite how convoluted his life would become because of the impulsive decision he'd made to come here after seeing Joe and Lauren off on their honeymoon.

He could almost hear Joe saying, "I told you so." After all, his brother had been warning him for years of the dangers of getting tangled up with others, even though Joe had finally succumbed to that temptation himself when he'd met and fallen in love with Lauren.

Joe hadn't thought Ryan's trip to Dallas was such a good idea. He was concerned about digging into a past that had been painful for both of them. Now Ryan found himself as fascinated by Taylor Simmons—and the decidedly odd way she behaved around him—as he was by the family who'd drawn him here in the first place.

This was all getting very strange, he thought with a shake of his head as he left the restaurant. He probably should have stayed in Colorado. Or taken another assignment for the security agency that had employed him for the past seven years. Joe's guidance had often proven valuable in the past. Maybe Ryan should have heeded his brother's advice again.

Chapter Three

Taylor was sitting at her desk later that afternoon, trying very hard to concentrate on work and put Ryan Kent out of her mind—and not being particularly successful at it—when she received another unexpected visitor. A tentative tap on her open door made her look up to find her longtime friend Michelle Trent D'Alessandro poised in the doorway. "Hi, Michelle. Come on in," Taylor said, setting down her pen and pushing a stack of paperwork aside.

Michelle walked in with the innate grace that Taylor had always secretly envied. "I don't want to keep you away from your work," she said, then held up a colorfully jacketed hardback book. "But you wanted to borrow the new Barbara Michaels novel when I finished it, and I thought you might like to read it this weekend. I had to come into town, anyway. I have a hair appointment this afternoon."

"Thanks. I have a feeling reading is all I'll feel like doing this weekend." With a rueful grimace, Taylor blew her nose and tossed the tissue into an overflowing wastebasket.

"Your cold isn't any better?" Michelle asked sympathetically, sinking into one of the two chairs in front of the desk.

Taylor shook her head. "I feel lousy," she admitted. "I've been trying to ignore it in hopes it will go away, but so far it's not working."

"You really should go home early. You need rest and liquids so you can get past this before it develops into something more serious. Do you have any vitamin C tablets at home?"

"Probably. But I think I'll try Grandma Cowper's favorite cold remedy—a shot of whiskey and ten straight hours in bed."

Michelle's smile was reflected in her dark-blue eyes, dispelling the illusion of cool distance her beautiful, serene face usually conveyed. "That might just work," she agreed. "Is there anything I can do for you?"

"Yes. Go away," Taylor said with a bluntness she emphasized with a finger pointed toward the door. "Tony will never forgive me if I expose you to my nasty germs in your delicate condition."

Michelle laughed and shook her head. "Don't be silly. I'm not delicate—just pregnant."

"And disgustingly proud of it," Taylor muttered only half-teasingly, eyeing her friend's rather smug smile with a nagging, uncomfortable touch of envy buried deep inside her. As delighted as she was that Michelle had married Tony and that they were now expecting their first child after trying for almost a year, Taylor couldn't help wondering at times if she'd ever have her own family, ever find someone to love her the way Tony obviously adored Michelle.

Her mind filled with the image of a man's face—but for once, it wasn't Dylan who occupied her thoughts. This time, for some wholly unexplainable reason, she'd thought of Ryan Kent, to her dismay. Why couldn't she rid her mind of that guy? She didn't even know him, for Pete's sake!

"Did Tony tell you I stopped by his office yesterday afternoon?" she asked Michelle, mostly to distract herself from her unsettling thoughts. "You talked so much yesterday about what a great job the decorator did with his offices that I just had to check it out for myself."

"Tony told me you'd dropped in. What did you think of the redecorating job?"

"It looked terrific. Very sleek and professional—great for Tony's image. You were right, that new decorator's good."

"Yes, we've all been quite impressed with her. Cassie even wheedled her into giving some free advice about color combinations for the nursery at the ranch."

Taylor chuckled. "Trust your sister-in-law to sweet-talk free decorating advice out of a professional decorator. Has anyone ever been able to refuse Cassie anything?"

"Certainly not Jared," Michelle answered, referring to her older brother, Cassie's husband. "Especially with their own baby on the way. Anything Cassie wants, all she has to do is hint and both Jared and Shane will knock themselves out getting it for her. Except for my Tony, I've never seen a more doting husband than Jared—or a more devoted stepson than Shane. Cassie's very lucky to have found them."

Taylor reflected that Michelle could well have used the word *found* in the literal sense, in this case. Cassie had been working as an apprentice investigator for D'Alessandro Investigations when she'd been assigned to locate Michelle's long-lost brother, Jared Walker.

Orphaned as a toddler, Michelle Walker had been separated from her six siblings and raised as an only child by the wealthy Dallas couple who'd adopted her. After her adoptive parents died, Michelle hired Tony to find the biological brothers and sisters she'd learned about while going through her mother's papers.

Michelle and Tony married only a few months after they met, while the investigation was still in progress. Cassie had found Jared and his teenage son in a little town in New Mexico, and had fallen in love with both of them before she'd returned to Dallas, bringing them with her to be reunited with Michelle and another sister who'd been located earlier.

Since then, yet another sister had been located and happily reunited with her birth family. They'd learned that one brother had died in his teens, leaving only twin brothers still unaccounted for, though Tony hadn't stopped searching for them.

Taylor had watched Michelle's family grow with an avid fascination, and had been delighted at Michelle's transformation from a lonely, withdrawn young heiress to a happier, more open individual. Taylor and Michelle had been friends since junior high school, and their relationship was a close, mutually supportive one. Taylor didn't know what she would have done without Michelle's friendship in those dark, desolate months after Dylan died.

Taylor started to say something else to Michelle about Cassie's winning personality, but her words were abruptly cut off by an explosive sneeze. She grabbed another tissue.

"Taylor, go home," Michelle ordered sternly. "You can't accomplish anything here when you're sick."

"She's right," Maxie agreed, appearing in the doorway in time to hear Michelle's suggestion. "Go home, Taylor. We'll struggle along without you for a couple of hours."

"I took yesterday afternoon off," Taylor reminded them from behind her tissue.

"Big deal," Maxie said with a shrug. "Go on. Get some rest. Just make sure you're well by Monday. We have that meeting with LuCon Industries Monday afternoon, you know."

Taylor sighed and tossed the tissue in the vicinity of the wastebasket, not even caring that it landed on the floor beside it. "I'll try to knock off a little early," she promised. "But I have a couple of things to finish here first. Of course," she added archly, "I could finish even quicker if you'd both stop lecturing me and let me get back to work."

Neither of her friends took offense at the less-than-subtle hint. Michelle stood with a smile. "I have to go, anyway. I'm due at my hair stylist in a few minutes."

"And I just need to get the First Commercial Bank file from you," Maxie said, rummaging through a stack of folders on one corner of Taylor's desk. "Here it is."

"Thanks again for bringing the book, Michelle," Taylor said, reaching for her pen.

"Sure. I'll call later to check on you, okay?"

A few minutes later, Taylor was alone, her head bent industriously over her paperwork. She muttered a curse when she realized that instead of ideas for striking visuals for a new ad campaign, her mind was filled again with images of a man with golden-brown hair, crystal-blue eyes, an intriguingly scarred brow and a sexier-than-hell walk. A man who bore so many eerie resemblances to the man she'd loved and lost—and yet was so very different in many other ways.

Why couldn't she stop thinking about this guy?

Ryan couldn't have explained why he was still hanging around the ad agency, his car parked at the curb where he could discreetly watch anyone who entered or departed. He'd sat lost in thought during most of the afternoon, trying to come to a decision about whether to leave Dallas now or make contact with the family who'd been searching for him.

He'd finally decided he should at least go to his motel when he spotted Michelle D'Alessandro entering the ad agency. His hand fell away from the ignition key. Maybe he'd hang around just a little longer, he decided. Rather reluctantly, he admitted to himself that he wanted to see Michelle just one more time before he made a decision about what to do next.

She didn't stay inside long. Twenty minutes later she reappeared, slid behind the wheel of a pearl-gray Lexus and disappeared down the busy city avenue. Ryan watched her car until it was completely out of his sight.

This was all getting very complicated. The way he reacted to Michelle. The strange draw Taylor Simmons exerted over him. He really should head straight for the airport, he thought irritably. Get the hell out of Dallas before he got himself into trouble—again.

But even as the thought crossed his mind, he knew he probably wouldn't follow through with it. Not yet. For one thing, he realized grimly, he really had nowhere else to go.

* * *

Taylor had been home only half an hour when her doorbell rang. Muttering at the inconvenience, she hauled her aching body off the couch, where she'd been lying in a moaning lump ever since she'd gotten home. "Who is it?" she called out huskily, shuffling to the door in her stocking feet.

"Ryan."

Now why wasn't she more surprised? She wished her head didn't feel as though it had been stuffed with cotton. It was hard to think clearly and rationally at the moment.

The guy's a stranger, she reminded herself, *and a disturbingly persistent one, at that. Send him away.*

She sighed and opened the door. "What now?"

He was holding flowers. Masses of them, in a rainbow of soft, cheery colors. A large paper bag dangled from one of his hands, and several appetizing aromas wafted from it. "I didn't think you'd feel up to cooking tonight, so I've brought you some dinner."

"You're either the most thick-skulled man I've ever met, or the most incredibly arrogant," Taylor said, shaking her head to express her disbelief at his refusal to take no for an answer.

"D'you mind if I come in while you decide which it is?" he asked politely. "Your food's getting cold."

She didn't know whether to blame her sudden acquiescence on her illness, his smile or her own tangled emotions, but she stepped aside and motioned him into the apartment.

Ryan passed her quickly—as though he was a bit concerned that she'd change her mind before he made it all the way in. "Where do you want this?" he asked, looking around at her blue and coral Southwestern decor with obvious approval.

She motioned toward the dining table visible through an arched doorway. "In there."

He set the flowers, which he'd brought in a clear glass vase, in the center of the table as a centerpiece, then began to unload the food, talking the whole time. "I hope you like Chinese. Chicken soup seems to be the age-old remedy for a cold, so I brought egg drop. And since you need to keep up your strength, I also got egg rolls, shrimp with vegetables, fried rice and twice-cooked pork."

She crossed her arms and watched in amazement as colorful cartons proliferated on her table. "Gee," she commented dryly, "you've provided enough for at least two people."

He grinned. "Yeah. I'm aware of that."

She groaned and threw up her hands. "Oh, hell. Would you like to join me for dinner, Ryan?"

"Yes, thank you. I'd love to," he replied, courteously holding a chair for her.

Ryan was quite pleased with himself for the progress he'd made thus far. It had taken nerve to march up to her door and all but push his way inside, but nerve wasn't something Ryan had ever lacked.

He made a special effort to be charming during the meal, knowing full well that charm was another trait he had in abundance. One he'd learned to use to full advantage during the past twenty-five years or so.

Taylor was rather quiet at first, picking at her food and giving him suspicious looks that he secretly found amusing. He urged her to eat all her soup, noting that the color was slowly returning to her face, which had been too pale when he'd arrived. He'd satisfied himself that she wasn't really ill, that her cold was more annoying than debilitating, but he could tell she felt generally rotten. Not above taking advantage of her present vulnerability, he exerted himself to entertain her and to weaken her formidable resistance to him.

Her job seemed like a safe enough topic for discussion. At his subtle questioning, she told him that she'd worked as a fashion photographer before buying into the ad agency. "Were you good at it?" he asked curiously.

"I was good," she answered without prevarication. "But I got tired of it. I guess I burned out."

"That happens," he said with a slight shrug.

"Yes." He noted the way her smoky eyes suddenly shuttered, as if her thoughts were focused on a distant and not particularly pleasant memory. Something had apparently triggered her burnout, he decided. Something that was still eating at her, haunting her. He wondered how long it would take him to inveigle the explanation from her.

"You like your work with the ad agency?" he asked, his tone deliberately casual as he reached for the hot tea they'd prepared from tea bags to go with their meal.

"Very much. Maxie and Jay are great partners. We all get along very well—most of the time—and our client list is growing even more quickly than we'd expected. I think I made a wise move."

"Good for you. I enjoyed meeting Maxie. She seems like a lot of fun."

"She is. She's also smart, competent, ambitious and creative. And she's a terrific single mom, as well."

"High praise."

"She deserves it. I admire her a lot."

"She's divorced?"

Taylor nodded, her smile fading. "Her ex was a real creep. Played around on her, then lied to cover up his running around. If there's one thing I detest, it's a liar and a sneak."

Ryan cleared his throat and appeared to give all his attention to the egg roll he was shredding on his plate.

"What about you?" Taylor asked, suddenly redirecting the questioning. "You said you're in sales? Security equipment or something like that, wasn't it?"

"Mmm." He told himself it was good that she was interested enough to ask, though he had no intention of revealing very much about himself yet. He still hadn't quite decided what to do about Michelle, and he was all too aware that Taylor and Michelle were connected, though he didn't yet know how strong that connection was.

"I've been thinking about making a career change," he added. That, at least, was true enough. Now that Joe was talking about getting out of the free-lance security business, Ryan had been forced to examine his own goals. He wasn't sure he wanted to stay in the business without his brother, who'd also been his partner.

"Really? What would you like to do?"

He shrugged. "I'm still considering options."

"Like what?" she persisted, studying him out of her huge, cold-blurred gray eyes.

He wished to hell he knew. "When I was a teenager, I wanted to be a rock star," he mused, hoping to both amuse and distract her. "Grew my hair out to shoulder length and started writing excruciatingly bad song lyrics."

"You're kidding."

"No. Want a sample?"

"Of course."

"Hmm." He pretended to think about it. "Well, there was one that went something like—'Lady with the copper hair, shining in the sun, Lady with the skin so fair, I think that you're the one.'"

Taylor shuddered. "I hate to tell you this—"

He grinned. "You don't have to. My brother didn't bother to mince words when he broke the news that I had no poetic talent. I think he finally snapped when I tried to rhyme sweet lovin' with wheat muffin."

Taylor laughed. It was the first time she'd done so with him, he realized smugly. Lord, she was beautiful! He was definitely making progress.

"Maybe you'd better not consider a career as a song writer," she advised.

"No doubt about it." Before she could ask another logical question—like what job he *was* considering—he said, "Have some more fried rice. There's plenty left."

She looked at the container without enthusiasm. "I'm not very hungry. The soup was good, though."

He swallowed another generous forkful of stir-fried vegetables. "Tell me more about yourself, Taylor," he said then. "Are you originally from Dallas? Do you have family here?"

"My family moved here when I was in junior high school. My parents retired to San Antonio a couple of years ago, and my younger brother is in the service and travels quite a bit, so I'm pretty much on my own now."

"You've never been married?"

He asked the question as nonchalantly as he could manage, but again her eyes went dark and sad. Someone had hurt her, he sensed immediately. The same someone he reminded her of? He found himself growing increasingly resentful of the guy—and he didn't even know that there'd *been* a guy!

You're losing it, Ry. Get a grip, he could almost hear his brother telling him.

"No, I've never married," Taylor answered, avoiding his eyes by pushing a small mound of vegetables around on her plate. "My mother's starting to panic that her only daughter is twenty-seven and still single, but I guess I've just gotten too accustomed to my independence."

Before he could say anything else on that subject, she quickly changed the topic. "You mentioned at lunch that your brother recently married."

"Yes. He's away on his honeymoon now."

"Do you like his wife?"

Ryan smiled as he pictured his first meeting with Lauren Caldwell. She'd had a gun trained on him at the time and had just ordered him to freeze. She'd been terrified that he was one of the men who'd been trying to kidnap her, and she hadn't had the foggiest idea how to use the gun, but she hadn't blinked an eye as she'd faced him down. "Yeah. I like her a lot."

"What's her name?"

"Lauren. She's a CPA from Chicago." And then he skillfully changed the subject again, leading into a discussion of recent movies and music, keeping the conversation light, amusing and impersonal. One of his specialities, he thought wryly—airy persiflage designed to extract the most information from someone else while revealing an absolute minimum about himself.

Disarmed by Ryan's casual tone and lazy charm, Taylor slowly relaxed during the meal. She'd expected to spend the evening alone, lying on the couch and contemplating her congested sinuses, but instead she was having dinner with a good-looking, flatteringly attentive man. She'd be a fool to complain.

She even found herself making a conscious effort to compare Ryan to her memories of Dylan, and she was encouraged by the differences she found. Oh, he still looked very much like Dylan. So much that at times her breath caught painfully in response to the way he tilted his head or smiled a bit crookedly. The few differences she could find—hair color, eye color, the thin scar through his left eyebrow, his rolling walk—still didn't change the fact that he could have been Dylan's twin.

The other differences were more subtle. Almost indefinable. Dylan had been more frivolous, quicker to laugh than Ryan seemed to be. His grin had held a cocky defiance of fate that had worried her almost as much as it captivated her. She'd once asked Dylan if anything frightened him; his candid reply had been that nothing could. She'd had the feeling that Dylan had never come up against an obstacle he hadn't been able to defeat.

But even in the brief time she'd known Ryan, she'd sensed that he had known fear, as well as defeat. That he'd had to confront his own mortality and vulnerabilities in a way Dylan never had. She didn't quite understand what had made her reach those sweeping conclusions or why she found herself drawn to the well-camouflaged pain in him.

She drew her lower lip between her teeth, warning herself against getting involved with this man. She was too vulnerable right now, she reminded herself. She'd been a bit lonely recently, envious of her married friends' happiness and contentment. And she was still uncomfortably drawn to the resemblances between Ryan and Dylan.

She had to be careful. Very careful.

Ryan sensed the moment Taylor began to withdraw from him again. Though her elusiveness frustrated him, he told himself to be patient as he helped her clean away the remains of their dinner. After spending time with her, he found himself more drawn by the minute. Unfortunately, patience had never been one of his virtues.

Taylor Simmons fascinated him. He was attracted to her as he hadn't been to any woman in a very long time. He was growing increasingly eager to find out where this attraction would lead them.

Taylor led him into the living room when the dining table had been cleared. She motioned him politely toward a chair, but he remained standing, close enough that she was forced to look at him. Seeing that her eyelids were growing heavier and faint lines had etched themselves around her mouth, he told himself reluctantly that she really wasn't up to dealing with him tonight. He could wait.

With a tenderness that surprised him almost as much as it seemed to startle her, he touched her flushed cheek, finding the skin warmer than it should have been. He didn't comment on the way she flinched at his touch. He decided to take her response as a sign that she was as physically aware of him as he was of her. "You feel as though you have a slight fever. You really should take something for it and go to bed. If there's nothing else you need, I'll leave now so you can get some rest."

A quick but unmistakable look of relief flashed across her face before she nodded. "Yes, I think I'll do that. Thank you for the dinner, Ryan—and the flowers."

"You're welcome." He leaned toward her, his gaze focused on her temptingly close mouth.

She drew back just before his lips touched hers. "You don't want to catch my cold," she warned him, her voice noticeably unsteady.

Patience, Ryan. He drew back with a faint sigh. "It would have been worth it," he murmured, touching her cheek again. And then he made himself leave. While he still could.

Made drowsy by a dose of cold medication, Taylor was almost asleep when she crawled into bed less than an hour after Ryan left. She was relieved that the medication was working so quickly, dulling her mind and easing her into a heavy, healing sleep.

She was in no condition to think about Ryan—or Dylan—tonight.

Chapter Four

Taylor slept later the next morning than she had in a very long time. She crawled out of bed and took a long, warm bath, then padded into the kitchen and made herself a cup of steaming hot tea. She had just taken the first cautious sip when the phone rang.

"How are you feeling this morning?"

She chided herself furiously for the juvenile leap of her pulse in response to the deep voice. When she answered, her tone was a bit stilted. "Much better, thank you."

"Good." Ryan sounded smug. "Must have been the TLC you got last night."

"More likely the cold has just run its course," she retorted.

"Whatever." He dismissed her suggestion without interest. "Think you'll feel up to seeing a movie with me tonight?"

Taylor hesitated, trying to decide how to answer, then sighed and settled on blunt honesty. "I don't know why you keep asking me out. It isn't as if I've given you any encouragement."

"No," he agreed wryly. "But I like you, anyway. I enjoy being with you. I don't know anyone else in Dallas, and I guess I'm a little lonely. Haven't you ever been lonely, Taylor?"

Her breath caught involuntarily. He couldn't know, of course, how intimately she had become acquainted with loneliness during the past two years. Nor could he possibly understand how she found herself almost clinging to that loneliness, how it had become her safety net, her security. How could he understand, when she couldn't have explained it even to herself?

A refusal trembled on her lips, but for some reason she couldn't say it. She thought of the evening before, when Ryan had been so charming, so casual, so unthreatening. What could another evening hurt? He probably wouldn't be in town much longer, anyway. And, darn it, she liked him, too.

"All right," she said abruptly.

His brief hesitation indicated his surprise at her sudden acceptance. "You will?"

"Yeah. Are you picking me up or do you want to meet somewhere?"

"I'll pick you up. Seven-thirty?"

"I'll be ready."

"Great. We'll have a good time, Taylor. You won't be sorry you said yes."

I hope not, Ryan, she found herself thinking as she cradled the telephone receiver. *I truly hope not.*

* * *

The film was a thriller based on a best-selling novel about a wealthy woman kidnapped by American terrorists and rescued by a dashing hero portrayed by a popular Hollywood movie idol. Taylor found the movie interesting, but she was intensely aware of Ryan sitting so close beside her. They shared a large bag of wonderfully greasy buttered popcorn, and he seemed to go out of his way to make sure their hands collided often. When the popcorn was gone, he dropped all pretense and captured her hand in his own, holding it snugly during the remainder of the film.

Taylor felt like a light-headed schoolgirl again, her attention equally divided between the movie and the feel of Ryan's warm, callused palm sliding against hers.

Sometime during the last twenty minutes of the film, it occurred to her that she'd started thinking of him as uniquely Ryan, his resemblances to Dylan fading from her thoughts. She wasn't sure if she was more relieved or concerned about that development.

They stopped at a nearby restaurant for dessert and coffee after the movie. Trying not to think about calories, Taylor ordered chocolate peppermint pie, while Ryan settled on chocolate cake with vanilla ice cream and hot fudge sauce. "Maybe we should go for a run later to work this off," he suggested, looking in mock dismay at the huge serving the waitress set in front of him.

"I think I'll just eat salad for a couple of days, instead," Taylor said, picking up her fork. "I hate running."

"Good. So do I. Tennis and swimming are my sports."

That didn't surprise her. He had the lean hips and well-developed torso of a swimmer and the natural grace and quick reflexes of a tennis player. She'd have been willing to bet he was also extremely good at indoor sports. She concentrated fiercely on her pie, not wanting him to see the intimate speculation in her eyes.

"What about you, Taylor? Any favorite sports?"

"I love ice skating. I wanted to be an Ice Capades star when I was a kid."

"What changed your mind?"

"I didn't have the dedication to put in the required hours of practice," she admitted. "And then I discovered in high school that I was pretty good with a camera, and that seemed a more practical career goal."

"Do you miss being a professional photographer?"

"No. I'd gotten really tired of f-stops and shutter speeds and light meters. It was never really in my blood— only something I was good at and was paid well for. I much prefer the work I'm doing now at the ad agency."

They ate in silence for a few moments and then Ryan changed the subject, asking what she'd thought of the movie.

"It wasn't bad. Definitely fast-paced and entertaining."

"But?"

She shrugged. "It had a few plot points that were a little hard to swallow. No more than most products of Hollywood, I suppose."

"Are you kidding? There were holes in that plot you could drive a truck through. No one with any training in antiterrorism would make some of the just plain stupid mistakes our so-called hero made, even if he did manage to come out on top in the end."

"I'll bet you read adventure novels," Taylor commented with a smile. "Those complicated, extensively researched ones that intelligent men seem to like so much."

Ryan frowned for a moment as though trying to decide whether she'd just complimented him, then admitted, "Yes, I read a lot. And I prefer well-written page turners."

She was growing increasingly curious about Ryan. She knew so little about him, and there were so many things she wanted to learn. "What was your major in college?" she asked, thinking that would be a good start in learning more about his interests.

A muscle twitched lightly in his jaw. "I never went to college. Finished high school with a GED," he admitted.

"Oh. I—uh—didn't mean to pry. I just assumed—"

He nodded. "I didn't have what you'd call a stable childhood. I've been pretty much on my own since I was a teenager. Dropped out of school, then worked at a series of odd jobs until I ended up where I am now. I don't have a criminal record, but I don't have a glowing résumé, either. I just do my best to take life as it comes."

She was startled by his words, which revealed so much more than she'd expected to hear. "You didn't have to tell me all that."

"I know." His expression was hard to read. "I just thought you should know."

"Why?" she asked involuntarily.

He lifted his coffee cup to his mouth, his eyes meeting hers.

She hastily decided to change the subject. "Um—about the movie—"

"Yes?" He seemed relieved that they were back to comfortable ground.

"I thought the kidnapping scene was well done. Believable enough. It closely resembled real incidents I've read about in the newspaper."

"Yeah. That part was okay," Ryan agreed. "It was similar to an experience my sister-in-law went through recently."

Taylor's eyes widened. "Your sister-in-law was kidnapped?"

"She was the target of an attempted kidnapping. Her father's a prosecutor and he was working up a case against some sleazy hate mongers in Chicago. A couple of the jerks thought snatching Lauren would give them bargaining power. Fortunately, they were captured before they could grab her."

Taylor studied Ryan's face, sensing that there was a lot more to the story than he'd told her. He'd been involved in some way, she suspected. But how?

Deciding he'd tell her more only when and if he was ready, she encouraged him with a story of her own. "Oddly enough, I know two people who have been kidnapped. They're sisters, actually, though their kidnappings were years apart. One was just a little girl, only eight years old. She was taken by a man who worked for her father, and held for five days in a closet while the louse negotiated for ransom. She was rescued by a private investigator who'd tracked her down."

Ryan's attention seemed equally divided between her story and his dessert. "Was she harmed?"

"No," Taylor answered gratefully. "Physically, she was okay. Emotionally—well, it took her a long time to get over it. I used to wonder if she'd ever learn to trust anyone again. Thanks to Tony—her husband—she's finally learned that—"

"Tony?" Ryan's interruption was sharp, his head coming up abruptly in response to the name.

She blinked at his vehemence, but explained. "He's a private investigator—the son of the man who rescued

Michelle. Tony and Michelle were married last year and they're blissfully happy together. They're expecting their first child soon, so the story has a happy ending, though it could have ended tragically when Michelle was eight.''

Ryan's knuckles had gone white from the force of his grip on his fork. His face was grim, utterly lacking the lazy humor that seemed more characteristic of the man she'd come to know.

''Ryan?'' she prodded when he remained quiet for several long, taut moments. ''What is it?''

His eyelids twitched and he seemed to force himself to relax as he looked at her across the table. ''Sorry. I just hate hearing about anyone who'd do something like that to a little kid. I hope they made the bastard pay.''

''He went to prison. Died there a few years later in a fight with another inmate,'' Taylor said. ''Tony found that out a couple of months ago when he looked up the guy's record. I think he wanted to reassure himself that the jerk wouldn't ever be showing up again to endanger Michelle.''

''I doubt that anyone grieved over the news of his death.''

''No one who knows and loves Michelle,'' Taylor admitted. ''As I said, it took her a long time to recover. She didn't deserve to have her childhood taken away from her that way.''

''But she's happy now?'' Ryan asked, looking into his coffee cup as he spoke.

''Very happy.''

''I'm glad to hear it. For your friend's sake, of course,'' he added, then asked in an odd tone, ''You said her sister was also kidnapped?''

''Yes. Only a few months ago, actually. Lindsay was grabbed by a disbarred lawyer who wanted revenge against Tony and Michelle because they'd provided evidence that he was embezzling from his clients—Michelle, for one. A whole gang of guys, led by Tony and Lindsay's fiancé—he's her husband now—rushed to the rescue, but Lindsay had already managed to escape on her own."

"Is she all right?"

"She was badly shaken up, of course, and suffered a few cuts and bruises, but she's fine now. Very happy with her new husband, who quite simply adores her. The whole incident was almost as hard for Michelle as it was for Lindsay, since it brought back that old nightmare of her childhood incident. But they're two strong, capable women, with lots of support from their husbands and families. They'll both be fine."

Ryan's expression was about as revealing as a closed door. He sat in silence for a few moments, then nodded toward her plate. "How was your dessert?"

"Delicious." She motioned toward his, which he'd left only half finished. "Wasn't yours as good as you'd expected?"

"I guess I'm not really as hungry as I thought I was. Must have been all that popcorn."

"Oh. Well, I'm ready to leave whenever you are."

His face still oddly set, he reached for his wallet.

Ryan's mood changed again during the ride to Taylor's apartment. By the time they arrived, he was smiling and teasing again, more like the man she'd come to know. She couldn't help responding to his good humor. Almost before she'd realized what she was doing, she'd invited him in.

They sat on the couch, cups of tea in front of them, the late news playing on the television. Neither of them watched it. Taylor plucked at a crease in the crisp khaki slacks she'd worn with a red silk camp shirt. She'd known as she dressed that the red looked good on her, contrasting becomingly with her dark hair and tanned skin. She'd found herself wanting to look her best for her date with Ryan, despite her firm self-assurances that she wouldn't allow herself to become involved with him.

She slanted a surreptitious look at him from beneath her lashes, wondering if he'd chosen his own clothes to best display his masculine assets. If so, he'd selected wisely. His blue-and-white-striped chambray shirt and closely fitting faded blue jeans made him look as though he'd just stepped out of a catalog advertising men's casual wear. With his intriguingly tousled golden-brown hair, striking pale blue eyes and mouth-watering physique, he could have had a successful career as a male model. Even though she was no longer in the business, she found herself almost itching to frame him in a camera's viewfinder.

The physical awareness between them was almost palpable. They fell silent. Desperately searching for something—anything—to say, Taylor fancied she could almost hear the tension humming in the charged air around her.

As though neither could stand the quiet any longer, they suddenly spoke in unison.

"Could I—"

"Taylor, I—"

They both stopped. Taylor smiled and waved one hand toward him. "Go ahead."

He shook his head. "What were you going to say?"

"I was going to ask if I could get you anything. More tea? Something to eat?"

"No, thanks. I'm fine."

"Oh. Good. So, um, what were *you* going to say?"

He twisted to face her, his smile a bit crooked. "I was going to ask if I could see you again. Tomorrow?"

She bit her lower lip. She wasn't surprised he'd asked, nor was she startled by the rush of pleasure that went through her at this indication that he wanted to spend more time with her. She couldn't remember ever feeling more torn than she was at this moment.

Part of her wanted to throw caution to the wind and jump at the chance to be with Ryan. He was charming and fun and attractive—why shouldn't she enjoy him while she could?

Yet another part of her—that deep, secret, somber part that still held the aching memories of another man—warned her that she risked being hurt if she allowed herself to get involved impetuously, for perhaps all the wrong reasons. And she dreaded the thought of going through heartache again.

"Is it really such a hard decision?" Ryan asked quietly, turning her averted face to his with a gentle hand on her chin.

She met his searching gaze with her own. "Yes."

"Why?"

"I don't think you'd understand."

"Try me."

"No. Not—not now."

He slid a thumb across her unsteady lower lip, his eyes following the movement. "I have to be honest with you, Taylor," he murmured. "You've been driving me crazy from the first minute I saw you at, er, in that discount store. I'm very strongly attracted to you. And it's not just that I find you beautiful or desirable or fascinating, though all those things are true. I'm attracted to your mind, your personality, your sense of humor. I want very much to get to know you better. I wish you'd try to help me understand why that bothers you so much."

"I—" She paused, emotionally staggered by his words, uncertain how to respond.

"Do I frighten you?"

"No." But she wasn't sure she was being completely honest. The way she responded to him—the way he was making her feel right now—scared her to death.

"Good. Because I would never hurt you, Taylor. Not intentionally. I want you to believe that."

Her gaze locked on his mouth, so very close to her own. Her mind went blank. What had he said? What was she expected to say in return?

His breath suddenly quickened, clearly audible to her. Her own had grown ragged. Temptation waged war with caution. His head lowered. Temptation won. She closed her eyes and tilted her face to his.

The kiss was light, almost tentative at first. Little more than a perfunctory first-date embrace. It quickly flared into more.

Taylor's lips parted automatically when Ryan's tongue swept across them. She was hardly aware of lifting her hands to his shoulders, though she was fully conscious of the solid, virile feel of him beneath her palms. He murmured something incoherent into her mouth and pulled her closer. Her arms slid around his neck, bringing her breasts into contact with his chest. Her entire body tingled in reaction.

Ryan had one hand buried in the short hair at the back of her head. He tilted her face to a new angle, allowing him better access to her mouth. The kiss deepened, heated. Taylor clung to him, feeling the sensual ripples begin deep inside her and surge outward until she was weak and trembling with needs she didn't want to examine too closely.

He felt so good, so warm and strong. So male. And he was kissing her with a skill that left her dazed and hungry, aching to experience more. If he could make her feel this good with no more than a kiss, she could just imagine what his lovemaking would do to her! And for one sharp, greedy moment, she wanted that lovemaking more than she wanted her next breath.

It had been so long. So very long since anyone had held her like this, kissed her like this, made her want this badly.

She hadn't experienced anything this powerful since— Oh, God.

Dylan.

With a gasp of anguish, she tore herself out of Ryan's arms. A moment later she was off the couch and standing halfway across the room, her arms locked defensively at her waist, her face averted. She was afraid he'd already seen the hot sheen of tears in her eyes.

When Ryan spoke, his voice was as unsteady as her hands. "What's wrong, sweetheart?"

"Nothing," she answered, staring blindly at the wall in front of her, trying to ignore the frivolous endearment.

She hadn't even realized he'd risen from the couch until he spoke from very close behind her. "Taylor, talk to me. What is it about me that scares you this way?"

She shook her head, drawing her arms more tightly around her, refusing to look at him. "You don't scare me, Ryan. I'm just . . . not ready for what was happening between us."

His hands settled on her shoulders, so lightly she didn't even flinch at his touch. "There's more to it than that," he insisted.

She remained silent.

After a moment, Ryan spoke again. "The day we met—when you first saw me standing in that store aisle, looking at you—you reacted so vehemently that I was afraid you were going to faint. I said you looked as though you'd seen a ghost. You said you thought you had."

She moistened her lips. "Yes."

"Who is it that I remind you of, Taylor? What did he do to you to make you so wary of me?"

"He died."

Ryan's fingers jerked reflexively on her shoulders in response to her stark whisper. "Who was he?" he asked after a moment.

"A man I once loved. Very deeply. He died very young, very unexpectedly."

His cheek rested against the back of her head. "I'm sorry. I didn't know."

"No."

"There hasn't been anyone else?"

"No."

Again there was silence while Ryan digested her words. And then he asked, "Do I really look like him?"

"You could be his twin."

Ryan's fingers twitched again, then squeezed warmly. "I'm sorry, Taylor," he repeated. "I didn't mean to make you so unhappy."

"It's not your fault. You couldn't have known."

"I'd better go now."

"Yes." She tried not to sound as anxious as she felt for him to leave. She needed to be alone for a while. She needed time to think. And she couldn't do that with him here.

If he was disappointed by her quick agreement, he didn't allow it to show. "I won't rush you, Taylor. You have my word. But I can't promise that I'll stay away from you, either. I'm not quite ready to concede defeat. Must be my pushy personality."

Wrapped in her confusion and misery, she couldn't respond to his gentle attempt to make her smile. She felt him press a kiss to the back of her head, felt his hands tighten on her shoulders for just a moment.

And then he was gone, leaving her alone in her achingly silent apartment.

She took a deep, shuddering breath and buried her face in her hands. "Oh, Dylan," she whispered, her voice tortured. "What have you done to me? Why won't you let me go?"

Ryan couldn't remember ever being more frustrated than he was that night as he paced the small confines of his motel room. Part of his problem was physical discomfort. It had been a very long time since he'd been with a woman, and he wanted Taylor more than he'd ever wanted anyone in his memory.

But even more uncomfortable was his awareness of his seething, savage jealousy of a man he'd never met. A man who'd died. He was eaten up with resentment—of a ghost.

Only then did he admit that the feelings he was developing for Taylor Simmons were a lot more than physical, much stronger than they should have been at this fledgling stage of their relationship. He thought of how quickly Joe had fallen in love with Lauren, and he wondered if the same thing was happening, to him. Had Joe felt this completely ill-equipped to deal with his feelings?

He groaned at how complicated this had all become—how complicated it was yet to become. After all, he reminded himself mercilessly, Taylor still didn't even know who he was. She wouldn't be pleased when she learned that he'd lied to her. When she found out his connection to her friend Michelle.

He really should have listened to Joe.

Wearing only a pair of unsnapped jeans, Ryan lounged on the hotel bed, unenthusiastically flipping channels on the TV with the remote control the hotel provided. There wasn't a hell of a lot to watch at two in the morning. Twenty-four-hour cable news, oddly colorized old movies, sitcoms that had been in reruns back when he was a kid, half-hour commercials posing as documentaries. He stopped at the shopping channel and idly considered placing an order for a complete Ginsu knife set for only twenty-nine ninety-nine. Never knew when he'd need to cut through a lead pipe and a tomato with the same knife.

The phone beside Ryan's bed rang. He answered it without bothering to mute the set, knowing who it was even before he heard the deep voice at the other end of the line. "Hi, Joe," he said. "How'd you know how to contact me?"

"Miller told me," his brother answered, referring to their supervisor at the security agency. "I knew you'd leave your number with him, in case of an emergency."

"*Is* this an emergency?" Ryan asked, though he sensed that nothing was seriously wrong. He'd already know if it was. "Why would you interrupt your honeymoon to call me? Need some marital advice?"

"My honeymoon is going quite well, thank you. And if I needed marital advice, I sure as hell wouldn't call you. What's that noise? TV?"

"Yeah. Home shopping channel. Want to order Lauren a nice set of knives for your one-month anniversary?"

"I think I'll pass, thanks." And then Joe grew abruptly serious. "How are you, Ry? Is everything okay?"

Ryan wasn't surprised that Joe seemed to know he was troubled. He and his brother had always had a connection that somehow let them know when the other was deeply upset or in danger. "I'm fine. You know, of course, that I'm in Dallas."

"Yeah. So, have you contacted them yet?"

It wasn't necessary for Joe to clarify who he meant by *them.* "No. Not yet. I still haven't decided whether I even want to. But I saw Michelle, from a distance. Twice."

There was a brief, tense pause at the other end. And then Joe asked quietly, "How does she look?"

"Beautiful," Ryan answered honestly. "And apparently very happy. She's pregnant."

He didn't mention the story Taylor had told him about Michelle's childhood kidnapping, or about the similar misadventure Lindsay had gone through more recently. He would tell Joe about both incidents eventually, but for now he was still too coldly furious at the bastards who'd callously risked two lives for their own evil purposes.

"So little Shelley's expecting," Joe said after a brief pause.

"Yeah. I checked her husband out, too. Seems like an okay guy. Successful, well-respected. From all reports, he's crazy about Michelle."

"I'm glad to hear it. So, if you haven't contacted Michelle, what have you been doing in Dallas?"

Ryan cleared his throat. "Well—I've met someone. A woman."

Joe groaned, and Ryan knew his brother had read more into the words than he'd intended for him to know just yet.

He couldn't help but speak defensively. "Okay, I've fallen kind of hard. But it doesn't look like it's going anywhere. She's carrying around a lot of old emotional baggage. It's really getting in the way." He had some baggage of his own, as far as that went, though he didn't bother to mention what Joe already knew so well.

"What's the problem?"

"There are a couple of problems, actually. First, she's a friend of Michelle's. A close friend."

"Oh. Does she know about—?"

"No."

"That could get awkward."

"It already has."

"What's the other problem?"

"Apparently, I remind her of a dead lover."

"Hell."

Ryan nodded grimly. "Yeah."

You could be his twin, Taylor had said.

Suddenly frowning, Ryan asked carefully, "Uh, Joe? You never met anyone named Taylor Simmons, did you? Dark hair, gray eyes, mid-twenties? Used to be a professional photographer."

"Doesn't ring a bell. And, anyway, you said the other guy's dead."

"Yeah," Ryan admitted. "She said he died very young. Apparently unexpectedly. I didn't ask the details—I guess I wasn't ready to hear them yet."

After a moment, Joe spoke again, choosing his words with care. "Ryan—don't forget what happened the last time you got involved with a woman when I wasn't around."

Ryan winced. "I'd rather not talk about that right now."

"Right. But be careful, okay?"

"I will." *If it's not already too late for caution,* he thought, though he kept the words to himself.

"You know how to reach me if you need me."

"And if I decide to contact the others?"

Joe hesitated, then said, "Give them my best."

Ryan was disappointed, but not surprised. "All right. Give Lauren my love."

They didn't bother to say goodbye before disconnecting. They never did.

That night it was Ryan who dreamed, who woke in a trembling sweat. His recurring nightmares were all the more horrifying because the incident about which he dreamed had really happened to him.

He'd awakened in a strange hospital bed, his movements restricted by straps and tubes and monitors and casts. The pain was so bad he'd almost screamed. Every inch of him throbbed as he lay staring at the unfamiliar ceiling. What was wrong with him? Why couldn't he move his legs? Was he paralyzed? Would he lie here staring at this same ceiling for the rest of his life?

He tried frantically to remember what had happened to him. Couldn't. He remembered nothing prior to waking in such horrible pain; he didn't know who he was or why he was here. Or who, if anyone, knew or cared where or how he was.

He always woke at that point in the nightmare, coming awake with a gasp of remembered pain and fear. But the dream—or rather the memories never ended there. He was always forced to relive the entire ordeal in his mind. The weeks of agonizing therapy. The frustratingly slow regaining of his memory—all but the few weeks leading up to his injuries. The nights he'd lain in bed, staring at the ceiling, desperately trying to recall those lost weeks, straining to remember what had happened to him, struggling to understand the few puzzling facts he'd been told. The months he'd spent getting back on his feet, building his strength. Slowly, painfully, determinedly recovering full use of his mind and his limbs.

His brother's voice—encouraging, supporting, nagging, sometimes yelling—had helped Ryan through that time, urging him on even when he wanted to give up, making him believe the pain would eventually be rewarded with success. Telling him he had to stop torturing himself over the weeks he'd lost and make the most of the time he'd miraculously been granted.

He didn't think he'd have made it if it hadn't been for Joe. But now Joe was married, his future bound irrevocably with someone else's, and Ryan was truly on his own for the first time in his life.

He'd come to Dallas because he hadn't been so sure he wanted to be alone. Yet he'd taken no real action since arriving because he'd been equally uncertain that he'd really wanted to change the way he'd been living for the past few years.

And now there was Taylor. A woman whose dark, expressive eyes haunted him, who pulled at him as no one had before her. And he realized that he couldn't leave Dallas. Not yet. He was hooked, and he didn't for the life of him know what he was going to do next.

Had that subconscious realization triggered the old dream of helplessness and vulnerability? Shouldn't that be a warning to him?

"Dammit," he muttered into the darkness of the nondescript motel room. "What are you going to do now, Ryan?"

This time he knew he was truly on his own. Joe couldn't help him now.

Chapter Five

Taylor opened her door the next morning to find Ryan standing on the other side, his finger still hovering over the doorbell, a look of sheer determination hardening his handsome face. He wore a black knit shirt with khaki shorts. His right knee was scarred, and there was another scar on his left calf, but they didn't detract from his great legs. Sports injuries, she guessed. He looked lean and tough and just a little dangerous.

He looked wonderful.

"I've been thinking about what you said last night," he said bluntly.

She smoothed her palms nervously down the front of the pleated turquoise shorts she wore with a hot pink and turquoise top. "You have?"

"Yes. And I've decided I'm not going to slip quietly out of your life. If I'm going to be rejected, it will be because of who I am, how you feel about me. Not because of some vague resemblance to a guy you used to care about.''

"It's more than a vague resemblance," Taylor retorted, oddly annoyed by the remark. "You're the very image of—"

"I don't want to talk about him," Ryan interrupted before she could say the name. "Maybe there is a strong resemblance." His mouth twisted into a wry smile she couldn't quite interpret when he added, "It's not the first time I've been mistaken for someone else, and it probably won't be the last, but I deserve the chance to be judged for my actions and not my appearance.

"Tell me," he challenged without pausing. "Am I really that much like him, in anything but the way I look?"

"There are similarities," she confessed, "and in more ways than looks. But—" She gave a slight shrug. "There are differences, too."

Ryan nodded in apparent satisfaction. "Give me a chance," he said enticingly, "and I'll convince you I'm not a ghost, but a real flesh-and-blood man who wants to get to know you better. Unless you aren't at all interested in getting to know *me?* The *real* me, not the outside packaging."

Her fingers clenched tightly in front of her. "I'm attracted to you, Ryan. You have to know that already, since you aren't stupid. But—" She hesitated, moistening her lips.

He rested a hand against the doorframe, leaning toward her, still standing on the walkway outside her apartment door. "But?"

"I'm worried about my reasons for being attracted," she admitted, though she knew he wouldn't like it.

She was right. His brows drew sharply downward. "I refuse to accept that you're confusing your memories with the present. *You're* not stupid, either. Give me a chance, Taylor. Let me try to make you forget anyone but me.''

A ripple of sadness coursed through her. ''I've tried to forget before,'' she whispered, looking at her hands. ''I can't.''

His hand on her chin brought her face up to his. His light-blue eyes burned into hers, looking far warmer than their icy color should have allowed. ''Give me a chance, Taylor,'' he repeated in a seductive murmur. ''One more day. If you still want me to get lost at the end of today, I'll do so.''

Holding her breath, she searched his face, wondering why her answer seemed so important to him, wondering if he really cared as much as he seemed to, hoping . . .

''All right,'' she said, the words little louder than a sigh. ''We can try.''

His smile was as brilliant as the July sun shining outside. ''You won't regret it,'' he murmured, then brushed her mouth with his own before he stepped back and urged her to get her purse so they could leave. He didn't want to waste another moment of this absolutely glorious day, he said.

It took him less than an hour to work his way past her initial reserve. Sometime during lunch at a popular, casual deli, Taylor realized she'd laughed more that morning than she had in a long time. She shook her head in silent admiration of Ryan's easy charm, which he used as effectively as anyone who had ever worked a natural talent.

As though aware that activity was called for to forestall more serious contemplation on her part, Ryan kept her very busy that day. They must have walked miles—at a park, a museum, a trendy, tourist-based shopping center on the west end of town. And they talked, so rapidly sometimes their words overlapped and tangled, underscored by shared laughter. Ryan was skilled at casual conversation, so good at it that several hours had passed before Taylor realized she'd told him nearly everything there was to know about herself without learning anything of any significance about him.

"How did you get this scar?" she asked late in the afternoon, leaning against a railing on the third level of the shopping center for a quick breather. Unable to resist, she'd lifted a hand to brush a heavy lock of his goldstreaked hair from his forehead, her fingers lingering at his scarred brow. She traced the four-inch length of the thin white line, thinking that it must have been a deep and painful cut, though the scar had faded to near insignificance, not at all detracting from his classic good looks.

"Car accident."

"Was it a serious one?"

"Serious enough." He turned to look over the railing, apparently studying the ground-floor food court two stories below, one sneakered foot resting on the lowest metal rung.

"Then you must have felt fortunate to escape with just this scar. Or is there some other lingering repercussion?"

He shrugged, still looking down. "I get migraine headaches sometimes, and I have a recurring back problem. Neither serious, but both are a result of the accident."

"Were you—"

He turned suddenly, his expression bland and totally unreadable. "Are you hungry? Watching those people eat down there is making me ravenous. How about an ice-cream cone or something?''

''Sure, if you want,'' she agreed, aware that he'd just deliberately brought the talk about his car accident to an end. Why was he so reticent about talking about himself?

They were sitting at a tiny table in the food court, enjoying their ice cream, when she tried again. ''Are your parents still living?'' she asked, remembering that he'd told her he'd been on his own for many years.

''No.''

''And you have no other family except your brother?''

''No one that I'm close to. What about you? Are you close to your parents and your brother?''

''In a funny way,'' she answered, frustrated with his evasiveness, but hopeful that her openness might encourage his. ''My father was a major workaholic and I didn't see him much when I was growing up. My mother was always busy with social clubs and volunteer work— real Junior League material. My brother's five years younger than I am—he's twenty-two—so we didn't have a great deal in common. But we all get along well enough, and enjoy seeing one another now when we get together for holidays or whatever.''

''So you spent a lot of time learning to entertain yourself as a kid.''

Taylor nodded to confirm his perceptive comment. ''That's why I took up photography, I guess. It gave me something productive to do. And I spent a lot of time with my friends, particularly Michelle—the one I mentioned yesterday,'' she reminded him.

He nodded. ''I remember. The one who was...um... kidnapped.''

"Yes. I met her after that, when we were in junior high. She was an only child—or thought she was—and a bit overprotected by her loving parents. We knew we were soulmates from the beginning. We've been close ever since."

Ryan was watching her closely, rather flatteringly interested in her words. "She *thought* she was an only child?" he repeated with a quizzical smile. "I suppose you can explain?"

Taylor took another lick of her ice cream before answering. "She was adopted by the Trents when she was just a toddler. She didn't remember anything prior to her adoption, and wasn't aware she'd had several siblings who were separated when their parents died. After her adoptive mother died, Michelle found a letter telling her all the details about her birth family in case she wanted to try to meet them."

"And has she found them?" Ryan asked casually, studying his half-eaten ice cream.

"A brother and two sisters, leaving two brothers unaccounted for. I've met the ones she located, and they're really nice people. The brother and one of the sisters live within thirty miles of here, and the other sister lives in Little Rock. They're all happily married, and seem to be quite content despite their divergent and not always happy backgrounds."

She shifted her weight on the hard plastic seat, hoping she wasn't boring him with her chatter about people he didn't even know. But he *had* asked. "Michelle and I have talked often about how lucky she was to have found them, and that she truly likes each one of them. In just over a year, they've become a real family—and they've sort of adopted me among them. I'm usually invited to the family gatherings, and I try to join them whenever I can, since my own family is so scattered.''

"They all get along pretty well, huh?''

"Surprisingly well. Of course, they've all made real efforts to do so. Being part of a family requires some compromise and adjustments, but I think it's worth it in the long run. I'd hate to think I wouldn't have anyone to turn to if I was in real trouble.'' And then Taylor stopped abruptly, wondering if her artless words would bother Ryan, who seemed so much alone himself. Or did he consider his brother all the family he needed?

He took a crunching bite of his sugar cone, apparently unfazed by any mental comparisons. "What would you like to do next?'' he asked, completely changing the subject. "Want to see another movie—maybe a comedy this time?''

She'd never learn anything more about him sitting in a quiet movie theater with many other people. Was that part of his intention? "Why don't we go back to my place and watch videos, instead?'' she suggested impulsively. "I'll make dinner and we can talk some more.''

Did the expression that flashed through his eyes indicate approval, surprise or wariness at her suggestion of more conversation? Or perhaps a mixture of the three? Whichever, he quickly masked it and pushed himself to his feet. "Sounds good to me. Ready to go?''

Spending another evening alone with him may not have been the smartest idea you've ever had, Simmons, she found herself thinking as she stood and tossed her napkin into a trash can.

She was already having serious doubts about whether she'd be willing—or able—to send him away when the evening ended.

* * *

Taylor sat on the floor after dinner, her legs tucked under her as she studied the dozens of video titles she kept neatly arranged in a cabinet in her living room. Ryan knelt behind her, looking over her shoulder. "You have a lot of movies," he commented.

"I'm a film freak," she admitted. "And not a particularly discriminating one."

"So I see," he commented, running a finger along the spine of a wildly silly coming-of-age comedy.

"That one makes me laugh when I'm in the mullygrumps," she said with a shrug. "Not all films have to be great art to be enjoyed."

"This is a very good film library," he said with a conciliatory smile. "A nice variety of subjects and styles. I was only teasing."

"You said you're in the mood for comedy this evening?" She skimmed past the action adventure, science fiction and dramatic films, concentrating on the shelf she considered her humor section. "See any titles that interest you?"

He leaned closer, ostensibly to better study the boxes. His warm breath caressed her bare nape, sending a shiver of awareness down her spine. "Pick one of your favorites. I'd like to see what appeals to you."

She told herself he surely hadn't meant the latter as a double entendre, and then decided he probably had. Sternly ignoring his proximity—or trying to, anyway—she ran a fingertip across the boxes, pausing at several she particularly liked.

What did she want to watch? What did she want to reveal to him with her choice?

An oldie? *Father Goose*? *Arsenic and Old Lace*? Anything with Hepburn and Tracy?

Something newer, delightfully absurd? *The Princess Bride*? *Airplane*? Anything with Peter Sellers or John Cleese?

Maybe humor laced with tears. *Ghost*. *Same Time Next Year*. Or the real killer—*Brian's Song*.

She bit her lip against a smile. Would Ryan burst into tears upon hearing Billy Dee Williams mutter, "I lo-o-o-ve Brian Piccolo," as Taylor's brother had the first time he'd seen the movie? Of course, Ryan had probably seen it already.

"Come on, Taylor, you're choosing a movie, not making a lifelong commitment," Ryan complained humorously.

She snatched out a box. "Have you seen this one?"

"*American Dreamer*? No. What's it about?"

"It's a ridiculous premise about a normally repressed woman who hits her head and wakes up convinced she's a dashing character from a series of women's adventure novels. Stars JoBeth Williams and Tom Conti. It's utterly preposterous, totally unbelievable and sometimes downright silly. I love it."

"Then by all means, let's watch it." Ryan stood and held out a hand to boost her up.

Ryan quickly concluded that it must be one of those women's movies. Oh, the film was amusing enough, but did the hero have to be so befuddled and tractable? Why didn't he just firmly shake the woman, tell her she was *not* Rebecca Ryan and then kiss some sense into her?

He glanced sideways at Taylor as she laughed aloud at another scene in which the wily, delusional Cathy evaded her beleaguered protector, and decided maybe he'd better keep his opinions—which she would probably consider chauvinistic and arrogant—to himself.

The only time he'd really squirmed during the film was close to the beginning, when Cathy-Rebecca was knocked down by a car while crossing a street, resulting in her mental confusion. That image hit just a little too close to home for Ryan's comfort.

Fortunately, the scene wasn't intended to be funny, so he didn't have to force a smile. Even Taylor had stopped smiling for a moment, her expression going distant and a bit sad, as though she'd forgotten about that scene and found it less amusing than she'd remembered. But her smile had returned quickly enough after Tom Conti made his appearance in the movie, finding himself drawn helplessly into a web of danger and confusion woven by a beautiful oddball.

The movie ended on a blatantly romantic note. "What did you think of it?" Taylor demanded as the credits rolled across the television screen.

Ryan cleared his throat. "Very interesting."

She made a face. "Men."

He chuckled and twisted on the couch to face her, reaching out to brush a strand of hair away from her eye. "What's that supposed to mean?"

"You have a totally different idea of what's funny than women do. You probably laugh yourself silly at wise-cracking men's adventure films, like *Die Hard* and those *Lethal Weapon* movies."

"Yeah. I like those," he admitted. "But you know what I really find funny? The interplay between Spock and McCoy of the original *Star Trek* cast. That's funny stuff."

Her eyes lit up. "That *is* funny," she said, seeming pleased that they agreed on something. "Didn't you especially like *Star Trek IV: The Voyage Home*? Remember that scene when Kirk was trying to explain to a twentieth-century female scientist that he's come back three hundred years to borrow a couple of humpback whales for the future? I laughed—''

Unable to resist a moment longer, Ryan covered her mouth with his before she could finish the sentence. Several long, pleasant minutes passed before he came up for air, though he remained where he was, his arms around her, his face only inches from hers.

Her cheeks flushed, eyes rather glazed, breathing ragged, Taylor blinked and stared at him. "I, uh—''

"You're beautiful," he murmured, caressing her features with his gaze. "Your eyes—''

He touched a fingertip to one quivering eyelid, letting her long, dark lashes tickle his skin. "So big and dark and mysterious. And your nose—''

He traced that same finger down her nose. "Perfectly shaped. Just the right size. Your mouth—''

His finger slid over her full, moist lower lip. "Sweet. Soft. Sexy.''

He leaned over and kissed her again, savoring the taste of her. His entire body tightened with need, aching to carry the embrace further. He told himself he could handle this, and hoped he wasn't being overly confident.

Taylor's arms slid slowly around his neck, her fingers burrowing into his hair. "Ryan," she whispered against his lips.

Hearing his name murmured so seductively—*his* name, he thought exultantly—weakened his already shaky willpower even further. He pulled her closer, sliding one hand into the soft, short hair behind her head to hold her still when he took her willingly offered mouth with a hot, hungry thoroughness. His tongue slipped between her parted lips and was eagerly greeted by hers.

Her arms tightened around him, and her smooth, bare leg slid against his harder, rougher one, making him glad they'd both chosen to wear shorts that day. He couldn't stop himself from reaching down to stroke her thigh, from knee to hem. He managed to restrain himself there, though his fingers itched to slide beneath the fabric and explore the soft secrets beyond.

Her full breasts were crushed sensually against his chest. He wanted to touch her, wanted to rid them both of the fabric that separated them so he could feel her, taste her. He plundered her mouth, his mind filled with images that made him shudder with needs too long denied. And she kissed him with an eagerness that made him suspect she wouldn't protest if he carried this further.

Desire slammed through him, robbing him of breath and strength. The temptation was almost more than he could resist. Almost.

It might have been the hardest thing he'd ever done to raise his head and force himself backward on the couch, putting several empty inches between them. "I guess I'd better go now," he croaked, his voice nearly unrecognizable.

Taylor opened her heavy eyelids to look at him in disbelief. "Go?" she repeated, her voice hoarse. "But—"

Still holding himself rigidly under control, he rested his forehead against hers. "I promised I'd give you time to get to know me," he reminded her. "I won't rush you into anything you aren't ready for."

She drew a deep, unsteady breath. "Oh."

And then she drew back, clasping her arms around her waist. "I'm grateful, of course, that you aren't trying to rush me."

She didn't sound grateful. She sounded as frustrated as he felt, but he nodded soberly. "We've only known each other a few days," he reminded her.

She pushed a hand through her dark hair, leaving it ruffled in endearing spikes around her face. "I've never believed in jumping into bed with a near stranger," she said bluntly.

"Nor have I," he assured her.

"That's—good."

"Yeah." He knew he had to stand up, had to make himself leave. Damn, he wanted to stay. "I'd better go," he said again, half hoping she'd try to change his mind.

She hesitated only a moment, then nodded firmly. "Yes. You probably should."

He wasn't disappointed, of course, since this had been his decision in the first place. *Yeah, Ryan. Sure.*

"Will you see me again?" he asked gravely, remembering his promise that he would leave her alone after this if she asked.

Taylor bit her lower lip, obviously remembering that vow herself.

He tensed as the silence lengthened. "Taylor?"

"I should tell you no," she whispered. "I know I should. But—"

He cupped her face between his hands. "Say yes." The words came out a husky cross between an order and a plea.

"Yes." It was little more than a sigh. "I'll see you again."

Relief almost stole his breath. "Thank you." He kissed her quickly, breaking the contact before the emotions could flare out of control again.

And then he stood, knowing he had to leave now, while he still could.

Taylor rose with him, moving too quickly. Caught off balance, she stumbled over the shoes she'd discarded when they'd settled onto the couch to watch the video.

Grinning at her sudden look of panic, Ryan twisted to steady her.

His laughter turned to a sharp gasp of pain.

A moment later he was sprawled on the floor. Taylor knelt beside him, clutching his shoulders, calling his name. "Ryan? Ryan, what it is? What's wrong?"

"My back," he grated out between clenched teeth. "Dammit, I've twisted it. I can't stand up."

Chapter Six

Ryan had gone pale and clammy, his eyes glassy with pain. Taylor knelt beside him, feeling terribly helpless. "What can I do? Should I call an ambulance?"

"No. I'll be all right."

"Can you stand?"

He shifted his weight, trying to rise on one elbow. What little color had been left in his face drained with the movement. Deep lines carved themselves into his forehead and around his mouth. Taylor caught his shoulders and lowered him to the floor. "I'm calling an ambulance."

"No." He caught her hand, holding her in place when she would have stood. "I've done this before. Please don't call an ambulance."

"But, Ryan, you should see a doctor."

"I don't like doctors. I had my fill of the medical profession after my car accident. All I need is a couple of days to rest and to take the muscle relaxers and pain pills I carry in my bag for when something like this happens."

She drew a deep breath, unable to resist the look in his eyes. "All right. You can stay here until your back is better."

"That's not necessary. I can—"

"You can what?" she interrupted flatly. "Drive yourself to your hotel when you can't even stand? Take care of yourself in this condition?"

He shrugged, then scowled at the resulting discomfort from the movement. "It wouldn't be the first time," he muttered.

"Well, this time you're staying right here. And since you're in no shape to take me on, I suggest you don't try to argue with me." She waited a minute, giving him a chance to demur. Satisfied when he remained silent, she gave a curt nod and said, "I'll go get your medicine and your bags, but I don't want to leave you lying here on the floor. How are we going to move you to the bed without causing you too much pain?"

He struggled to sit up. "I can walk. Just give me a shoulder for balance."

"Are you sure you should be moving this much?" she fretted. "What if you hurt yourself worse?"

"I won't." He sounded confident, so she decided he knew what he was talking about.

She didn't like hearing his breath catch when he dragged himself to his feet, knowing how badly he must be hurting. She wrapped her arm around his lean waist, supporting his weight as best she could during the slow walk to her bedroom. She was as relieved as he was when she stripped back the covers and finally lowered him to the bed.

He glanced around the bedroom, which continued the Southwestern decor she'd utilized in the living room. "This wasn't the way I'd planned to get my first look at your bedroom," he grumbled.

She managed a smile and brushed his hair away from his clammy forehead. "Are you sure you'll be all right while I'm gone?"

He tried to smile in return, though the effort was heartbreakingly weak. "Yeah. Just bring me my pills and I'll be eternally in your debt. The hotel room key is on the ring in my pocket." He named the hotel, then added, "I'm in room 218. I only have one bag and a shaving kit, neither of which are unpacked. Might as well bring it all."

She draped the Hopi-print comforter over him and tucked the edges around his shoulders. "I'll hurry."

"Just drive carefully."

"I will."

She cast one worried look at him as she left the room. Hating to leave him alone, she was tempted to call Michelle, ask her to come stay with Ryan while she went after his things. But, she reasoned, by the time Michelle arrived—if she was even free to do so—Taylor could have been to the hotel and back. She decided Ryan would rather have his pain pills sooner, and wouldn't appreciate a baby-sitter, anyway. Biting her lip, she turned and all but ran from the apartment.

Ryan's hotel room looked like thousands of others Taylor had seen—bland, colorless, clean. His bag sat on a luggage rack at the foot of the made bed. There were no personal items sitting around the room.

She found his shaving kit in the bathroom, nothing but a toothbrush and tube of toothpaste sitting on the counter. She packed them, spotting several prescription bottles in the kit as she did so. She hoped those were the ones he needed. She couldn't help noting the labels. Odd. The directions for use of the medications had been typed onto the labels, but the space for the patient's name had been left blank. She wondered why.

Tucking the shaving kit under her arm, she headed for the door, snatching up his bag on the way. She hadn't realized the bag was unzipped until it opened and several items spilled out at her feet. Cursing her clumsiness, she knelt and stuffed the garments inside.

And then froze at the sight of the gun lying at her feet.

She stared at the weapon for some time before reluctantly picking it up. She held it between thumb and finger as she gingerly slipped it into the bag and secured the zipper.

She was probably the world's biggest idiot to allow an armed man who was still basically a stranger to spend the night in her bed. As secretive as he'd been about himself, Ryan could be a homicidal maniac, for all she knew. And then she pictured his smile—the one that had turned so abruptly to a grimace of pain—and she knew she trusted him. Without any reason, without any justification, she trusted him.

"You probably are a fool, Simmons," she said aloud in the empty room.

She stood, carrying the bag and its deadly contents, and left the motel, anxious to get back to the man she'd left in her bed.

She found Ryan lying exactly as she had left him, his eyes closed, his skin still much too pale. The deepened lines between his brows made her suspect that his head was hurting, as well as his back. When she asked, he reluctantly admitted that it was, that back pain occasionally triggered the headaches he suffered. "The pain medicine will help both," he assured her when she brought him a glass of water to take the capsules with.

"It's getting late," Taylor said when he'd swallowed the pills. "Why don't you get some sleep? I'll be in the other room if you need anything."

"Where are you going to sleep?"

"On the couch."

"I don't want to put you out of your bed."

"The couch is perfectly comfortable. I'll be fine. Do you want me to, uh, help you out of your clothes or anything?" she asked, trying to speak matter-of-factly.

His mouth twitched in a near smile. "No. I think that would be more painful than beneficial right now. I'll just sleep in them tonight."

"Whatever you think best," she agreed, knowing she spoke just a bit too quickly. She cursed her sudden awkwardness and took a step backward, toward the door. "Yell if you need anything."

"I will. Thanks, Taylor. I'm sorry about being so much trouble."

"Don't be stupid," she said brusquely, her hand on the door. "Good night, Ryan."

"Good night, sweetheart."

She snapped off the light and escaped into the hallway, closing the door behind her.

She slipped into the room a couple of hours later, holding her breath as she tiptoed to the bed. The bright security lights outside her bedroom window filtered into the room through her thin curtains. It wasn't necessary for her to turn on the bedside lamp to see that Ryan was sleeping deeply. She thought the medication had probably made him drowsy.

He moved restlessly against the pillows, and she guessed sympathetically that he was still in some pain from his strained back. She couldn't resist reaching out to smooth his hair away from his forehead. Funny. She couldn't remember having these vaguely nurturing feelings about any man before—and it seemed especially odd that she was feeling them now, for a man as tough and self-sufficient as Ryan.

Standing very still, looking down at him with her lower lip caught firmly between her teeth, she made herself think of Dylan, deliberately looking for similarities. But it was Ryan she saw, Ryan who filled her thoughts.

Maybe the similarities weren't as strong as she'd convinced herself they were, she thought with a touch of hope. After all, it had been two years, and she hadn't even had a photograph to remember Dylan by. He'd refused to allow her to take pictures of him during their brief time together, telling her he was painfully camera shy. She'd hoped to convince him otherwise, but hadn't had a chance before the accident.

Maybe the resemblances were really only superficial— maybe she was simply attracted to similar types and needn't be so concerned that her developing feelings for Ryan were influenced by her lingering emotions for Dylan.

Maybe it was safe to allow herself to start caring for this man on his own merits.

A ripple of unease went through her—premonition? She scolded herself for her paranoia and stepped silently away from the bed. She was careful not to make any noise when she pulled a nightshirt out of a drawer and left the room. She left the door ajar an inch or so, just in case Ryan called out to her during the night.

As comfortable as her couch was, she slept only fitfully that night. She didn't know if her restlessness was due to the unfamiliar bed—or to her constant awareness that Ryan lay so close by. Sometime during the early hours of the morning, she gave in to exhaustion and fell into a heavy, dreamless sleep that wasn't disturbed until sunlight streamed fully through the living room window.

She woke with a gasp, making a grab for her watch. She was relieved to see that it wasn't much later than she usually awoke, so she wouldn't be very late for work. She didn't have to be right on time this morning, she thought, sitting upright with a yawn and a slow stretch, but she had a meeting she couldn't miss that afternoon.

She looked toward her bedroom. The door was still ajar and she couldn't hear anything, so she assumed Ryan was still sleeping. She wondered if she should wake him. He probably needed to take another muscle relaxer.

Tugging her oversize nightshirt down over her thighs, she decided she was decent enough to be seen by him. The shirt covered as much as her shorts had the day before, she reminded herself as she stood and headed for the bedroom, running a hand through her disheveled hair on the way. She fretted that she must look like a hag after her night on the couch. He'd probably take one look at her and run, his back magically healed. She pushed the door open and stepped cautiously into the room.

Ryan wasn't in the bed. Frowning, she looked around and saw him standing in the doorway of the tiny connected bathroom. He wasn't wearing his shirt, and his low-slung khaki shorts weren't buttoned. His chest was tanned and sleek, with only a sparse scattering of brown hair in the center, arrowing down to his intriguingly loosened shorts.

Her mouth went dry.

And then she saw the scars that crisscrossed his chest and rib cage. "What did you *do* to yourself?" she blurted, shocked into tactlessness by the number and apparent severity of the old wounds.

"Good morning to you, too," he said, pushing away from the bathroom doorframe to walk slowly to the bed. He held himself very stiffly, his steps small and tentative, and he lowered himself very carefully to the edge of the bed, proving he was still in pain.

Taylor walked toward him, her gaze still on his scarred chest. "Did those all come from the accident?"

"Yes. There are more on my back, if you're interested," he answered rather crossly. "Want me to model them?"

She pulled her gaze to his face. "I'm sorry. I didn't mean to stare. I just didn't realize you'd been injured so badly."

"I told you it was bad."

"Yes." She just hadn't realized exactly *how* bad. Shuddering at the unpleasant mental images, she wondered if he'd been thrown through a windshield. But he obviously didn't want to talk about the accident, so she let the subject drop. "Are you hungry?" she asked instead.

"No. I was just about to take another pill."

"Let me get you some fresh water," she said, grabbing the glass he'd used the night before and hurrying to refill it.

"Thanks," Ryan said gratefully when she returned.

She noted that the skin around his mouth was taut, the furrows back between his brows. "Ryan, are you sure you don't want to see a doctor?" she couldn't help asking.

The look he gave her was all the answer she needed.

She sighed at his obstinance and took a step away from the bed. "Then I guess I'll have my shower and get dressed."

He only nodded.

Taylor was fully dressed, made up and accessorized when she stepped out of the bathroom half an hour later. She approached the bedroom cautiously, remembering the mood Ryan had been in earlier. He was lying propped against the pillows, his eyes closed, the lower half of his body covered with the comforter. The khaki shorts he'd been wearing earlier were lying on the floor beside the bed.

His eyelids twitched, then opened as she stood beside the bed. "You look very nice," he murmured, studying the cherry-red suit she wore with a white silk shell.

"Thanks." She wondered if it was the medication slurring his voice, and decided it probably was. She suspected the muscle relaxers he was taking were a strong dosage. She hated the thought of leaving him alone like this. "I don't have to leave for the office immediately, but there's a meeting this afternoon I really shouldn't miss," she said. "Maybe I could have a friend come stay with you while I'm gone. I'm sure Michelle—"

"No!"

Taylor started in response to the explosive interruption.

Ryan winced at the sharp sound of his own voice, then held out his hand to her. "I'm sorry," he said when she placed her hand in his after only the slightest hesitation.

"I know I've been a real grouch this morning. I don't mean to snap at you. Especially after you've gone to so much trouble for me."

"I understand," she said, hearing the sincerity of the apology. "You're obviously in a lot of pain."

"That's no excuse. I wouldn't blame you if you threw me out on my ear."

She smiled and gave his fingers a slight squeeze. "Tempting as the thought may be, I'll let you hang around a bit longer."

He smiled at the teasing and tugged on her hand to urge her to sit on the edge of the bed. "I guess I'm mad at myself, more than anything," he explained rather sheepishly.

She lifted an eyebrow in question.

He moved his free hand to indicate his horizontal position. "I feel like a fool, throwing my back out like this. And right after I was trying so hard to impress you with my nobility and willpower," he added wryly.

She bit her lip against a smile.

"Anyway, I'm sorry I've snapped at you this morning. I won't do it again," he promised, holding her hand in both of his. "I want you to go to work. I'll be fine here by myself. I've managed on my own when I was in worse shape than this, I assure you. Another couple hours rest and I'll be able to get up and move around a little more comfortably. I really don't need a baby-sitter."

"I just thought—"

"I know," he cut in again, though more gently this time. "You were concerned about me. And I appreciate it." Another tug on her hand brought her forward, her face close to his. He wrapped a hand around the back of her neck and urged her the rest of the way, his lips taking hers with a tenderness that made her insides melt.

Taylor was flushed and flustered when she finally drew back, strongly tempted to crawl right into that bed with him. Not that he'd be able to do anything about it if she did, she reminded herself sternly. Where was *her* willpower? "I'll be right back," she said, standing a bit too quickly and leaving the bedroom with more haste than dignity.

Ten minutes later, her delinquent hormones firmly under control, she returned to the bedroom carrying a tall glass of pulpy orange juice and a plate holding a microwave-warmed and buttered blueberry muffin. The morning newspaper was tucked under her arm.

"I thought you should try to eat something, since you're taking all that medicine," she said, setting the dishes on the nightstand within easy reach of Ryan. She laid the newspaper on the bed beside him. "I've written my work number down on the pad on the nightstand, if you need to reach me today. Is there anything else I can get for you?"

He shook his head against the pillows, smiling at her. "I'll be fine, Taylor. Thank you."

"You're welcome." She hesitated a moment longer, shifting her weight from one foot to another. She found it even harder to leave him than she'd expected.

His smile deepened. "Go to work, Taylor. I'll be fine."

She made a face and gave a slight, self-conscious laugh. "I'm hovering, aren't I?"

"Yes. But I appreciate the concern."

Knowing it was time, she nodded briskly. "All right. Call if you need me."

"I will."

Impulsively, she leaned over the bed and brushed a kiss against his mouth, though she didn't linger long enough to allow him to respond. She was halfway out the door when she paused one more time and looked at him over her shoulder. "Ryan?"

He hadn't taken his eyes off her as she'd walked away. "Yes?"

"About yesterday... last night..."

"What about it?"

"I just want you to know," she said rather woodenly, feeling her cheeks burning and cursing herself for it, "I knew who I was kissing. I wasn't confusing you with anyone else."

His smile might have made her want to hit him, if he hadn't already been temporarily incapacitated. "I know," he said and his tone was just a little too smug.

Taylor was scowling when she left, closing the apartment door with more force than necessary as she stepped outside. *Should have kept your mouth shut, Simmons. That man definitely doesn't have any ego problems!*

Maxie and Jay were in the middle of a heated argument when Taylor reached the agency. It didn't particularly bother her, since those two seemed to enjoy arguing more than anyone she'd ever known. "I suppose you've forgotten we have a big client meeting this afternoon that we should all be getting ready for? LuCon Industries?" she reminded them dryly.

Maxie stopped glaring at Jay and turned to Taylor. "How are you feeling?"

"Fine. The cold's all but gone."

Maxie's auburn brows knit as she continued to study Taylor's face. "So what did you do this weekend?"

Taylor tried to look nonchalant as she inched toward the security of her own office. "Nothing much. Took in a movie, watched some videos, did a little shopping."

"Alone?"

Taylor frowned at Maxie's speculative question. "Why do you ask?"

"Oh, I don't know. Maybe because you're looking just a bit dreamy-eyed this morning."

Taylor hated herself for flushing. Maxie laughed. "You *were* with someone. And I'll bet I know who it was!"

"I don't suppose it's occurred to you that this is none of your business?" Jay inquired, sounding as though he didn't expect to be heeded.

He wasn't, of course. "You were with Ryan Kent, weren't you?" Maxie demanded of Taylor.

Taylor sighed in exasperation at the well-intentioned but discomfiting prying. "As a matter of fact, he was still lying in my bed when I left for work this morning. There. Does that make you happy?"

She was fully aware that her partners were staring open-mouthed after her as she turned and stalked into her office. She closed the door sharply behind her, just in case either of them was tempted to follow. Honestly. Couldn't a person have any privacy around here?

Michelle called that afternoon to make sure Taylor was feeling better. Taylor assured her friend that she was much improved, then asked, "How are *you* feeling?"

"I had a rough start," Michelle admitted. "This morning sickness bit is worse than I expected! But I'm over it now. Until tomorrow, at least."

Taylor murmured sympathetically. "How long is this part supposed to last?"

"It differs with everyone, apparently. And Cassie's no help at all. She claims she hasn't been sick even once during her five months of pregnancy."

"How unfair."

"I thought so," Michelle answered gravely, though Taylor could tell she was smiling. "I talked to Lindsay yesterday," Michelle said, changing the subject.

Lindsay was Michelle's youngest sister, the newest addition to the reunited family, having been located in Little Rock, Arkansas, eight months earlier. Less than a year old when the Walker siblings had been orphaned and separated, Lindsay had been adopted by a couple with two sons. Very close to her adopted family and quite content with her life in Little Rock, Lindsay had been hesitant about a reunion with siblings she'd never known about. The man she'd been dating at the time, now her husband, had tried to talk her out of it, as had her adopted brothers, who'd felt threatened by the appearance of her long-missing biological siblings.

Since then, however, both families had formed a tentative, positive relationship, their mutual affection for Lindsay proving a strong bond between them. Lindsay seemed quite capable of happily balancing two very nice families.

"How is Lindsay?" Taylor asked.

"She's fine. She and Nick are talking about becoming a foster family, though they'd also like to have children of their own, eventually."

Taylor could easily picture Lindsay, a junior-high teacher, and Nick, a pediatrician and former foster child himself, providing a disciplined, yet loving and secure home for troubled children with nowhere else to go.

"Now that the pleasantries are out of the way," Michelle continued casually, "why don't you tell me about this fascinating man you spent the weekend with. And then explain, if you can, why you haven't told me, your best friend in the whole world, anything about him before this."

Taylor jerked the receiver away from her ear and stared at it in shock. *How on earth...?*

Very slowly, she brought it back and asked, "How did you know?"

"Erika was on a coffee break, so Maxie answered the phone when I called. She said I should ask."

Mentally promising all sorts of horrible retributions to her wickedly mischievous business partner, Taylor tried to think of a way to explain Ryan. "I just met him last Thursday. There hasn't been anything to tell."

"C'mon, Simmons, this is me you're talking to, remember? Who is he? What's going on? When do I get to meet him?"

"His name is Ryan, he's a salesman, and we went out a couple of times during the weekend. You'd like him, I think."

"Taylor, this is great! It's been so long since you've been interested in anyone. I can't wait to meet him!"

Taylor winced at her friend's enthusiasm. "Now, wait a minute. As I said, I hardly know him. He seems nice enough—" *Nice? Can't you do better than that, Simmons?* "—but it's a little too soon to start planning bridal showers, okay? Give me a chance to get to know him better."

"Is he cute?" Michelle asked teasingly, and Taylor had to smile at a sudden memory of their teen years, when boys had been the subject of so many of their lengthy telephone conversations.

"He's cute," she said lightly, picturing Ryan lying against her bed pillows. "Gold-streaked hair, crystal-blue eyes, a body to die for."

"This is getting better all the time."

Taylor's smile faded a bit. "He looks quite a bit like Dylan, actually, except for his hair and eye coloring. A *lot* like Dylan."

Michelle's pause was a startled one, full of unspoken concerns. "Does he?"

"Yes. It bothered me at first. I was a little—no, I was very much concerned about the inevitable comparisons."

"And now?"

"Now...I think of him as Ryan, not Dylan. The similarities are still there—disturbingly so, at times—but it's getting easier to keep the past distinguished from the present. Maybe, in time, it won't be a problem at all."

"I hope you're right," Michelle said slowly, and all the teasing had left her voice.

Taylor wasn't encouraged by her friend's tone. "Listen, Michelle, I'd love to talk longer, but we have a big meeting coming up in a few minutes, and I..."

"I'll let you go, then," Michelle said quickly. "You'll call?"

"I'll call. Don't worry about me."

"Right. Just like you've never worried about me, hmm?"

She had her there. Wincing, Taylor murmured something noncommital and disconnected the call.

She called to check on Ryan shortly before the client meeting was to begin, knowing she wouldn't be able to concentrate on work without knowing Ryan was all right. He sounded groggy, but assured her he was better.

"Have you had anything to eat?"

"I ate the muffin you brought me this morning."

"Nothing since?"

"I'm really not very hungry. Don't worry about it, Taylor. I'm fine. But thanks for caring."

Only slightly reassured, she hung up. And then spent the remaining time before the meeting worrying about how much she did care.

She'd known him only a few days. It was much too soon to be this deeply involved.

The last time she'd fallen this hard, this fast, it had ended in disaster. She couldn't help being afraid this relationship would end just as traumatically. And this time she might not recover at all.

Chapter Seven

The meeting lasted longer than Taylor had expected. It was after six when she finally walked through her door. She expected to find Ryan still flat on his back. Instead, she found him in the kitchen, dressed in jeans and a knit shirt. He stood at the stove, stirring a pan of bubbling, fragrant mixture with a wooden spoon.

"I made spaghetti sauce," he said when he noticed her standing in the doorway. "Hope that's okay with you."

"What are you doing up?" she demanded. "You should be in bed. You shouldn't be cooking dinner!"

"My back is much better," he assured her, though he still held himself a bit more stiffly than he had before. "I told you all I needed was some rest and a few muscle relaxers."

"But—"

"You probably want to change into comfortable clothes," he suggested, turning to his cooking. "I'll put the spaghetti and garlic bread on to cook. Dinner will be ready in about twenty minutes.''

"At least sit down and let me finish cooking dinner,'' she fretted.

He gave her a look that made her go silent. "I'll take care of it,'' he said, his tone quiet, pleasant and utterly emphatic.

Must be one of those male pride things, she decided, beating a hasty retreat to her bedroom. Far be it from her to impinge on his ego. Even if he *was* being ridiculous about it!

Ten minutes later she found herself standing in front of her closet, staring into it in indecision. Should she wear the new taupe vest and slacks set? The royal-blue silk camp shirt with black slacks? Or the hot pink knit romper she'd ordered from the Eddie Bauer catalog? Or . . .

She caught herself with a muffled exclamation of disgust. What the heck was she *doing?* She was about to eat spaghetti in her own kitchen. She didn't really expect the fashion police to make an unexpected appearance.

She chose the sleeveless madras dress because it was comfortable, she told herself firmly as she slipped it over her head. She smoothed it over her hips, noting only in a passing glance at the mirror that the bright plaid was quite flattering to her dark coloring, and that the loose, fluid garment nicely displayed her full bustline and slender hips. So what? She dressed to please herself, she argued silently, sliding her feet into brown leather huaraches. She was *not* dressing to please Ryan.

She paused on her way out of the room to throw one contemptuous glance at the full-length mirror. "Liar,'' she muttered to the shamefaced reflection there.

"You look nice,'' Ryan said the moment she joined him in the kitchen.

"Thank you. That sauce smells delicious. Do you cook often?"

"Only when I'm hungry," he quipped, scooping spaghetti onto two of her blue and coral stoneware plates. "How about you?"

"Only when I'm hungry and there's no one else to cook for me," she retorted, smiling as she slid into her seat. "It's not one of my favorite hobbies."

He ladled thick, fragrant red sauce over the pasta. "I don't mind it so badly. It's the cleaning up I don't like."

"Then I'll take k.p. tonight, since you did the cooking."

He slid carefully into his chair and picked up his fork, his posture still suspiciously straight. "You've got a deal."

Taylor resisted asking him again about his back. She knew how badly she hated being hovered over when she wasn't in top form, and suspected Ryan felt much the same way about it. Not to mention that pesky male ego thing.

Instead, she started to talk, telling him about her day, sharing a few amusing anecdotes about her spirited coworkers, finding herself conversing as easily with him as she had during their outing the day before. Why did it feel so right, so natural to be talking to Ryan over a casual dinner in her apartment?

As skillfully as he had before, Ryan kept the conversation focused on Taylor and her life, proving as evasive as ever about his own. He seemed particularly interested in hearing more about her friend Michelle and her recently reunited siblings, casually explaining that he'd heard a lot lately about families reunited after many years and he'd always wondered how such reunions worked out. "Always seemed to me," he added, "that it would end up being a bunch of strangers awkwardly trying to act like family."

"The reunions don't always work out," Taylor admitted. "Michelle and I have both read quite a bit about the recent trend you've noticed, and at first we were dismayed at the unhappiness that resulted from so many of the reunions."

She shrugged and added, "But then we decided that maybe those people expected too much. Michelle just wanted to meet her siblings, find out what they were like, see if there was any chance they could become friends after so many years of separation. She wasn't expecting instant love and devotion, didn't even know if she'd like them all. So, for her, it was a pleasant surprise when she and her brother and sisters grew so close, so quickly and relatively easily."

"Are there any family resemblances? Strange coincidences, that sort of thing?"

"Their coloring is strikingly similar—dark-brown hair, eyes such a dark blue they're almost navy. The sisters strongly resemble each other, especially Michelle and Lindsay. The oldest sister, Layla, has an old family portrait, and they all favor their mother, even Jared, though he's a very masculine version."

"So you've met all of them."

"Yes. And I like them."

"What are they like?"

Taylor looked up from her spaghetti, puzzled by his apparent interest in people who were strangers to him. "Why?"

He shrugged. "I want to get to know you better. Hearing about your friends tells me more about your life."

She supposed that made sense—in a rather odd sort of way. Not that she minded talking about her friends, of course. That seemed a safe enough topic to pursue with Ryan. Much safer than talking about themselves. So she chattered for a while about the Walker siblings.

Jared, the tough ex-Navy-seaman-turned-rancher. Gruff-natured, slow to smile, but utterly devoted to Cassie, his pregnant wife of less than a year, and Shane, his fifteen-year-old son from a previous marriage.

"Shane's a sweetheart," she added with a smile. "I'm seriously crazy about him. He had a rough childhood with an alcoholic mother while Jared was at sea, but he's turned out amazingly well. Funny and smart and polite. Michelle thinks he developed his charm as a means of getting attention when his mother and stepfather ignored him and as a way of avoiding trouble when he was old enough to be on his own."

And then there was Layla, the oldest Walker sister. A real estate agent married to an accountant, she lived in Fort Worth with their three young children. "She's very nice," Taylor said. "The sentimental, maternal type. She was the one who suffered most from being separated from her brothers and sisters, I think, though it was hard on Jared, too, since he says he always felt responsible for his younger siblings."

She mentioned Michelle's devotion to her pet charities and her joy in being reunited with the siblings she'd always longed for while growing up. Then Taylor gave him a quick verbal sketch of Lindsay and her husband, Nick.

There'd been three other brothers, she added—Miles and twins Joey and Bobby. Miles had died in a car accident several years before the others reunited; no one yet knew what had become of the twins, though Tony was still searching for them.

"Sounds like a pretty average family," Ryan commented, having said little else during the past fifteen minutes. "Your friend was lucky that the ones she found turned out to be respectable. It could have been a lot different."

"She's aware of that. It worried her a great deal, at first. Michelle has confided to me that she doesn't know how she would have felt about meeting either of her biological parents, had they still been living. She thinks that would have been much more difficult than meeting siblings who'd had no more control over their future than Michelle had."

Ryan's expression was distant, set. She wondered if he was remembering his own parents. "How old were you when your parents died?" she asked, wishing he'd tell her more about the unconventional childhood he'd hinted at before. She wanted so badly to know more about him.

Funny, she thought without any corresponding amusement, family was one thing Dylan would never talk about, either. He had always brushed off her questions about his home life, usually by reminding her that they'd have plenty of time to discuss all the "mundane details" in the future. The future they hadn't been allowed to share.

She'd always wondered if he'd planned to tell her all about his family and his past over dinner at the Vagabond. He'd said he had a lot to tell her. What would it have been? Would it have made any difference in their relationship? Had he...?

But she forced herself to push those old, futile questions away. This was Ryan, not Dylan, she reminded herself ruthlessly. And he still hadn't answered her question. Why did she seem so oddly drawn to such stubbornly reticent men? "Ryan?"

He made a show of swallowing a bite of spaghetti, as though he'd delayed answering only because he'd been otherwise occupied, rather than because of any reluctance to tell her more about himself. "I was very young when my parents died. Just a kid."

"Do you remember them?"

"I remember certain things."

"Pleasant things?" Taylor asked softly, sympathetically.

"Not particularly. Not about my father, anyway. As for my mother—" He paused, then shrugged. "It was a long time ago. I can hardly remember what she looked like."

There was a lot of pain and bitterness hidden behind Ryan's charming exterior, Taylor realized abruptly. Old hurts and more recent ones. Did he ever share them with anyone? Would he ever share them with her?

"Do you want any more to eat?" Ryan asked abruptly, bringing the personal conversation to an end. "There's plenty more sauce."

Accepting defeat—for the moment—Taylor politely refused, assuring him that she couldn't eat another bite. She sent him into the living room to rest and watch TV while she cleaned up the kitchen. She performed the familiar chores automatically, her mind spinning with questions about Ryan Kent.

Who was he, really? What had his past been like that he was so reluctant to talk about it? What did he want to do with his life? Had he ever been in love? Other than the obvious, exactly what—if anything—did he want from her?

So many questions. So few answers. So many strong, disturbing emotions in such a short time.

Oh, God, was it happening all over again?

* * *

Though Ryan insisted that she sit beside him on the couch after dinner, Taylor kept a careful distance between them as they watched the Monday night summer reruns. Ryan was unusually quiet, as well, though Taylor wasn't sure if he was reacting to her mood, his physical discomfort or troubling thoughts of his own.

As a noisy commercial blared from the set, Ryan stretched carefully and shifted on the couch. "It's getting late," he said, turning to face her. "Guess I'd better be going."

"You're leaving?" she asked, surprised.

"I still have a hotel room," he reminded her. "And, as you can see, my back is much better."

"Will you be taking another muscle relaxer tonight?"

"Probably. One more couldn't hurt."

"I don't like to think of you staying alone when you're taking that strong medication," she fretted.

"It wouldn't—"

"—be the first time," she finished with him, impatiently. "I know. But there's no need for you to be alone this time. Why don't you just stay here another night? I really don't mind sleeping on the couch again."

"I don't want to be any more trouble to you," Ryan argued stubbornly.

"Ryan, you're hardly any trouble. You're so independent, it's almost annoying—heck, you even cooked dinner. There's no reason for you to leave tonight."

"There is one," Ryan said, his eyes narrowed, jaw tight.

She cocked her head, searching his face with wary eyes. "What?"

"This," he murmured, and reached for her.

Startled, Taylor stiffened at first, her hands coming up to his chest. To push him away, or draw him closer? Even she didn't know for sure. Her lips clung to his, and she responded to the kiss with a hunger she'd been trying to repress all evening—without a great deal of success, apparently.

He finally lifted his head, drawing a deep, ragged breath. "That's why I'd better go," he muttered, his hands tight on her shoulders.

Her breathing was no steadier than his. "But your back—"

"Right. I don't want to start something I'm not entirely sure I can finish. It was hard enough to stay away from you last night—and I could hardly move then."

She wasn't sure whether to be gratified by the unmasked desire in his eyes or dismayed by the arrogance of his assumption that something *would* happen if he stayed tonight. Didn't he give her credit for willpower of her own?

And then, glancing down at the way she'd plastered herself against his chest during that one long kiss, she ruefully admitted that she couldn't really blame him if he didn't. It had proven impossible for her to resist Ryan from the beginning, as hard as she had tried.

She drew herself abruptly out of his arms, putting several cautious inches between them. But the thought of him driving himself to a lonely hotel room, taking a strong pill and falling into a drugged sleep with no one there to check on him made her bite her lip anxiously. "I don't want you to be alone tonight," she repeated. "Stay, Ryan. Nothing will happen."

He raised a skeptical eyebrow. Something about the way he looked at her made her chin lift defiantly.

"Nothing will happen," she repeated firmly, "because we won't let it. Will we?"

His mouth twitching in response to her stern challenge, he shrugged one shoulder. "If you say so."

"I say so."

He nodded. "Then I'll stay, if it makes you feel more comfortable. But I really would be fine on my own."

"I'm sure you would," she said coolly. "But there's no need to put that to the test tonight."

"Whatever you say, sweetheart."

"And *don't* call me sweetheart," she snapped, shoving herself to her feet. "I'm going to get my things out of the bedroom. I think I'll turn in early. You should, too."

"Yes, ma'am," he murmured, unable to disguise the amusement he was trying to hold back.

She was too annoyed that he was laughing at her to be gratified that the smile had finally returned to his beautiful eyes.

Taylor talked to Michelle again the next afternoon. Michelle had called the office on the pretext of inviting Taylor to a family dinner on Sunday, though her real objective soon became clear. "Why don't you bring Ryan with you?" she asked a bit too casually. "I'd love to meet him."

"I'm sure you would," Taylor responded wryly, shaking her head in exasperation at Michelle's well-intentioned prying. "Are you going to get his name, bank balance and past job history while he's there?"

"Why, Taylor, I don't—"

"Just tell me you haven't got that private-eye husband of yours doing a background search on him," Taylor begged, only half teasing.

"Don't be silly. Of course I haven't," Michelle retorted, then added, "you haven't given me enough information about him to start a background check."

Taylor groaned.

Michelle laughed. "I'm sorry, Taylor. I know I'm being overprotective. But I'd like to meet the guy who has you acting so uncharacteristically bemused."

Bemused. Yes, Taylor thought, that pretty well summed up her current condition. Bemused, bewitched, befuddled, bedazzled. Was there a "be" word that meant terrified? Because she was that, too. "I don't know, Michelle. He might not want to come. He might not even be in town by Sunday. He hasn't said how long he plans to stay."

"Well, if he's still around, maybe you'll want to bring him. The invitation remains open."

"All right. Regardless of whether Ryan's with me or not, I'll be there," Taylor promised with a smile, looking forward to another afternoon with Michelle and her nice family.

But her smile faded soon after she'd hung up the phone. *Would* Ryan still be around by Sunday?

And how much would she miss him if he'd moved on by then?

Just how deeply had she already gotten involved with this man? How badly was she going to be hurt this time?

Ryan guided the beige rental car aimlessly through the streets of Dallas, no destination in mind, no reason to be wasting gasoline except that he couldn't have stayed cooped up in Taylor's apartment any longer and hadn't wanted to return to his hotel quite yet. A heavy bank of gray clouds rolled in from the west, dimming the afternoon light, seeming to match his mood. His mouth was set in a grim line, his fingers clenched tightly around the steering wheel.

He was still furious with himself for stupidly wrenching his back and putting Taylor in the position of having to take care of him for two days. It didn't do much for his ego to have been all but incapacitated in front of a woman he'd been trying to impress! But Taylor had handled the situation beautifully, reacting with such generous sympathy and acceptance that he'd fallen even harder for her.

He knew the smartest thing to do would be to head for the outskirts of town, get out of Dallas and out of Texas without giving himself time to change his mind. He'd stirred up enough trouble here already, landed himself in a big enough mess as it was. How much worse would it get if he stayed? How much more painful would it become? For himself—for Taylor—for the others?

Yet each time he found himself getting close to the Dallas city limits, he turned the wheel, still aimlessly driving but remaining in town, held there as though by an invisible force screen in one of the science-fiction thrillers he enjoyed reading. Every time he tried to leave, the thought of Taylor drew him back.

Dammit. What was he going to do? How was he going to tell her the truth? How badly would she hate him when she found out he'd been lying to her?

"If there's one thing I detest, it's a liar and a sneak," she'd said. And Ryan was both.

He scowled more deeply when he realized that his haphazard twists and turns had brought him into Michelle's exclusive neighborhood. An accident? Surely he knew himself better than to even try to believe that.

He slowed on her street, and braked at the curb, staring glumly at the imposing Tudor. Why the hell didn't he just stop, knock on the door, get this whole thing out in the open? For everyone?

He'd never realized he was such a coward. Funny, Joe had always accused him of being *too* reckless and impulsive.

He doubted that even Joe would recognize his behavior now.

Muttering a curse between clenched teeth, he slammed his foot on the accelerator and sped away, still uncertain of his destination but resignedly certain he'd end up on Taylor's doorstep.

He didn't see the curtain move in one of the many gleaming windows of the mansion he left behind.

Taylor was disappointed to return home that evening and find Ryan gone. She was even more perturbed at the extent of that disappointment. She'd known him only a few days, after all, and he'd spent only a couple of nights in her bed. Her apartment really shouldn't feel so empty without him in it.

The worst part was the nagging fear that she'd never see him again. Was he gone? Would he have left Dallas without a goodbye? He wouldn't have been that rude, that thoughtless. Would he?

Her breath escaped in a sigh of relief when she walked into her bedroom and saw the bag sitting on the floor at the foot of her bed. He wouldn't have left without his things. He'd be back.

It really shouldn't matter so much.

She'd just changed into navy slacks and a jaunty, nautically styled top when the doorbell chimed. Taking a deep breath, she smoothed suddenly damp palms over her slacks. "Who is it?"

"Ryan."

She opened the door. He stood on the doorstep, holding flowers again—coral-colored roses, this time. A dozen of them. She couldn't resist burying her face in them when he handed them to her. "They're beautiful."

"I wanted to do something to show you how much I appreciate your taking care of me the last couple of days."

"It wasn't necessary, but thank you."

"You're welcome."

They stood there, looking at each other, an awkward silence growing between them. Taylor hurried to fill it. "I'll just put these in water," she said, taking a quick step backward. "It will only take a minute. Can I get you anything while I'm in the kitchen?"

"No. Thanks."

She'd expected him to stay in the living room. Instead, he followed her into the kitchen, which seemed to shrink when he entered it. Taylor felt suddenly awkward as she fumbled in a cabinet for a cut glass vase, filled it with water and arranged the roses and greenery in it. Ryan watched her silently.

"How's your back?" she asked, anxious to break the mounting tension.

"Much better."

"Good. Are you hungry? I'm sure I can find something..."

"Why don't we go out for dinner tonight?"

Going out sounded like the best idea she'd heard in a long time—preferably some place busy and noisy. "Sure. Fine," she said heartily. "I'll get my purse."

She moved toward the kitchen doorway. He stood in her way. He didn't step aside as she approached. She looked at him in question, wondering if there was something else he wanted to say. She started to ask, but the question was abruptly smothered beneath Ryan's mouth.

The kiss was long and heated. Thorough. By the time it finally ended, Taylor thought it was a miracle that her knees hadn't buckled. She didn't feel at all steady as she pulled herself out of his arms.

"I'll, uh, I'll go get my purse," she said again, and hurried past him into the safety of the other room.

Taylor directed Ryan to a trendy, popular seafood place close to her apartment. The rain that had threatened all day finally let loose just as they got out of the car. Ryan grabbed Taylor's hand and they dashed across the parking lot, laughing as they entered the noisy, crowded lobby.

Ryan ran a hand through his hair, dislodging shimmering drops of water; Taylor blinked raindrops from her eyelashes, knowing her short haircut would quickly dry. Their breathless laughter eased the tension between them, giving them a chance to relax and enjoy their dinners.

Because of the noise level in the popular restaurant, conversation was necessarily light and impersonal, consisting mostly of brisk banter and shared laughter. The food was excellent—rather surprisingly so in view of the decor, which could only be called "tacky tropical." Plastic palm trees, pink flamingos, gaudy flower prints. When she slid into her chair, Taylor swallowed a gulp at the uncomfortable reminders of her time in the Caribbean with Dylan.

Had she chosen this restaurant deliberately—if subconsciously—to remind herself of what had happened the last time she'd gotten involved with a dangerously attractive, stubbornly mysterious man? Was this her way of keeping a safe distance between herself and Ryan, at least until she knew more about him, better understood her powerful responses to him?

Or was it just a bizarre coincidence, after all? She put the questions firmly out of her mind, determined to enjoy the evening and Ryan's charming companionship.

A large screen TV in one corner of the room played back-to-back *Gilligan's Island* reruns, eliciting occasional hoots of amusement or derision from diners. Taylor laughed until she had to wipe her streaming eyes at Ryan's exaggeratedly grave analysis of the program and its social ramifications—especially his interpretation of the relationship between the Skipper and his "little buddy."

"I always thought it strange that the only woman getting any action on that island was the old society matron," Taylor quipped. "Especially considering how attractive the other two women were."

"You can bet I wouldn't be as noble as the professor if you and I were stranded on a deserted island," Ryan assured her with a rakish smile.

Laughing, she plucked a hot pink plastic orchid from the center of the tiny table and held it up to her ear. "Think you'd like me in a grass skirt and coconut shells, do you?"

Ryan started to make a teasing retort but suddenly went quiet, his gaze riveted on the flower in her hand, his brow creasing in a frown.

Taylor lowered the flower in confusion, wondering why he'd suddenly stopped smiling. "Ryan? Is anything wrong?"

He blinked and shook his head, as though shaking off a disturbing feeling. "No. Nothing. You just—"

"Can I show you our dessert tray?" a perky waitress inquired from beside him, interrupting whatever he might have said.

Ryan and Taylor both declared themselves much too full for dessert. Ryan paid for their dinners—Taylor offered to pay this time, which he firmly refused—and they made their way to the lobby, where they discovered that the rain was still falling steadily outside. "I'll go get the car," Ryan offered. "No need for both of us to get wet."

So, maybe it was sexist and outdated—but Taylor liked the pampering, anyway, just as she always secretly appreciated having doors opened for her and chairs held. The convoluted workings of the modern, liberated female mind, she thought wryly as she waited for Ryan's beige sedan to pull up at the front of the restaurant.

Since there was no umbrella in Ryan's rental car, they both had to brave the elements again to reach Taylor's apartment. Damp and disheveled, they entered in a rush, Ryan closing the door behind them. The apartment seemed very quiet and empty after the clamor of the restaurant.

"Guess I'll get my things and head back to the hotel," Ryan said after a moment. "I have a few phone calls I need to make tonight."

Taylor was aware of strongly mixed feelings of relief and disappointment as Ryan disappeared into the bedroom to get his bag. She told herself it was better for him to go tonight. She couldn't help remembering how empty her apartment had seemed earlier; how much worse would it be after he'd spent even more time there?

"Do you have everything?" she asked when he reappeared, bag in hand.

He nodded. "I think so."

"Even your gun?" The question left her mouth before she'd realized she was going to ask it. Biting her tongue, she berated herself. That gun had apparently been nagging at her subconscious more than she'd realized.

Ryan's eyebrows lifted.

"I wasn't going through your things," she hurried to assure him. "Your bag wasn't zipped when I picked it up and several things spilled out. I couldn't help noticing the gun. It's, um, not something I could have overlooked."

"When was this?"

"In your hotel room, when I went for your medicine."

"And you're just now asking me about the gun? That was two days ago. You hardly knew me."

She didn't point out that she knew little more about him now. It didn't really seem necessary.

Ryan sighed and shook his head. "I hope you're not always this trusting."

"I'm not," she said curtly, stung by the unspoken accusation of naïveté. "Why *do* you carry a gun?"

"For security. I travel a lot, spend time in a lot of big cities and strange hotel rooms. I figure it never hurts to be cautious."

The mention of his traveling reminded her of another question that had plagued her that day. "How long will you be in Dallas, Ryan? You haven't said."

He made a vague gesture with his free hand. "I don't have any concrete plans. Since meeting you, I haven't been in any hurry to leave," he confessed. He stepped closer, raising that same hand to her cheek. "I want to get to know you better, Taylor. Give you a chance to get to know me. I don't want to interfere with your plans, but will you make time to spend with me if I stay in Dallas for a while?"

She bit her lip, looking mutely at him.

He smiled reassuringly. "I'm not trying to push for anything more than a few dates, if that's all you're interested in. I know you still have reservations about getting involved with me, and I'll try not to rush you into anything you aren't ready for. I just want to spend more time with you, Taylor. Is that okay with you?"

"Yes," she said, because she couldn't bring herself to send him away, even if she did still have too many questions and too few answers about this intriguing man.

He kissed her quickly, breaking the contact before it could develop into anything more tempting. "Good. Is it okay for me to call you at your office tomorrow?"

"Yes."

He nodded and stepped toward the door. "Good night, Taylor. Sleep well—I'm sure you'll be glad to spend a night in your own bed again."

She thought wistfully of how much nicer that bed would be if Ryan was still in it.

He sighed lightly, as though thinking something along the same lines, then gave her a crooked smile and let himself out.

"Oh, Simmons," Taylor murmured into the lonely silence left behind him. "What the *hell* are you doing?"

She couldn't answer her own question, of course. She simply didn't know the answer.

Chapter Eight

"Well, it's about time. I've been trying to reach you for the past three days."

The telephone had been ringing when Ryan had let himself into his hotel room. "Hello, Miller," he said without enthusiasm, dropping onto the edge of one of the beds.

"That's all you're going to say?" his employer demanded. "'Hello, Miller?'"

"How's the weather in Denver?" Ryan asked politely, just to annoy the usually unflappable security expert.

Miller's gusty exhale proved Ryan had succeeded. "All right, forget it. How's it going for you?" he asked, more conciliatorily. "Have you made contact with the Walker family yet?"

"No."

"You've found them, haven't you?"

"I know where they all are. I just haven't decided whether I should do anything about it."

"Joe's still opposed to a meeting?"

"Joe thinks it's a mistake to dig up the past. He thinks it would only get sticky and awkward."

"And you?"

"I'm still making up my mind," Ryan answered, deciding not to mention that he'd been too deeply distracted lately to give much thought to a meeting with the Walker siblings.

"Think it's going to take you much longer to decide?"

"Why? What have you got?"

"Another possible insurance fraud case. Guy claims he lost a couple million dollars worth of paintings and sculpture in a fire, but rumor has it he's got the stuff stashed to sell on the black market. Right up your alley."

"Maybe you'd better get someone else this time. How about Kajinski? She's good."

"She's good. But you're the best."

Ryan's mouth twisted at the frank assessment. "Why, gee, Miller. I didn't know you cared."

Miller's rejoinder was curt and mildly obscene.

Ryan laughed, then grew serious again. "I need a few more weeks, Miller."

Miller could have insisted, of course. He *was* the boss, though Ryan considered himself a free-lance employee. Ryan wasn't surprised when Miller sighed and muttered, "All right. Let me know when you're ready to come back to work. I'd hate to lose both you and Joe."

Ryan didn't have any reassurances to offer. He couldn't be absolutely certain that he *would* be returning to work for Miller. There were several variables involved. He suspected that Taylor was an all-too-important one of those variables. Would she be interested in becoming involved with a man who spent so much time on the road, who never knew where he'd be assigned from one project to the next? Who'd been known to risk his life on more than one occasion in pursuit of those assignments?

But if not this career, then what? What else was he qualified for? What did he have to offer *any* woman— especially a smart, successful, independent businesswoman like Taylor Simmons?

The phone rang again only minutes after Miller disconnected. This time Ryan knew who was on the other end.

"Where the hell have you been?" Joe barked.

"Out," Ryan answered succinctly. "Why?"

"How the hell am I supposed to enjoy my honeymoon when you keep disappearing?"

"I can take care of myself, Joe. You just concentrate on taking care of Lauren."

Typically, Joe ignored Ryan's peevish tone. "Are you all right?" he asked more quietly.

Ryan shook his head. Joe was a natural worrier, and had always considered it his duty to watch out for his only slightly younger brother. Ryan appreciated his brother's concern, but it did get exasperating at times, as even Lauren had discovered when Joe had first taken responsibility for her—first as her bodyguard, then as her husband. Ryan and Lauren had discussed Joe's tendency toward overprotection—and had come to the rueful conclusion that there was absolutely nothing they could do to change him, even if they wanted to.

"I twisted my back again Sunday," he finally admitted. "It was painful—kept me off my feet for a day or so—but it's better now. I had my muscle relaxers with me."

"Dammit, I knew you were hurt."

"It wasn't serious."

"I knew that, too."

Ryan wasn't surprised. They'd always known, somehow, when the other was in trouble. "Then why the third degree?"

"Guess I just needed to hear you say it wasn't serious."

What could Ryan say in response to that? He knew it wasn't easy for Joe to express his feelings. "I'm okay, Joe."

"Good. So where *have* you been?"

"With Taylor."

"Michelle's friend."

"Right."

"You still remind her of the dead boyfriend?"

Ryan winced at the blunt question. "I don't know. We don't talk about it."

"Maybe you should."

"Yeah. Eventually," Ryan agreed reluctantly. It wasn't something he looked forward to, though he knew it was inevitable if he and Taylor were to have any sort of a future together.

"What about the others?"

"I still haven't made contact. I was trying to decide what to do about them when I threw my back out."

"Find out anything more about them?"

"Some." He outlined what Taylor had told him about the Walker siblings, finding it quite easy to remember almost word for word what she'd said about each of them.

"So both Jared and Shelley are about to become parents" was all Joe said when Ryan finished.

"Yeah. Jared for the second time. And Layla's got three of her own. The family's getting bigger all the time."

"Wonder what the old man would think about that?"

Ryan's mouth twisted. "Who knows what the old man thought about *anything?* Mama would have been pleased, though. Maybe."

"Yeah. Maybe."

"We're going to have to see them, Joe. You know that, don't you?"

He half expected Joe to argue. Instead, his brother sighed and said, "You're probably right."

Ryan blinked. "What was that again?"

"Lauren's still pushing to meet them. She seems to think it's important for me—for us—to face our past so we can get on with our future."

"I'm beginning to agree with her," Ryan murmured, his mind filling with old, painful memories he'd tried to suppress for twenty-five years. Memories that had haunted him through many long, disturbing nights. Memories that had made him wary of getting close to anyone else for so long, that seemed to shadow every relationship he'd tried to establish.

Would a reunion with his long-separated siblings enhance his budding relationship with Taylor—or destroy it?

"Have you told Taylor yet?" Joe asked, as though reading Ryan's mind. Ryan was relieved that their rapport didn't extend quite that far.

"No. As far as she still knows, I'm Ryan Kent, a security consultant from Colorado. She's probably going to be furious when she finds out I haven't been completely honest with her."

"What are you going to do now?"

"I don't know," Ryan confessed, wearily rubbing his aching forehead.

"Lauren and I were planning to leave here late next week. We can come to Dallas if you want, face them together."

That would give Ryan another week to further his relationship with Taylor, maybe find a chance to break the truth to her in his own time and his own way, with hopes of minimizing the damage. "Yeah. I think that would be best," he agreed slowly. "We'll face them together."

While he would face Taylor alone.

Taylor had been given a couple of tickets to a local comedy club. She mentioned them to Ryan when he called her office Wednesday afternoon. "Would you like to go tonight?" she asked, already looking forward to seeing him again.

"Sounds like fun. I enjoy stand-up comics," he said.

"So do I. Want me to pick you up at your hotel?"

"No. I'll meet you at your place."

"All right. See you at seven, then."

She disconnected the call with an unsettling mixture of anticipation, nervousness and excitement. She hadn't felt like this since she was a schoolgirl, she thought with a rueful shake of her head. She really should hate it—but it felt quite nice, actually. "You've definitely lost it, Simmons," she muttered, reaching for a pen.

"What have you lost this time?" Jay asked, entering her office just in time to overhear her self-directed comment.

She shook her head. "Nothing. What's up?" she asked, studying his expression curiously. It wasn't unusual for Jay to look glum—Maxie claimed that Glum was his middle name—but this time he looked more troubled than usual. "Is something wrong with one of the accounts?"

"No. Business is booming," he said, dropping into a chair. "We're meeting with more success than I could have even imagined this time a year ago."

"Then why don't you sound happier about it?"

He scowled. "It's Maxie."

Taylor rolled her eyes, not surprised at the reason for his bad mood. "What about her? Have you two been fighting again?"

"Are you aware that she's promised LuCon a full-blown campaign by the first of next month? How the hell does she expect us to do that, hmm? Do you know what will happen to the great reputation we're developing if she goes around blithely making promises we can't possibly keep? I've told her over and over that she's too impulsive and too impractical, but will she ever listen to a word I say? No. And not only that—"

"We'll make the deadline, Jay. It's going to be a fairly simple campaign. Maxie and I have already discussed several ideas with Mr. Lueken and he's—"

"Not to mention the way she's been spending money. I told her to get a small, practical coffeemaker for the office. Have you *seen* that ostentatious yuppie monstrosity she hauled in here?"

"'Yuppie' is getting outdated, Jay. You really should stay current on your slang." Taylor didn't expect to have her murmur heeded, so she wasn't perturbed when Jay continued with his diatribe for several more minutes. Sometime during the middle of it, she picked up her pen, pulled a legal pad in front of her and began to write, her thoughts divided between her job, Jay's complaints and her date with Ryan that evening.

Of the latter two, Ryan threatened to be the more serious distraction from her work.

"That man drives me insane!" Maxie announced later that afternoon, as Taylor was tugging her purse out of her desk drawer and preparing to leave the office for the day.

Taylor tried not to be too obvious about looking at her watch as Maxie stormed through the doorway. She didn't want to be rude to her partner, of course, but she wanted to get home in time to change before Ryan arrived. "I assume you're talking about Jay."

"Of *course* I'm talking about Jay! Who else is so utterly, completely, stubbornly infuriating? Can you believe the way he's carrying on about that stupid coffeemaker?"

"Maxie, we did agree that Jay would be responsible for office management, including budgeting and expenses. He's only trying to do his job."

"One would think I'd cleaned out the bank accounts, the way he's acting. We're turning a profit, Taylor. We can afford a decent coffeemaker."

Taylor started to point out that there was a difference between decent and extravagant, but decided not to waste her precious time. Maxie would never agree.

"Maybe Jay should handle the purchases himself from now on," she suggested instead. "Or suggest a maximum amount to pay for a particular item, so it wouldn't be such a nasty shock to him. Remember, he's used to thinking of us as a struggling new agency—which we are, by the way, despite a few early successes—and he doesn't want us to overextend. I agree with him that it's better to take it slowly and carefully at first."

"But a *coffeemaker,*" Maxie wailed. "It's not exactly a major purchase."

Taylor bit her tongue to keep from pointing out that Maxie had paid more for that coffeemaker than some people paid for a month's rent. She looked again at her watch.

"You're in a hurry," Maxie said abruptly, proving she wasn't as oblivious as Taylor had hoped.

"Well—yes, a little," Taylor admitted.

"You have a date with Ryan?"

"Uh, yes, I do."

Maxie cocked her copper head in blatant speculation. "Sounds like this thing is getting serious."

"Don't be ridiculous. I hardly know him."

"Hmm."

Taylor's fingers tightened defensively around her purse strap. "What's that supposed to mean?"

Maxie looked innocent—or tried to.

"Nothing."

"Look, it's just a date, okay? Even *you* have dates occasionally. Do I carry on like this when you do?"

"*I'm* not the one who's carrying on," Maxie pointed out. "All I said was *hmm.*"

"It was the way you said it," Taylor muttered, realizing her overreaction was providing her friend with a great deal of amusement at her expense.

Maxie stopped smiling. "It *is* getting serious, isn't it, Taylor?"

Sighing, Taylor ran a hand through her short hair, not caring that she left it in rumpled spikes around her face. "Yes. I think it is."

It was the first time she'd admitted aloud that her feelings for Ryan were growing more intense and more complicated with each passing day. Just hearing her own words terrified her.

Maxie patted her hand. "Don't look so worried, Taylor. Everything will work out."

Taylor wished Maxie had sounded just a bit more confident.

"I still think the second comic was the best," Taylor insisted as she and Ryan entered her apartment much later that evening. "That whole routine about mothers giving their daughters the birds-and-bees talk for the first time was really funny."

"Yeah. She seemed to appeal strongly to the women in the audience. But that Sledge guy was a riot," Ryan rebutted. "His characterization of a sleazy, fast-talking nineteen-forties private eye was really great."

"Okay, so he was more of a man's comic. But—"

Ryan's long, thorough kiss made her argument fizzle into a muffled moan of pleasure.

"What was that for?" she asked breathlessly, when he finally raised his head.

His grin was just this side of wicked. "Because you look so cute when you argue. And because I haven't kissed you in hours."

"Cute?" she repeated, planting her hands on her hips. "I *hate* being called cute."

He chuckled and pulled her close again. "How about gorgeous? Or sexy? Or wildly desirable?"

"Only if you mean it," she murmured, sliding her arms around his neck and giving him an exaggeratedly coy smile.

He slid one hand to the small of her back to press her against him. "I mean every word of it," he assured her deeply, then kissed her again.

A quiver of excitement rippled through her as the embrace heated. Her body throbbed with needs she'd denied too long, desires Ryan stirred so expertly. It had been so long since she'd felt like this, so long since she'd wanted this badly.

She could resist physical temptation—she had been resisting for a long time. Having known real love, she hadn't been able to settle for casual sex. But this wasn't casual. And it was much more than physical.

For two years she'd thought it impossible that she'd ever care for a man again. Now she realized she'd been wrong. Ryan had come to mean a great deal to her in the brief time she'd known him. Just as Dylan had become so desperately important to her in the few weeks she'd spent with him.

Why did she fall so hard, so fast? Was this affair destined to end as unhappily, if not as tragically?

Very slowly, she pulled her mouth from his, racked with doubts about the wisdom of carrying this relationship further, aching with the need to do so. Her gaze met his, and she made no effort to hide her turmoil from him.

"Taylor," he murmured, his voice raw. "I want you."

"I know," she whispered.

"I know it's too soon—"

"Probably."

"I'll go, if you want."

Her eyes didn't waver from his. "I don't want you to go." She was proud of the steadiness of her voice, despite her nervousness.

His eyes widened, then narrowed. "You're sure?"

"Yes." She tightened her arms around his neck, pulling herself closer to him, her mouth inches from his. "I want you."

His fingers clenched convulsively at her hips. "Say my name," he muttered hoarsely, his breath warm against her face.

"Ryan." She brushed her mouth against his. "Ryan." She touched the tip of her tongue to his lower lip, savoring the taste of him. "Ryan. I want you. I want—"

He crushed her mouth beneath his, lifting her so tightly against his chest that she could hardly breathe. She didn't care.

She gasped when he swung her into his arms, her feet dangling inches off the floor. "Ryan!" She clutched his shoulders. "You'll hurt your back."

He was already moving toward the bedroom. "I know what I'm doing."

That she could believe. Never in her adult life had she fantasized about being carried to bed—but she found herself loving every minute of it. And when he lowered her to the pillows, she tugged him down with her with an eagerness that rather startled her.

"I want to take this slow," Ryan muttered, kissing her cheek, her ear, her throat. His hands swept restlessly over her body, her thin turquoise silk blouse and short black skirt proving little barrier to his seeking touch. "I want to make it last all night. But I don't know if I can."

"I don't know if I can wait, either," Taylor admitted ruefully, burying her fingers in his thick, gold-tipped brown hair "I want you so much."

"I want you, too. More than I've ever wanted anyone." His fingers worked skillfully at the buttons of her blouse. "It's been a long time for me, Taylor. A very long time. I guess you should know that."

"For me, too," she whispered, surprised by his admission, but not questioning his honesty. She was glad that this wasn't something he took lightly, either. "There's been no one for me since—"

He kissed her quickly, smothering the name. "Tonight, it's just us," he said, sliding a hand inside her blouse to cup one full, aching breast. "Taylor and Ryan."

She loved the sound of their names coupled on his lips. "Yes." She drew him closer, tugging at the fabric that separated them. "Just us."

Ryan took it as slowly as he could, undressing her one item at a time, pausing to thoroughly explore each area he uncovered before moving on to the next discovery. His clothing fell piece by piece to the floor beside the bed, discarded by Taylor's avid hands.

Ryan's self-control lasted only until the last garment had been tossed aside. And then, as though driven beyond control by that first full-length press of skin to skin, he shuddered and abandoned all effort to prolong the torment. His hands unsteady, his firm, tanned skin covered with a thin film of sweat, he caressed her feverishly, his lips and fingers racing over her writhing body. Taylor was with him all the way, her lips as hungry, her hands as greedy.

Made clumsy with passion, he fumbled with protection, muttering beneath his breath when the foil package proved stubborn, making Taylor laugh breathlessly at his impatience. And then her laughter turned to a gasp of delight when he surged into her.

She clung tightly to his shoulders, her body rocked by his fiery possession, her mind whirling with overwhelming pleasure, her heart filled with emotions she couldn't have vocalized had she tried. She couldn't even say his name, could only wrap herself around him and blindly follow as he led them both over the edge of sanity.

* * *

Ryan had begun to wonder if his heart rate and breathing would ever return to normal, if he'd ever fully recover from making love to Taylor. Had anything ever felt like that? Had *he* ever felt like that? If he had, he'd forgotten. And then he mentally flinched away from the unintentional reminder of those lost weeks in his past. His arms tightened around the warm, soft woman lying against him.

As if sensing his need for closeness, she snuggled closer, dropping a kiss on his shoulder. "Are you okay?" she asked, her voice deliciously husky.

"Better than okay," he assured her. "*Much* better."

"Your back?"

"Not even a twinge." Not that he'd have noticed if there had been.

"Good." She smoothed her hand lazily over his chest.

He liked having her touch him, liked having her next to him this way. This could definitely become addictive, he mused, toying with the short, soft hairs at her nape. Her fingers paused at a ridge of scar tissue just above his rib cage. He wondered if his scars bothered her. Not that she'd seemed repulsed by them earlier, he reasssured himself, uncharacteristically concerned about his appearance. His throat tightened when she bent her head to press a fleeting kiss on the scar, then nestled into his shoulder.

This was most definitely serious, he thought as his heart began to beat rapidly again in response to the tender gesture.

"Ryan?"

"Hmm?"

"Have you ever been in love?"

The question startled him. His thoughts turned again to those lost weeks before he'd been hurt, and the reports that he'd been deeply involved with a woman during that time. So deeply involved, so totally distracted from his assignment, that he'd almost gotten himself killed.

He flinched when Taylor's fingers brushed another scar, another physical reminder of those forgotten weeks. "I don't know," he answered as honestly as he could.

"You don't know?" She sounded puzzled.

"No." *Had* there been a woman? *Had* he loved her? Why the hell couldn't he remember her? How many hours had he struggled to see into those dark, hidden corners of his mind, only to be frustrated again and again by a total lack of recall of those weeks?

Taylor stirred against him, and he realized that his fingers had tightened on her shoulder, probably painfully. With a murmured apology, he quickly loosened them. "Why don't you know?" she persisted, lifting her head to look at him.

"Maybe because I just don't know what love is supposed to feel like," he said, brushing his knuckles against her soft cheek. "All I know is that I don't remember ever feeling for anyone else the way I feel about you. You're very special to me, Taylor. I'm crazy about you."

Was this love? Had he felt anything like this for the woman he'd forgotten? Would he ever feel like this again with any other woman? Somehow he doubted it. At the moment, he couldn't imagine being with any woman other than the one in his arms. Taylor.

Her eyes locked with his, Taylor brushed a strand of hair from his forehead, her fingertips lingering against his face. "I never thought I'd feel like this again," she whis-

pered, the words barely loud enough for him to hear.
"I'm a little scared to be feeling this much, this soon."

"I know," he murmured, understanding her fears all
too well.

"Just promise me one thing."

He moistened his lips. "What?"

She didn't look away, and her smoky gray eyes were
huge, vulnerable. Open. "Be honest with me. Whatever
you feel, whatever you want from me, tell me. I don't
want to have to guess, or to worry, or to try to read your
mind. I don't want to play games. I can't deal with that
now. Not with you."

Oh, hell. He swallowed hard, coming close to hating
himself at that moment. Why hadn't he just told her the
truth from the beginning? When had deception and subterfuge become such a part of his life that he hadn't even
considered honesty as a first option? Could she accept
that he'd been forced to live that way from the time he
was a kid, struggling to survive, rebelling against a huge,
slow-moving system that had not worked for him? That
he'd had so many names, so many identities, so many
roles to play that he no longer knew quite who he was or
what he wanted?

Could she understand his reluctance to confront a past
that held a great deal of bitterness and pain in addition
to those frightening blanks in his memory?

"Ryan?" She sounded wary, disturbed by his silence.

He tugged her head down to his for a long, tender,
soothing kiss. "I won't hurt you, Taylor," he promised
her, telling himself that he wasn't lying now. He would
never intentionally hurt her. He would make every effort
to find a way to tell her the truth without destroying
whatever confidence she'd found in him.

He felt as though he'd been looking for her all his life. He wasn't going to let her go without making every effort to convince her to give them a chance.

She was his now. And Ryan fully intended to convince her of that, no matter what it took.

Giving her no further opportunity for talk, he pulled her on top of him, his hands sweeping down her back to cup her bottom and fit her more securely against him. She gasped at the discovery that he wanted her again. Now. And then she threw herself wholeheartedly into cooperating with him, to their mutual satisfaction.

Ryan felt as though he'd had a very narrow escape. Yet he knew the respite was only temporary. The truth would have to come out before his relationship with Taylor could go much further.

Chapter Nine

It was Friday night before Taylor tentatively brought up the invitation to Michelle's house for lunch on Sunday. After two more evenings of being with Ryan, and two more blissful nights in his arms, she was beginning to feel just a bit more optimistic about their relationship. Not that anything had actually been said about their future, of course. But Ryan had treated her so specially, made love to her so tenderly and so passionately. He seemed content to be with her, in no apparent hurry to leave her. Surely his feelings for her were almost as serious as hers were for him.

Maybe this time, she thought with the first stirrings of wistful optimism. Maybe this time . . .

Oh, great. Now she was starting to think in Kander and Ebb song lyrics! What was this man *doing* to her?

"You've heard me talk about my friend Michelle," she reminded him as she sat next to him on her couch Friday evening, the late news blaring from the television screen.

"Several times," he agreed.

"She'd love to meet you," Taylor said, watching closely for his reaction.

She didn't miss the way he stiffened, though he tried to mask his reaction. "You've, uh, told her about me?" he asked, throwing her a quick, searching look.

"Of course. She's my best friend, Ryan. I told her I've been seeing someone very special. It's not as though we're trying to keep our relationship a secret—is it?"

"No. Of course not." He agreed just a bit too quickly. "I just didn't realize you'd mentioned me to your friends."

"Only Michelle and Maxie and Jay. They're my closest friends. And you've already met Maxie, so Michelle's getting impatient to meet you, too. She's invited us to lunch at her house Sunday. Her brother and sister and their spouses will also be there. I've already told you that they're all very nice. I think you'll enjoy meeting them."

"I'm not sure I can make it, Taylor. Maybe another time."

Her stomach tightened. "Why can't you make it this time?"

He shrugged, his attention apparently focused on the weather forecast currently airing on the television. "I have some things I need to do. This will give me a chance to get them done while you're visiting with your friends. Maybe you and I can get together Sunday evening."

He didn't want to meet her friends, she realized abruptly. Why?

Taylor's hands clenched in her lap as several unpleasant possibilities flashed through her mind.

He'd sworn he wasn't married, but his apparent reluctance to make their relationship more public was suspicious.

He'd said he didn't regard her as a temporary fling to amuse him while he was in town, but he wasn't acting as though he intended to become a permanent part of her life.

He'd said he was taking a few weeks' leave from his job, but now he claimed to have some things he needed to do. What things? Where did he go when they weren't together? Who was he with?

Dammit, she'd just started to trust him. He'd promised he wouldn't lie to her or play games with her. That he'd be honest with her. So why was he being so vague and evasive now?

He looked at her and sighed. "Taylor—"

She shrugged away when he would have touched her arm. "Forget I said anything. If you don't want to go, I'm certainly not going to insist."

"Don't be mad, sweetheart. It's nothing personal. I'm, uh, not very good in crowds of strangers," he explained, sounding as though he was hastily improvising. "I think it would be better for me to meet your friends one at a time. Why don't we have lunch with Maxie again—and Jay Stern, maybe. Then I'll meet Michelle and the others."

And when would Taylor meet Ryan's friends? As far as she knew, he didn't even have any. Certainly no one he'd ever mentioned, other than his brother, of course. Come to think of it, he'd never said anything about her meeting his brother, either. Nor had either of them suggested a meeting between Ryan and Taylor's parents.

She reminded herself hastily that she and Ryan had been seeing each other for only a week. Hardly long enough to start meeting family and making long-range plans. She wasn't quite ready for that next step herself.

Ryan was right, of course. Everything was moving too fast. They needed more time to get to know each other, to find out where their emotions were leading them before bringing other people into this.

She swallowed a sigh and touched his hand, noting that he was looking worried. "It's okay," she said with a forced smile. "I understand. I won't push you, Ryan. I promise."

She didn't miss the relief that flashed through his eyes. "Thanks, Taylor. I'm glad you understand."

She didn't fully understand. But she could be patient. For now.

Losing interest—feigned or otherwise—in the weather report, Ryan distracted her with a long, leisurely kiss. By the time they were forced to come up for air, Taylor had managed to overcome her disappointment with his refusal to join her Sunday.

He made love to her with a new urgency that night, and held her so tightly afterward that she almost wondered if she'd be bruised the next day.

No, she didn't completely understand him. Not yet. But she was trying.

They didn't leave her apartment Saturday. They hardly left the bed.

With no pretense of holding meaningful conversations or making any sort of plans beyond the present, they enjoyed each other with a deep, mutual hunger that seemed to have no limits. Driven to the kitchen by another sort of hunger late that afternoon, they raided the refrigerator, laughing like giddy teenagers as they constructed enormous sandwiches and wolfed them down greedily. And then they made love again, starting in the kitchen and slowly working their way back to the bed.

They spent the evening playing board games, swapping silly jokes, listening to the stereo. Later they shared a long, lazy bath—to Ryan's exaggerated dismay, Taylor insisted on adding scented bubble bath to the water—which, of course, led them back to bed.

Taylor had never felt more decadent, more sensual, more thoroughly enjoyed. It was as if the rest of the world had disappeared for the duration of that day, leaving her and Ryan in blissful solitude. If either of them thought of anyone else during those enchanted hours, no other names were mentioned. Taylor didn't even refer to her plans for the next afternoon, unwilling to let anything detract from this time with Ryan.

She would face tomorrow, and any worries that accompanied it, only when it became absolutely necessary.

Sitting on the end of the wildly rumpled bed, Taylor watched wistfully as Ryan fastened his belt around his slim waist Sunday morning. "You're sure you won't change your mind about going with me?" she couldn't resist asking. "I really think you'd enjoy it."

Ryan hesitated a moment before answering, and she thought she saw temptation mirrored in his expression. At least, she wanted to believe she did. But then he shook his head. "I don't think it's a very good idea today. But I'll meet your friends soon, sweetheart. That's a promise."

She wanted to argue, wanted to ask why he was being so stubborn, wanted to know what it was about a simple luncheon invitation that had him acting so jumpy and

strange. But she swallowed the words and told herself
again that she must be patient, as difficult as it was for
her.

Maybe he was simply shy about meeting a group of
strangers who'd probably submit him to a pretty close
inspection to judge if he was right for Taylor. She could
certainly understand that—if Ryan was the shy type.
Which he wasn't.

She sighed.

He leaned over and brushed his mouth across hers.
"I'm sorry, Taylor."

She managed a fairly nonchalant shrug. "It's okay."

"I'll make this up to you."

She smiled and touched his cheek. "I'm pretty sure you
already have," she replied with a meaningful look at the
bed.

His smile was bright, yet still faintly apologetic. "I
haven't even begun," he assured her deeply, and then
kissed her again.

He drew back with obvious reluctance. "I'd better go
and let you get ready. I'll be back this evening—unless
you'd like some time to yourself tonight." He ended with
an upward inflection, making it a question. "I'd certainly understand if you—"

"I'll see you tonight," she cut in firmly. Already she
hated the thought of spending a night without him.

*You are in such trouble, Simmons. How did you ever
let this go so far?* But she had no answer to her mental
question, of course. All she knew was that she'd fallen in
love for only the second time in her life. And, also for the
second time, she'd fallen for a man who was rather mysterious, definitely unpredictable and unlike any of the
other, more ordinary men she knew.

Was she a glutton for punishment, or what?

* * *

Michelle opened her front door in response to Taylor's ring, not waiting for Betty, the housekeeper, to answer the summons. "Hi, Taylor. Oh—you're alone."

Taylor frowned. "You could at least try to hide your disappointment."

Michelle laughed and drew her friend through the doorway. "You know I'm delighted to see you. I was just hoping to meet this mystery man in your life."

Taylor managed not to wince at the term "mystery man." She didn't want Michelle, an admitted worrier, to know quite how little Taylor really knew about the man with whom she'd become so deeply involved in such a short time. "Ryan had other plans for today," she explained casually. "He wanted me to thank you for the invitation and to assure you he's looking forward to meeting you soon. I've told him a lot about you, of course."

"So why haven't you told *me* more about *him?*" Michelle demanded.

"Now, *tesoro*, you assured me you weren't going to pry into Taylor's love life today," an indulgent male voice chided, making both women look around—Michelle with a guilty smile.

Tall, dark-haired, dark-eyed Tony D'Alessandro greeted Taylor with an affectionate smile and a light kiss on the cheek. "I'm glad you could make it today," he said. "You look great. New outfit?"

"Yes." Taylor did a runway turn to show off the white T-shirt dress, which sported colorful sequined flowers across the front. "Like it?"

"Very much. Maybe Michelle can borrow it sometime—when she has a waistline again."

Michelle gasped in exaggerated outrage and punched her husband's arm, heatedly pointing out that she had not yet begun to show signs of her early pregnancy. Taylor laughed, grateful to Tony for distracting Michelle from questions about Ryan and suspecting that he had done so deliberately. Maybe Tony sensed that Taylor wasn't quite ready to talk about her tentative new love affair.

It turned out that Taylor was the last of the invited guests to arrive. Michelle ushered her into the large den where the others waited. Taylor greeted each of them fondly. "It's good to see you, Cassie," she told a petite, copper-haired, obviously pregnant woman about her own age. "How are you feeling?"

"I've never felt better," Cassie assured her with a brilliant smile, patting her bulging stomach. "Jared says pregnancy must suit me."

"It certainly seems to," Taylor agreed, eyeing the happiness reflected in Cassie's glowing face and mirrored in her lean, tanned husband's possessive navy eyes as he slipped an arm around his wife's shoulders and greeted Taylor. What would it be like, Taylor wondered, to share that sort of commitment, and to be facing that awesome responsibility of parenthood? Would she ever know for herself?

She tried to hide her unsettling thoughts as she chatted for a moment with Jared and his engaging teenage son, Shane, then turned to Michelle's older sister, Layla Samples, and her quiet, friendly, endearingly chubby husband, Kevin. "How are the children?" she asked them.

"They're fine," Layla replied with a mother's pride. "They're spending a week with Kevin's parents in Waco. We miss them, of course—but we've enjoyed having some time to ourselves for a change," she added with a smile for her husband, which he returned warmly.

Would any man ever smile at her in quite that way? Taylor couldn't help asking herself. Would Ryan?

And then she irritably chided herself for being so obsessed with him that she couldn't even spend a few hours with her friends without dwelling on thoughts of him. Honestly, what had happened to her independence? Not to mention her pride!

There was one other guest for lunch. Taylor greeted the handsome, dark-haired young man with a smile. "Well, if it isn't the young doctor. How's it going, Joe?"

"What's this I hear about you getting involved with some other guy behind my back?" he returned with a dramatic scowl. "I thought you were going to wait for me to finish my internship and residency so I could support you in style!"

Taylor couldn't help laughing, despite the pang that went through her at this reminder of Ryan. She was very fond of Tony's youngest brother, Joe D'Alessandro, who was two years her junior. He enjoyed teasing her and flirting with her, though neither of them had ever taken the flirting seriously. They were friends, nothing more. As handsome and charming as he was, Joe had never made Taylor react with the same flustered, sensual awareness she'd felt for Ryan from the first.

She evaded Joe's teasing question about the new man in her life by asking about his work as a medical intern, a topic he never seemed to tire of discussing. A few minutes later, Betty summoned everyone to the large, elegant dining room for lunch. Determined to enjoy her meal and the time with her friends, Taylor made an effort to put thoughts of Ryan out of her head.

It annoyed her greatly that she wasn't entirely able to do so.

They lingered for a long time over the excellent lunch, then drifted into the den for more pleasant conversation. None of the others seemed in a hurry to leave, and Taylor made no effort to break away, either. She needed this time away from Ryan, she told herself firmly. Needed to remind herself that she had a life apart from him, a life that had been quite fulfilling and satisfactory before he'd come into it. Or at least, most of the time.

But would she still be content with her life if Ryan left it as suddenly as he'd entered it? Somehow, she didn't think so.

Trying not to let her anxiety about her relationship with Ryan distress her again, she brought her attention to the present, just in time to hear part of a low-voiced conversation between Tony and Jared. She immediately forgot her problems when she realized what they were discussing.

"Are you sure someone's been watching Michelle?" Jared was asking Tony, his deep voice grave.

"I wish I *could* be sure," Tony answered, equally somber. "I haven't seen anyone, and neither has anyone else I've asked. But Michelle says she has seen the same beige sedan parked at the curb on more than one occasion and she thought she saw it following her downtown once when she was on her way to a hairdresser's appointment. She says every time she tries to get a look at the driver, he disappears."

"Damn. Michelle's not one to be paranoid without good reason."

"No."

"So what are you doing about it?" Jared demanded, looking as though he'd like to do something himself.

Tony made a frustrated gesture with one hand, an unconscious habit that made him look very Italian, despite his Texas drawl. "I've got Chuck looking into it. He hasn't seen anything suspicious, but he's only been watching for a couple of days. That's as long as I've known about it."

"How long does Michelle think the guy's been watching her?"

"A week. Maybe a little longer. She said she wanted to be sure before she mentioned it to me. She didn't want to worry me."

Jared muttered something incoherent and shook his head. Unable to stay out of it any longer, Taylor clutched Tony's arm. Like them, she kept her voice low so as not to be overheard by the others in the room, who were all engaged in laughing conversations of their own. "Someone's been watching Michelle?"

Tony winced at being overheard, but nodded honestly in response to her worried question. "Apparently."

Taylor thought of the man who'd snatched Michelle when she was a little girl and held her for ransom, an ordeal that had haunted her friend for years afterward. And then she remembered the family's horror when Lindsay was kidnapped a few months ago in Little Rock, an unpleasant episode that could have ended much more seriously had the revenge-driven abductor succeeded in his plan to kill Tony during the ransom drop. Was another slimy lowlife planning some sordid way of getting his hands on some of Michelle's money?

"What's happened?" she demanded, her fingers tightening on Tony's arm.

He repeated what he'd told Jared. "She's seen the car on three, maybe four occasions," he added. "Too many times to dismiss it as coincidence."

A beige sedan, Taylor thought with a frown, thinking inconsequentially of the beige rental car Ryan had been driving since she'd met him.

"There was one other incident that may or may not be connected to this," Tony said.

Both Taylor and Jared looked at him in question.

"A man apparently spent some time watching me from the coffee shop by my office last week—Thursday afternoon. Wanda, one of the waitresses who works there, mentioned him to me because the guy acted so suspicious after she'd told him my identity in response to his questioning."

"Did she get a description?" Jared asked.

"Youngish. Light brown hair, very light blue eyes. She said he was the type of man most women would notice."

Taylor shivered. Light-brown hair. Very light blue eyes. A beige sedan.

No. It was too ridiculous to even consider. Why would Ryan have been watching her friends? He was a security equipment salesman, which certainly made wealthy Michelle and private investigator Tony potential clients—but salesmen openly approached their would-be customers. They didn't sneak around and watch them.

She couldn't help thinking of all the questions Ryan had asked about Michelle—and then of his flat refusal to join her today.

No, she thought again, involuntarily shaking her head. It was merely a coincidence. It had to be.

"Taylor?" Tony was watching her oddly. "What is it? Do you know something about this?"

"No," she assured him firmly. "I was just . . . I'm just worried," she added, stumbling over the explanation.

He nodded, apparently accepting her concern, since he knew how close she was to Michelle. "So am I," he assured her. "We've started taking some extra precautions. Michelle won't be left alone and vulnerable until we know for sure whether something's going on."

"If someone's trying to hurt her again . . ." Jared growled, his strong, callused hands clenching into fists at his sides, his navy eyes glinting with barely suppressed fury.

"I'll take care of it," Tony finished, his usually smiling face set in a hard cast that made him look suddenly dangerous.

Taylor glanced across the room to where Michelle was laughing delightedly at something Shane had just said. At least she could reassure herself that Michelle was being well guarded by people who loved her deeply.

If only she could rid herself of her suddenly renewed doubts about Ryan. She crossed her arms at her waist and swallowed hard, trying to convince herself again that he couldn't possibly be involved in this in any way.

"Taylor," Cassie called out suddenly, moving as quickly as possible toward her, her steps made more awkward than usual by her pregnancy. "Did you remember to bring that mail-order furniture catalog you mentioned last week? I really want to see that big oak rocking chair you described. It sounded exactly like what I've been looking for to go in the nursery."

Taylor clapped her hand to her head. "Of course! I put it in my car that very afternoon—thank goodness, or I never would have remembered to bring it today. It's still in my back seat. I'll go out and get it."

"Want me to run get it for you, Taylor?" Shane offered politely.

She gave him a smile. "No, thanks, Shane. It's stuck in a file with some other papers I've been hauling around for a week. I'll have to find it myself. But it was sweet of you to offer."

"That's me," Shane said smugly, his expression exaggeratedly angelic. "Just one sweet guy."

A roomful of groans responded to his teasing self-praise.

Taylor was still chuckling at Shane's shenanigans when she walked out to her car. Her smile turned to a disgruntled mutter when she dropped her key ring as she was fitting it into the lock of her car door.

"Honestly, Simmons, you can be such a klutz sometimes," she complained, bending over to retrieve it.

She didn't know what made her turn her head sideways while she was still crouched by her car. Had she been standing, she wouldn't have been able to see the car across the street, almost hidden by the flowery shrubbery decorating the open gate to the estate. But she knew the man sitting behind the wheel of the beige sedan probably had a clear view of the front of Michelle and Tony's house.

Her fingers clenched in sudden anger around the key ring. She acted in sudden, impulsive decision, moving surreptitiously away from the car and toward the brick wall surrounding the house.

She intended to find out for herself just what the hell was going on here.

Chapter Ten

He was an idiot. No question about it.

Sitting behind the wheel of the beige rental sedan, Ryan pulled at his lower lip and stared blindly at the console in front of him. Lost in his disturbing thoughts, he'd allowed his attention to wander from the house he'd been watching for the past half hour or so.

He shouldn't be here, of course. It was stupid. But he'd had nothing else to do except sit in a quiet hotel room and miss Taylor, so he'd gone for a drive. Just to kill some time. He should have known he'd end up here—parked wistfully beside the house where Taylor and the others were spending the afternoon, unaware that he sat alone only yards away.

He was so deeply immersed in his glum, rather self-pitying thoughts that he was totally unprepared when the passenger door of the sedan abruptly opened. It was only the second time in his adult life he'd been caught so un-aware. The first time he'd ended up in a hospital bed.

"What the hell are you doing here?" Taylor de-manded angrily, plopping into the passenger seat to glare at him. "Just what are you up to, Ryan Kent?"

"Taylor, I—" He paused, searching his mind for a hasty, credible explanation. Funny. The glib lies had al-ways come so easily to him in the past. Why was he hav-ing such a hard time coming up with one now?

Maybe because he just couldn't bear the thought of lying any more to Taylor.

"Don't you dare try to bluff your way out of this," Taylor warned him flatly, making him wonder if she'd somehow read his thoughts. "Why are you here? Why have you been following Michelle?"

Startled by her phrasing, he eyed her warily. "What makes you think I've been following Michelle?"

"She told Tony a beige sedan's been following her around for the past week. I told myself it couldn't pos-sibly have been your car—but now I think it must have been. I want the truth, Ryan. Now. What is your con-nection to Michelle D'Alessandro?"

Well, hell. Stunned by the knowledge that Michelle had spotted him several times—he'd never blown a surveil-lance this badly in his entire career!—Ryan took a deep breath and answered honestly. "I'm her brother."

The silence that followed his announcement was so complete he could almost hear his own heavy heart-beats. Taylor stared at him in open disbelief, her hands clenching and unclenching in her lap. Finally, she spoke, seeming to force the words out. "You're her *what?*"

"Her brother," Ryan repeated. "Robert Ryan Walk-er." He hadn't used that name in so long that it sounded strange to him now.

"I don't believe you."

He shouldn't have been hurt by her mistrust. After all, he'd been lying to her from the beginning. She had every right to doubt him. But it hurt, anyway. "Believe it," he said curtly. "It's true."

"Why haven't you said anything before this?"

He made an ineffective gesture with one hand, wondering how to explain what he didn't quite understand himself. "I wasn't sure I was ready to be reunited with the others. I didn't want to say anything until I made up my mind."

Taylor was looking at him now like a suspicious stranger—hardly the way she'd looked at him during the night, he thought regretfully. Would she ever trust him again? Ever forgive him for deceiving her? "So you're the last missing brother," she murmured.

"One of the last," he corrected, sensing that she was trying to find a flaw in his story. "I'm a twin. My brother Joe is in Mexico on his honeymoon. Joseph Brian, if you're interested."

"You know quite a lot about the family," Taylor conceded. "I suppose you're also aware that Michelle is quite wealthy?"

Ryan's eyes narrowed as his rare temper flickered to life. He'd grant that Taylor had every right to be angry with him. But there was a limit to his indulgence of her pique. "Are you accusing me of running a scam?" he asked very softly.

She swallowed visibly in response to his tone, but managed a casual shrug. "You wouldn't be the first to try something like this. Tony has worried all along about impostors hoping to capitalize on Michelle's search for her missing siblings, but he probably never imagined anyone would use me to get to her."

"Dammit, Taylor!"

"Well, what the hell do you expect me to think?" she shouted. "You've lied to me. You've sneaked around watching Michelle, and you haven't given me one believable explanation. Do you really think I'm stupid enough to believe every word you say now just because we've shared a bed a few times?"

He was forced to pull in a long, deep breath before he could trust himself to speak. "We've shared a hell of a lot more than a bed," he said finally, the words flat and deliberate. "And, yes, I would have expected you to give me the benefit of the doubt, based on what I thought we'd found together."

Her gaze fell to her white-knuckled fists. "For Michelle's sake, I can't take that chance," she whispered. "You're going to have to come up with some proof."

Ryan had a great deal of personal experience with physical pain. He'd learned to handle it, when necessary. Now he discovered there were some hurts worse than physical ones.

Apparently he'd been deluding himself that he and Taylor had found something real and lasting. She couldn't possibly share his feelings if she really believed him to be a man who'd stoop to seducing her as part of a plan to bilk her wealthy friend.

He looked at her for a long time in silence, until she finally looked at him. And then he held her gaze with his own. "Taylor," he murmured, reaching out to her. "Do you really think so little of me? Haven't you gotten to know me any better than that during the past week?"

For one unguarded moment, something flashed in her eyes. Hope, perhaps. Maybe even a tentative, wishful trust.

And then the driver's door opened, breaking the spell. *Dammit,* Ryan thought in frustration. It had happened again!

"What the hell is going on here?" Tony D'Alessandro demanded, leaning into the car and looking suspiciously from Ryan to Taylor. A lean, tanned cowboy in jeans and boots stood behind Tony, fists on his hips, braced for trouble. Ryan hadn't seen or heard either of them approach the car.

He really was going to have to change careers. It seemed he'd lost the constant mental alertness necessary for the job he'd been in for the past seven or eight years.

Ryan glanced at Taylor. Whatever he'd seen in her eyes was gone now, replaced by the dull suspicion of before. She looked at Tony when she spoke, avoiding Ryan's gaze. "He claims to be one of the missing twins," she said, no expression evident in her voice. "I think you'd better talk to him, Tony."

Tony's dark eyes narrowed. "Yes," he said silkily, standing back from the car and motioning for Ryan to get out. "We should definitely talk."

Ryan sighed, gave Taylor one last look of reproach and slid out from behind the wheel.

It appeared that he wouldn't be waiting for Joe to join him for the family reunion, after all.

Ryan resisted an impulse to clear his throat and shift his feet on the plush carpeting. It took all his self-control to make himself stand with apparent ease in front of what appeared to be dozens of probing, accusing eyes.

Michelle was there, of course, watching curiously as her husband led Ryan in. Beside her stood a dark-haired, dark-eyed young man who looked very much like Tony— so much that he had to be a relative, probably a brother.

A copper-haired, obviously pregnant young woman and a teenage boy rose from the couch they'd been sharing, while another woman and a sandy-haired, rather chubby man stepped close behind Michelle.

Taylor stood by herself on one side of the crowded room, her hands tucked under her elbows, her expression shuttered. She had clearly distanced herself from Michelle's family—but she wasn't with Ryan, either. Taylor looked very much alone at the moment. Just the way Ryan was feeling.

"Michelle, this seems to be the guy who's been following you around lately," Tony announced. He stood close to Ryan's right side, while the cowboy—Jared, Ryan assumed—was stationed on his left, both obviously ready to act if Ryan should try anything funny. "He was parked out at the curb in a beige sedan, apparently watching the house."

Michelle looked at Ryan with a puzzled frown creasing her lovely face. "Who *are* you?" she asked him. "Why have you been watching me?"

Ryan studied her for a moment, trying to match her even, pretty features to an old, hazy memory of a curly-haired toddler. "Hello, Shelley," he said after a moment. "Do you still like jelly sandwiches or have you long since outgrown that?"

The brown-haired woman standing near Michelle gasped at the question, drawing Ryan's attention. Though she was several years older than Michelle, probably in her mid-thirties, the resemblance between them was marked. Ryan knew who she must be. "Layla," he murmured. "Do you sing 'I See the Moon and the Moon Sees Me' when you tuck your kids into bed, the way you did when you tucked us in?"

Layla's dark-blue eyes widened, one hand rising to her throat. "How do you know about that? Who are you?"

"You used to call me Bobby," he answered gently, smiling rather sadly at the memory of a serious little girl who'd taken such good care of him and the other children while their overworked young mother had struggled to put food on the table. "I started using my middle name when I was nine years old—do you remember it?"

"Ryan," she whispered. "Robert Ryan."

Michelle started and glanced quickly toward Taylor. "Ryan?" she repeated, taking a step toward her friend. "Is he the one who—"

Taylor nodded. "He told me his name was Ryan Kent," she said, her voice still oddly uninflected. "He asked a lot of questions about you, but I never figured out why. I didn't know about this, Michelle, I promise." She still refused to meet Ryan's eyes.

Layla's pretty face glowed with her smile. "Bobby," she said, moving impulsively toward him.

Jared moved between them. "Wait a minute, Layla. We don't know for sure that this *is* Bobby. He hasn't provided any proof."

"What proof do you want, Jared?" Ryan challenged him. "I could come up with papers, but we all know how easily papers can be faked. Want me to answer questions? Want me to remind you that you once told me I'd never live to see junior high school? Or talk about how many nights we ate canned pork and beans for dinner because it was all Mama could afford? We ate them cold. We couldn't heat them up because she couldn't pay the utility bills and our electricity was usually cut off.

"Or maybe," he continued coolly, "you want to hear about our old man, the cold, surly drunk who sat in a broken-down recliner while Mama waited on him hand and foot and the rest of us tried to stay out of his way."

He sensed the startled reactions of the others, though he didn't take his eyes from Jared's deeply tanned, roughly carved face. He wasn't sure how he felt about facing Jared again. He still remembered how he and Joe had idolized their older brother, how sharply they'd grieved for him—and the others—after the siblings had been so cruelly separated by fate and misguided social workers. Laughing, irrepressible Miles had been their buddy; Jared had been their hero.

"You do know a lot about the family," Jared conceded grudgingly. "But—"

"You still have doubts," Ryan finished for him.

Jared shrugged, not bothering to deny it.

Ryan looked briefly around the room, then at Tony. "Did you question all the others like this when you found them?"

Tony watched him steadily. "I carefully verified the identity of each one of them. You, however, are the first to approach the family before being located by me or one of my operatives. So I have some questions. How did you find Michelle? Why did you introduce yourself to Taylor as Ryan Kent, and why did you ask so many questions without telling her who you really are? Where have you been for the past fourteen years, ever since you and your twin brother disappeared from your last foster home without leaving a trace of your whereabouts?"

"Look, I'm not the one who started this search," Ryan snapped, losing patience with the inquisition. "You're the ones who have been tracking me for almost a year. Had I chosen to do so, I could have stalled your search indefinitely—you never would have found me, no matter how good a P.I. you might be. So you can either take my word for who I am or move out of my way so I can get the hell out of here. Your choice.''

"He sure *sounds* like a Walker," the pregnant redhead murmured, looking ruefully at Jared as she spoke.

Layla had moved closer, despite the protective efforts of her husband and brother. She searched Ryan's face, her navy eyes full of hope. "You *are* Bobby, aren't you?"

"I used to be, Sissy," he answered wearily. "Lately, I don't know who the hell I am half the time."

"Sissy," she whispered, covering her mouth with one hand. "Oh, Bobby—it is you!"

"You really are Bobby?" Michelle asked finally, studying him intently.

He figured he'd answered that question enough. He only looked at her, waiting for her to reach her own conclusion.

After a moment, she smiled tentatively. "I don't know why, but I believe you. It's just a feeling I have. . . ."

"Trust your feelings, Shelley," he murmured. "I am your brother. I don't remember much about you as a kid, but I do recall having to crawl under the house to rescue you when you'd gone in after a kitten and then got stuck. I was the only one small enough to reach you and drag you out."

Jared made a sound low in his throat. "I'd forgotten about that," he muttered. "Miles tried to go in after her and almost got stuck himself. I had to pull him out by his ankles."

Ryan nodded. "Shelley was screaming bloody murder, Layla was crying, Joe and I were fighting over which of us got to crawl to the rescue, and Miles was laughing his head off about the whole thing. As I remember, you were pretty disgusted with the whole bunch of us."

Jared had started to smile, his hard mouth tilting upward at the corners, his navy eyes trained intently on Ryan's face. "Yeah. I was. And we never told anyone about the incident, because we didn't want Mama to worry and we knew the old man wouldn't care one way or the other."

"No," Ryan agreed. "We never told anyone. So there's no way I could know about it without having been there, is there, Jerry?"

"Not unless the real Bobby told you about that incident and you're using it now for your own reasons."

Ryan gave a short laugh and shook his head. "There is that possibility, of course," he conceded. "All you have is my word that I was really there."

The room was very quiet while Jared considered Ryan's words. "I believe you," he said finally, making his sisters sigh in relief. "I guess you *are* Bobby."

Ryan smiled. "Yeah. But would you mind calling me Ryan? It would be real hard for me to get used to answering to Bobby again."

"Only if you quit calling me Jerry. It's Jared these days."

"You've got a deal," Ryan said, and held out his hand to the man who still seemed so much bigger and tougher, even though Ryan had grown some five inches taller than his once-idolized older brother.

Jared gripped Ryan's hand firmly. "Good to see you again, Ryan."

"You, too, Jared."

It was as if Jared's endorsement freed the others to accept Ryan, as well. They immediately surrounded him. Layla gave him a tearful hug and then introduced her husband, Kevin, adding that he was an accountant and that they lived in nearby Fort Worth with their three children. "Your nieces and nephew," she added.

Ryan shook his head in wonder at the thought of being an uncle—he didn't yet *feel* like anyone's uncle—but shook Kevin's hand with a polite smile.

After her own introduction, Cassie pumped Ryan's hand and told him how nice it was to have a new brother. Ryan liked the bubbly redhead immediately. And then Jared introduced his teenage son, Shane, who greeted Ryan with a curious smile. "You're the first one who doesn't look like the others," he commented, though he seemed to have no doubts about Ryan's identity. "Wonder how come?"

Layla had been standing close beside Ryan, looking at him closely. "He looks like our father," she said, glancing at Jared as if for confirmation. "I never really noticed in that old photo we have, but now that he's here, all grown up, I see the resemblance. Don't you agree, Jared?"

Jared frowned in memory, then nodded. "Yeah. I guess he does. I remember Dad's eyes being that pale blue color, and his hair *was* a lot lighter than Mama's."

Ryan couldn't bring himself to smile. "I wouldn't have chosen to take after him," he said without enthusiasm.

Jared shrugged. "People were always talking about him being a good-looking devil. But that was pretty much all he had going for him. Guess Mama found something else in him to care about, though. She never said a bad word about him, and Lord knows she grieved for him after he was killed in that industrial accident."

"What about your twin?" Shane asked. "Do you know where he is?"

"Joe's in Mexico," Ryan explained. "On his honeymoon. I talked to him Tuesday. He and Lauren will be here later in the week."

Layla clasped her hands in delight. "He's coming here? With his new bride? Oh, I can't wait to see them!"

Ryan's smile deepened as he realized that his older sister was the emotional, sentimental type. He was already feeling very fond of her. "Lauren's looking forward to meeting all of you, too. She's an only child and says she's always wanted brothers and sisters." He glanced at Layla's husband. "She's in your line of work, Kevin—she's a CPA. She has an accounting practice in Chicago. Or at least she did. I'm not sure where she and Joe are going to settle now."

"Isn't that a coincidence," Layla marveled. "To think that Joey and I both married accountants. Isn't that interesting, Kevin?"

Ryan hid his smile, thinking that Layla must be easily entertained.

"And how does Joe feel about the reunion?" Jared asked.

With a slight shrug, Ryan gave him a look that he knew was a bit rueful. "He's no more sure about it than I was. You have to admit, this is sort of strange, getting back together after all these years apart. Neither Joe nor I knew quite what to expect, or even whether we wanted to get involved."

Jared nodded in apparent understanding. "I felt the same way," he admitted. "Cassie had to talk me into coming here. I wasn't sure I wanted any reminders of a childhood that was far less than ideal. But now—" He slipped an arm around his wife's shoulders and glanced around at the room full of people. "Now I'm glad I did," he finished simply, the unemotional statement saying volumes.

"You'll be glad, too, Ryan," Layla assured him, patting his arm. "And so will Joe, once he gets to know everyone. It's so nice to be a family again, to know you have people who care about you, no matter what."

Vividly aware of Taylor, who was still standing so quietly apart from the others, Ryan managed a genial nod for Layla. "I'm sure it will be nice, once we get used to it."

Layla touched his arm again, as though still trying to reassure herself that he was really there. "You and Joey were such sweet little boys," she murmured, her dark-blue eyes misty with memories. "Do you remember my tenth birthday? You and Joey and Miles collected cans and bottles on the streets and cashed them in to buy me a tiny little bottle of inexpensive perfume because you couldn't afford anything else."

He chuckled lightly. "As I remember, it was *very* cheap perfume. Midnight in Bulgaria, or something like that, wasn't it?"

She laughed softly, the sound young and happy. "I didn't care what it was called. I treasured it anyway. It was from my little brothers." And then her smile faded. "Do you know about Miles?"

Ryan covered her hand with his own. "Yes, I heard. I'm sorry he didn't live to see everyone again."

She wiped the corner of one eye with her fingertips. "So am I."

"Oh, Ryan, you haven't met Joe," Michelle said suddenly, as though becoming aware of her duties as hostess, dispelling the momentary sadness. She held out a hand to the dark-haired young man who'd been standing beside her when Ryan had entered the room. "This is my other brother Joe," she added with a smile. "Tony's brother, actually, Dr. Joe D'Alessandro."

"Just think, Michelle, your baby's going to have two Uncle Joes," Shane remarked cheerfully as Ryan and Joe shook hands. "That could get confusing." Before anyone had a chance to respond, he turned to Ryan, obviously fascinated by the new addition to his ever-growing family. "Must be cool to have a twin, huh? Does he look like you?"

"We're identical," Ryan explained. "He looks exactly like me."

"Dad told me how one of you was born before midnight and one after, so you have different birthdays. I think that's funny, considering you're twins and all. Which one's older?"

Ryan sensed the others were waiting for his answer—that they had accepted his identity, but still welcomed further confirmation. "Joe's older, by ten minutes," he replied clearly. "According to our birth certificates, he was born at 11:55 P.M. on a Thursday, while I came in at 12:05 A.M. on a Friday."

"You probably don't remember, but all seven of us were born on different days of the week," Layla murmured to Ryan. "We—"

"I remember," he interrupted her gently. "It's one of my few memories of our mother. She used to recite that little poem about Monday's child and Tuesday's child while she rocked the baby to sleep. I couldn't tell you who was born on what day, except for the baby—I think she was born on a Sunday—but Joe and I tried hard to remember the poem during the first couple of years after we were separated, so we wouldn't ever forget either our mother or our brothers and sisters."

"And after that?" Jared asked.

"After that, it was easier to forget than to remember."

Again, Jared seemed to fully understand the sentiment. Ryan sensed that Jared, too, had spent many years trying to forget the family he'd been taken from, as a means of dealing with the raw pain of loss. A flicker of the old anger and resentment resurfaced, but Ryan shoved it down. The past was over, couldn't be changed. Now the future faced him.

He glanced again at Taylor, wishing he could read her closed expression and wondering just what the future held for him now.

Tony waited until Michelle had seated everyone and had the housekeeper serve drinks all around before he brought up something that had apparently been nagging at him. "How did you know I've been looking for you for a year?" he asked Ryan. "And what makes you think you could have evaded my search indefinitely if you chose to do so?"

Ryan was rather amused that his words had so rankled the private investigator. So he'd piqued Tony's professional pride, had he? Good. "For the past seven years, I've worked as a free-lance operative for a private security agency. American Security," he added for Tony's benefit. "My privacy was well protected by my employer. You wouldn't have found me."

Tony's left eyebrow shot upward. "I know of them, of course," he said. "They work very closely with the government, handle some major insurance investigations, provide bodyguards for a lot of big-name clients. They claim to employ only the very best in the business."

"They do," Ryan replied coolly, not bothering to feign modesty. He and Joe had both been very well trained during the past seven years. It had helped, of course, that they'd had a natural aptitude for the work, probably developed during long years of taking care of themselves when no one else seemed interested in doing so.

"What sort of work have you done for them?"

Ryan shrugged. "Whatever they've needed. Bodyguard, investigator, undercover work, courier services. Joe works for them, too. Or at least he did, until he married," he added.

"And what does he do now?"

"He hasn't decided yet."

Ryan could almost see the wheels turning in Tony's head. "I can always use well-trained operatives in my agency," Tony commented. "Especially now that Cassie's decided to quit to become a full-time mom and rancher," he added with a smile for his former employee, who smiled contentedly at him.

"Tell us about your childhood, Ryan," Layla commented, sitting close beside him on the couch where Michelle had urged him to be seated. "We know from Tony's research that you and Joe tended to run away from the foster homes where you were placed. Were you very unhappy in them?"

"We were a handful," Ryan admitted. "Mad at the world for taking us from our family, certain we didn't need anyone but each other. Every time someone tried to make us conform to behavior we didn't approve of, we took off. We were usually found within a few days, but we weren't easy to deal with. There was even talk of separating us for a while. Fortunately, it was decided that separating us would do more harm than good. We wouldn't have stood for it, of course. They wouldn't have been able to hold either of us separately. We'd have risked everything to get back together."

"You've been that close?" Layla asked.

"Yes." He didn't bother to elaborate. He figured that none of them could truly understand what it meant to be an identical twin, particularly twins separated from everyone they cared about except each other.

"And when you were sixteen, you ran away for good," Jared commented, subtly urging Ryan to continue.

He nodded. "We were fed up with the system, and the system was fed up with us. I'm not sure they ever even looked for us. We worked odd jobs after that, taking care of ourselves until we stumbled into the security business. We started training, finished high school with equivalency diplomas, and that's been our life until recently, when Joe met Lauren during an assignment."

"Do you have a permanent home anywhere?" Layla asked.

"Joe built a cabin in Colorado a few years ago. The two of us have sort of made that our base, though officially he's the one who owns it." It had been in that secluded cabin that Ryan had recuperated from his nearly fatal injuries two years ago, the two brothers spending whole weeks alone there while Ryan had worked to recover his strength and mobility with Joe's encouragement and insistence. "I've got an apartment in Denver, but I'm not there much," he added.

He noticed that Taylor and Michelle were leaving the room, their heads close together, Taylor still avoiding Ryan's eyes. His hand clenched on his knee. Was she leaving? Was it going to be necessary for him to follow her home and pound on her door until she let him in or had him arrested? Because that's what he would do, if he had to, to convince her to give him another chance to explain his actions.

He just wished he knew how the hell he would explain what he still didn't fully understand himself.

It was with some effort that he dragged his attention to Layla, who was asking him another question about his life during the past twenty-five years that they'd been separated. He answered mechanically, part of his mind busy trying to prepare his defenses for the inevitable confrontation with Taylor.

Chapter Eleven

"Taylor, are you okay?" Michelle asked in concern as soon as they were alone in the wood-paneled, wood-and-leather-furnished room that had been her father's home office and now served as Michelle's office.

Taylor ran a hand through her short hair, massaging her aching scalp. "I don't know for sure," she admitted, feeling oddly battered and wearied by the events of the afternoon.

Michelle took her hand and led her to a deep leather sofa, where they sat side by side. "He never told you who he really was? Never gave you any clue why he was in Dallas?"

"He said he was a salesman, here on business," Taylor answered with a trace of bitterness. "He lied to me from the very beginning."

"I'm sorry."

"So am I," Taylor whispered through a tight throat. "I was just beginning to trust him."

"I think it was more than trust," Michelle commented perceptively. "You care about him, don't you?"

"Maybe I was beginning to," Taylor admitted, her chin lifting defiantly. "But that's over now. It ended the minute I realized that he's been lying to me and using me from the day I met him."

"You really think he was just using you to find out more about me and the others?" Michelle asked with a frown.

"What else can I believe? All the lies he told me. All the questions he asked about you. All the chances he had to tell me the truth, if he'd wanted to do so. How can I ever trust him again?"

Michelle looked grave. "I don't know. I agree that what he did to you was reprehensible. Yet I find myself trying to find excuses for him. I don't know why."

"Because he's your brother."

Michelle shrugged. "I suppose so. It's worked out so well with the others that I guess I think Ryan should turn out to be as nice and honorable as they are."

"That's understandable."

Michelle's delicate jaw hardened, showing the stubborn temper Taylor had come to know so well during their years together. "It doesn't matter if he *is* my brother, he's still basically a stranger to me," she said flatly. "You're my friend. My *best* friend. You've been there for me when I wasn't sure there was anyone I could trust, and you'll always be as important to me as my own family. I just want you to know that I'll never forgive him for hurting you, and I never want you to doubt that my first loyalty will always be to you."

Touched, Taylor squeezed Michelle's hand. "Thank you. But I don't want to come between you and your family, Michelle. You've worked too hard to find them for that."

"And I've known you too long to let anything come between *us*," Michelle insisted. "I intend to tell Ryan exactly what I think about the way he's treated you."

"I'll tell him myself." Eventually. It wasn't something she looked forward to.

"So, um, you are going to talk to him? Give him a chance to explain, if he can?"

"I'll talk to him. But I can't imagine any explanations he can give that will make up for the way he lied to me."

Michelle sighed her implicit agreement.

Taylor stood abruptly, suddenly unable to sit still any longer. "I've got to leave now, Michelle. I need some time alone."

Looking worried, Michelle rose more slowly. "Are you sure you'll be all right?"

"I'll be fine," Taylor reassured her with a weak attempt at a smile. "I always am, remember?"

But Michelle didn't look convinced.

Taylor wasn't even sure she'd convinced herself.

Ryan knew when Michelle entered the den alone that Taylor had left without telling anyone goodbye. It wasn't hard to figure out that he was the one she'd wanted to avoid.

He was going to have his work cut out for him convincing her to listen to him.

"I'd like to talk to you," Michelle said in a low voice meant only for him. Her eyes were serious, not particularly friendly. "Alone, please."

Ryan suppressed an impulse to wince and nodded instead. "Now?"

"Now."

He motioned toward the door with one hand. "Lead the way."

"If you'll excuse us a moment, Ryan and I have something to discuss," Michelle told the others, who looked at them curiously. Tony moved as though to join them, but Michelle stopped him with a shake of her head. "This won't take long," she told him.

Tony nodded reluctantly, giving Ryan one long, searching, and rather warning look. *Be very careful with her,* that look implied. Ryan sensed that Tony was protective of Michelle. Remembering the things Taylor had told him about Michelle's childhood, Ryan understood Tony's desire to protect his obviously adored wife from any unpleasantness.

And something told him Tony wasn't a man he wanted to cross.

Michelle led Ryan outside, into a beautifully landscaped garden behind the house. It was a beautiful July afternoon, clear and hot, and the garden was filled with colorful, fragrant flowers. Any other time, Ryan would have enjoyed being out on a day like this. As it was, his attention was fully captured by the slender young woman walking so quietly at his side.

He was the one who finally broke the silence between them. "This is about Taylor, isn't it?"

Michelle slipped her hands into the pockets of the short-sleeved yellow linen jacket she wore with a creamy blouse and loosely pleated slacks, making her look as fresh and summery as the flowers surrounding them. Her expression, however, was anything but warm. "Yes. This is about Taylor. She's been my friend for a very long time, Ryan. I love her like a sister."

"I realize the two of you are very close."

Michelle stopped walking to turn to face him, her eyes narrowed. "Is that why you were so persistent about worming your way into Taylor's life? Because she and I are close? Were you using Taylor to find out more about me, Ryan?"

"No," he answered flatly, without a moment's hesitation. "My relationship with Taylor has absolutely nothing to do with you, Michelle. It was only by chance that I got to know her, only a coincidence that you and she are friends. Whatever I feel for her, it is in no way related to the reason I came to Dallas in the first place."

"Which was?"

"To satisfy my own curiosity. I knew you and the others were looking for me, and I was at a loss for something to do after Joe left on his honeymoon. I just wanted to see for myself how you'd all turned out, even though I wasn't sure I wanted to get involved in a family reunion. I stayed in Dallas after locating you and seeing you because I'd met Taylor and wanted to get to know her better, not because I was using her to find out more about you. Any information she let slip about you during the past few days, I could have just as easily gotten through my agency or through public records."

Michelle shook her head. "I still don't understand. Why did you—?"

He interrupted by placing a hand on her shoulder. "I know you don't understand, Michelle. Just believe me when I say that I never meant to hurt Taylor—or you. And believe, as well, that you have nothing to fear from me or from Joe. We don't want your money—wouldn't take it if you tried to give us any. We've always gotten by on our own, taken care of ourselves, and that's not going to change just because we've suddenly become part of a large family. I'd like to get to know you all better, and I'm sure Joe will, too, but I don't expect anything from you other than your friendship, if you choose to give it.''

Michelle bit her lower lip, and Ryan suspected sympathetically that she was torn between her desire to become better acquainted with her brothers and her loyalty to her best friend. "Taylor comes first with you," he said. "I understand. And, for her sake, I'm glad. I promise you I'll do my best to make her understand why I kept my identity from her—'' if he ever quite figured it out himself of course ''—and I hope she'll be able to forgive me.''

''If you hurt her again, *I'll* never forgive you,'' she warned him, suddenly fierce.

''I wouldn't blame you,'' he replied honestly.

''She's very vulnerable right now, Ryan. She told you about the man she loved two years ago?''

He hadn't known the time frame, but he nodded to indicate he knew there'd been another man.

''She was devastated when he died. I didn't think she'd ever care that much for anyone again. I was so pleased when she told me she was seeing someone again—you. She seemed so excited and hopeful, even though she was scared. Now she's feeling used and betrayed and very deeply hurt. It breaks my heart for her.''

He already felt like a worm. Michelle's words carried him even further down the food chain. ''I'll try to make it up to her, Michelle. I promise.''

''It won't be easy.''

''No.'' He didn't even try to delude himself that his practiced charm would be enough this time.

Michelle nodded as though suddenly reaching her own private conclusion. "Go after her, Ryan. And good luck."

He lifted a questioning eyebrow. "Are you saying you forgive me for deceiving her?"

"It's up to Taylor to forgive you," Michelle returned gently. "But I'll stay out of it from now on. For your sake and for Taylor's, I hope you can work this out. She's been alone long enough—and so have you, I think."

"Yeah," Ryan said with a sigh. "I think you're right. It's good to be back with the family, Shelley."

She smiled and rose on tiptoe to press a fleeting kiss to his cheek. "It's good to have you back, Bobby."

Taylor drove for hours. She considered going home, but knew Ryan wouldn't be far behind her. She wasn't quite ready to face him.

She'd thought of going to Maxie's but wasn't quite ready for that, either. She knew Maxie would want to hear the whole story. Maxie would be sympathetic and properly indignant on her behalf, of course, ready to take Ryan on with her bare hands for daring to hurt her friend. But for now, Taylor just needed some time to be alone.

It hurt so badly to think that Ryan had lied to her. Repeatedly. About his name, his job, his reason for being in Dallas.

Had he also lied about his feelings for her, led her to believe he was interested only in her when it was really her connection to Michelle that intrigued him?

She'd never forgive him for doing this to her, just when she'd been trying so hard to get over the loss of Dylan.

The low-fuel warning light was flashing on her dashboard when she finally pulled into the parking lot of her apartment complex. It was dark out, a quiet, uneventful Sunday night in Dallas, for once relatively free of the sounds of sirens and car horns.

Walking toward her apartment, her head down, steps weary, Taylor found little pleasure in the rare peacefulness of the evening. She shoved her key into the lock of her front door and pushed it open, only marginally aware that the living room lights were already on.

"I've been worried about you," Ryan said from the couch.

She hadn't given him a key. The front door had been locked when she'd left that morning, just as it had been locked when she'd returned moments ago. She sighed, not even bothering to ask how he'd gotten in. After hearing about his job—his *real* job—she figured he had all sorts of interesting talents.

"As you can see, I'm fine. You can stop worrying," she said, tossing her purse onto a chair.

He stood, watching her warily. "Where've you been?"

"That's really none of your business, is it?"

"No. I suppose it's not."

She nodded and headed for the bedroom. "I'm going to change. I'd like for you to be gone when I come out."

He followed her down the short hallway. "Taylor, we need to talk."

She paused just inside her bedroom, one hand on the door as she glared at him. "Why bother? I wouldn't believe anything you'd say, anyway."

She slammed the door before he could answer, locking it with a loud, final-sounding click. And then she sagged against it, her forehead pressed despairingly to the wood. Dammit, she thought with a moan of self-reproach. As angry as she was with him, as deeply as he'd hurt her, she'd still found herself wanting to burrow into his arms and have him hold her until the pain left her.

Had she completely lost her mind?

He didn't leave, of course. She hadn't really expected him to. She didn't even pretend to be surprised when she walked into her kitchen, the white sequin-splashed dress exchanged for an oversized gray Dallas Cowboys T-shirt and blue knit shorts, and found Ryan pouring steaming tea into two cups.

"I thought you could use this," he said, handing her one of the cups. He was smiling, but his jaw was set in a stubborn cast she'd learned to recognize from the beginning, when he'd been just as obdurate about her initial refusals to go out with him.

Ryan was not a man who gave up easily.

Fortunately, Taylor had a great deal of stubbornness of her own.

She took the tea without bothering to thank him. It was, after all, her tea, her kitchen. And Ryan an uninvited guest there.

He motioned toward the table. "Why don't we sit down and talk."

"You're not going away until you've had your say, are you?"

"No."

She sighed loudly and settled into a chair, her posture one of exaggerated, patronizing patience. "All right, let's get it over with. It's getting late, and I have to work tomorrow."

A hint of temper flashed briefly in his eyes, but he quickly banked it. "You're not going to make this easy for me, are you?"

She shrugged. "Why should I?"

He slid into a chair across the table, his tea sitting untouched in front of him. "You have every right to be furious with me, Taylor—"

"How gracious of you to grant me that privilege," she muttered into her cup.

"*But,*" he added repressively, "you could at least give me the courtesy of letting me try to explain."

"What's to explain? You lied to me, you spied on my friends, you used me to find out more about them. I understand completely."

He drew a deep, sharp breath. "You're beginning to make me angry," he warned.

She slapped a hand down on the table, not caring about the tea that splashed over the sides of the two cups. "Good!" she snapped, her frayed temper finally spilling over. "Because I'm mad as hell! How *dare* you do this to me? What gave you the right to use me that way? How could you let me think you cared about me when all along you were only using me for your own twisted purposes?"

"Taylor, it wasn't like that."

"You mean you didn't deliberately deceive me?" she taunted.

Chagrined, he frowned. "Yes, I lied to you," he had to admit. "But—"

"Then why should I believe anything you say now?"

"Because I'm not lying now, dammit! And I've never used you. Everything I said about us, about the way I felt—the way I feel about you—that was all true."

"Oh, God. I can't take this tonight." She stumbled to her feet and headed blindly for the doorway, trying to escape the words that were so painful to hear, so difficult—yet so very tempting—to believe.

He caught up with her before she could leave the room, his hands gripping her shoulders from behind to pull her gently to a stop. "Taylor," he murmured, his mouth close to her ear. "Don't do this to us."

"Don't you understand?" she whispered through a painfully tight throat. "There *is* no 'us.' I don't even know you. The man I thought I knew—the man I thought I was starting to care for—didn't even exist."

"You're wrong," he insisted, wrapping his arms around her from behind, his cheek against her hair. "I exist, Taylor. I'm very real. I lied to you only about my name and my job—and I've told those lies so many times, I hardly know the truth myself anymore. But I meant every other word I said. I wanted you from the first moment I saw you. Every minute I've spent with you since just made me want you more. I've never fallen as hard for anyone as I have for you. You have to believe me, sweetheart."

Oh, she wanted so badly to believe him. The very strength of that longing shook her. She was so afraid of being hurt again, so frightened of trusting him again. He wasn't making any promises about the future, wasn't offering anything more than desire. How could she risk everything with nothing more than his seductive words to reassure her?

His lips were soft against her cheek, his breath warm. "I wish I could go back and change the way I handled this whole mess, but I can't. All I can do is tell you that I'm sorry I hurt you. I promise I won't ever lie to you again."

She could feel her anger slipping away from her. She tried to cling to it—where was her spirit? But his arms were so warm, so strong. And she was so tired of fighting him—and herself. "Ryan," she whispered, closing her eyes for a moment.

His arms tightened. "Give me another chance, Taylor. I promise I'll make it up to you."

She needed to look at him, needed to see his eyes when she asked the next question. She turned in his arms, her searching gaze locked on his face. "You swear you weren't using me? That you didn't insist I go out with you just so you could learn more about Michelle and her family?"

"I swear," he said, his deep voice throbbing with apparent sincerity. "I asked you out because I wanted to be with you, get to know you. No other reason."

Her willpower slipped another notch, but she made herself ask, "So when you saw me in that discount store, it was just a wild coincidence? You didn't know then that I had any connection to Michelle?"

His obvious hesitation brought back her frown. "I saw you with Michelle earlier that afternoon—and later with Tony," he admitted finally. "I followed you to the discount store, sweetheart.

"But—" he added firmly when she started to pull out of his arms, "it was only because even then I was attracted to you. I know this sounds crazy—hell, maybe it *is* crazy—but from the very beginning you...well, you mesmerized me. At first I thought you looked familiar, as if I'd met you before. Even after I realized I didn't know you, I knew you were someone I wanted to know. I had to meet you. Once I did, I was hooked."

There was something very seductive about being told she'd had a mesmerizing effect on him. Taylor had never thought of herself as an irresistible siren, though she'd always considered herself attractive enough. But she made herself hold on to her frown. "You stole my wallet," she accused him.

"Borrowed it," he confessed ruefully. "How else could I have found you again?"

She shook her head. "You really have no compunction about sacrificing ethics to achieve your goals, do you, Ryan?"

"For most of my life I've been too busy trying to survive to worry much about ethics or noble principles," he answered evenly. "I told you once I didn't have a spotless past or traditional background. Now you know I've been pretty much on my own, except for Joe, since I was just a kid. I'm not particularly proud of my actions during the past week, Taylor, but I never set out to hurt you."

She thrust out her jaw, giving him one more glimpse of her righteous anger. "If you ever lie to me again, I'll—I'll—"

"Sweetheart, you can shoot me with my own gun," he promised with an enticing smile. "Just tell me you'll give me another chance."

"I'm probably the world's biggest idiot," she muttered, "but you've got your chance, Ryan. I won't refuse to see you again. But," she added hastily, when his arms tightened reflexively. She pressed her hands flat against his strong chest to hold him a few inches away. "I want you to go back to your hotel tonight. From now on, we're taking this... this relationship, or whatever it is, more slowly. I want you to stop rushing me."

He didn't look particularly enthused, but he nodded. "I'll give you all the time you need, Taylor."

"And all the space I need?" She had no intention of falling into bed with him until—or unless—she knew exactly where their relationship was heading from this point on. It was time for Taylor to start using some of that common sense she'd always taken such pride in, as far as Ryan "Kent" Walker was concerned!

Ryan nodded again.

She took a deep breath. "All right. Just so you know I'm not quite the gullible idiot I must have appeared so far."

"I never thought you were," he assured her, then brushed his mouth over hers.

She pulled back quickly, knowing her emotions were still too raw to make her impervious to temptation. And Ryan was, most definitely, the most tempting man she'd ever met. Look at the way he'd already talked her into forgiving him, at least conditionally, for deceiving her about his identity and his purpose for being in Dallas.

Speaking of which... "Why were you so hesitant about meeting your sisters and brother?" she asked, absently reaching for a paper towel to wipe up the tea spills on the table. "Why did you spend so much time watching them without letting them know you were here?"

Ryan picked up his teacup and took a sip of the lukewarm beverage before answering, apparently taking that opportunity to mentally phrase his explanation. "At first I wasn't sure I wanted to meet them again," he said finally. "You heard me explain that to Michelle and the others. I wasn't sure digging up a painful past was such a good idea. When I realized a reunion was probably inevitable, especially after I'd gotten involved with you, I decided to wait until Joe got here to face them. I guess I was a little nervous about facing them alone," he admitted ruefully.

Knowing now that Ryan and the brother he'd mentioned so often were identical twins, she realized that the bond between them must be very strong. She supposed she could understand that Ryan had wanted to wait until his brother joined him before facing the others. It was one of the few things he'd explained that actually made sense!

But hearing him talk about his feelings made him all too appealing again. And she was still much too vulnerable to him tonight. She tossed the paper towel into the trash can and looked meaningfully at the wall clock. "It's getting late."

Ryan's mouth twisted. "Is that a hint for me to leave, by any chance?"

She didn't return the faint smile. She couldn't remember being so drained and tired in a long time. "I'll see you out."

Ryan followed her obediently enough to the front door, but paused there for a moment to look at her. "You'll see me tomorrow?"

"Call me at the office. We'll talk about it."

A quick frown creased his brow, but he nodded. "All right. Good night, Taylor."

"Good night."

He put a hand on the doorknob, stopped and turned suddenly to pull her into his arms. The kiss was long and hard, deep and hungry. They were both breathing heavily when he finally ended it. "I'll miss you tonight," he murmured huskily. "I've gotten used to sleeping with you in my arms."

He left before she had regained enough breath to reply. Which was just as well, since she didn't know what she would have said.

She had a nagging suspicion that she might have begged him to stay, despite her sensible talk about needing more time and space.

* * *

Ryan prowled the hotel room restlessly, his pacing taking him from one blandly papered wall to the opposite one in only a few brisk steps. He was too wound up to sleep, his thoughts too unsettling to allow him to relax.

The unexpected reunion with his brother and sisters had put him through an emotional wringer. For so long, he'd thought of himself as alone in the world, except, of course, for Joe, whom he'd always considered as another part of himself. Now there were all these others, who seemed to expect him to become part of their lives, who wanted something from him he wasn't sure he was ready to give.

His family. Quite a concept for a man who hadn't considered himself part of a real family since he was five years old.

And then there was Taylor, of course. He'd hurt her badly. He hated himself for that. He felt as though he'd had a very narrow escape when she'd told him she would see him again. Not that he didn't have a long way to go in regaining the trust she'd tentatively given him. He didn't try to convince himself that the truth hadn't put new obstacles between them, obstacles he would have to carefully, warily navigate or risk driving her away completely. And that was one outcome he couldn't even bear to consider.

He was down for the count. Head over heels. Roped and tied. All those other clichés that meant he'd found the one woman for whom he was willing to work, fight— or even grovel.

He felt no more prepared for a permanent commitment to one woman than to being part of a large, extended family.

It seemed as though he was going to have to start preparing himself for some serious changes in his thinking and his life-style. Because now that he'd rediscovered his family, he wasn't sure he could ever permanently leave their lives again. And now that he'd found Taylor, he knew there was nothing on earth that would make him willingly walk away from her.

He swallowed hard, finally facing the emotional cowardice that had kept him footloose and uncommitted for so many years during which he'd prided himself on his physical courage. What a fool he'd been!

Trying to distract himself long enough to allow him to get a few hours' sleep—something told him he was going to need all his wits about him during the next few days—he threw himself onto the bed and turned on the television with the remote control. The set was still tuned to the shopping channel. An overly madeup blonde in a spangled dress was modeling a genuine fake fox jacket for only sixty-nine ninety-nine.

His mouth twisting, Ryan wondered if Layla would like it for her next birthday. Or maybe he could find a quart-size bottle of Midnight in Bulgaria.

His brief, somewhat confused bark of laughter echoed eerily from the empty corners of the hotel room as the television quietly played to its uninterested audience of one.

Chapter Twelve

True to his word, Ryan made no effort to rush Taylor during the next few days. He seemed content to be with her in the evenings after she left her office, taking her to dinner, to a piano concert, to another movie. Though he didn't even try to hide his reluctance to do so, he went to his motel room every night, leaving Taylor to sleep alone. But each night, before he left, he kissed her with a thoroughness and intensity that made sleep very difficult for her.

She could only hope he was aching as badly for her as he made her ache for him.

He used the hours while she worked getting to know his brother and sisters better. He spent Monday afternoon with Michelle and Tony, Tuesday at Jared's ranch some thirty miles out of Dallas. On Wednesday, he had lunch with Layla and Kevin at their home in Fort Worth. Thursday he spent several hours at Tony's place of business, looking over the investigation agency Tony had established three years earlier.

"So what do you think of them?" Taylor asked over dinner at her apartment Thursday evening, the first night they hadn't made plans to go out. They'd talked each night about Ryan's hours with his siblings, and he'd told her his initial impressions of them as individuals, but now she was interested in knowing how he reacted to them as a group. As a family.

Ryan swallowed a forkful of steamed fresh vegetables and reached for his iced tea. "They've all turned out amazingly well, considering our background," he admitted. "From everything they've told me about Lindsay, she's very nice, too. It's good to know none of them has ended up in prison or alone on the streets."

"Are they beginning to feel like family to you, or do they still seem like pleasant strangers?" she asked curiously, trying to read between his words.

He looked thoughtful. "Good question. Since I don't know what family is supposed to feel like—after all, it's been so long since I really belonged to one—I'm not sure how to answer. I do feel a . . . oh, a connection of sorts to all of them. Not like the bond I have with Joe, of course."

"You weren't separated from Joe for twenty-five years," Taylor reminded him unnecessarily.

"There is that."

"Will you try to maintain a relationship with them?"

"D'you mean, am I going to disappear from their lives for another twenty-five years?"

She nodded.

"No. I don't think it's possible. Now that I've met them, gotten to know them all as adults, I don't want to lose track of them again. I don't know if I'll ever be as close with them as some families seem to be, but I'm willing to give it a try."

"I'm glad," Taylor said with a smile and a ripple of relief that he had no plans, at least for now, to quietly disappear again. "For their sake and for yours."

Ryan helped her clear away the dishes after they'd eaten. They worked companionably in her small kitchen, the silence between them a comfortable one. Taylor couldn't help thinking about how accustomed she'd gotten to having him around—how much she would notice his absence if he left her life now.

They were still quiet when they went into the living room. Refusing her perfunctory offer of after-dinner drinks or coffee, Ryan turned to face her, lifting one hand to her cheek. His eyes held hers with an expression that made her swallow hard when he asked quietly, "Are you going to send me home again tonight?"

She knew she should say yes. After all, nothing had been settled between them. She opened her mouth to tell him so—but the words wouldn't come out. She could only stare mutely at him, vividly, achingly aware of his nearness. How long it had been since she'd felt him fully against her. How badly she wanted him.

Very slowly, he drew her closer, his movements gentle and unthreatening. She could have stopped him, could have broken away at any time, and they both knew it. But she didn't.

His arms closed around her and his breath left him in a long, expressive sigh as he rested his cheek against her hair. Pressed so closely against him, Taylor felt the arousal he made no effort to hide and knew he hungered as badly as she did. "Taylor," he murmured. "Sweetheart, I want you so much. If you ask me to leave, I will. But if you're going to ask, do it now, while I still can."

It felt so good to be in his arms again. She wasn't able to resist the impulse to press her cheek into his shoulder, her arms locked around his waist, her hands splayed across his strong back. A heavy throbbing began in her breasts and spread throughout her body, centering deep between her thighs. She wanted him. How much longer was she going to punish him—and herself—for deceiving her?

Yet how could she find the courage to really trust him again?

His lips moved against her cheek, his voice a warm, soft whisper against her heated, sensitized skin. "Taylor. Sweetheart . . ."

She turned her head so that their mouths met in a kiss that rocked her all the way to her toes. Ryan groaned deep in his chest and hauled her closer, almost squeezing the breath out of her in his ardor. She didn't care. She held him just as tightly.

He finally broke the kiss with a gasp for air. "I hope this means you're not sending me away tonight."

"No," she whispered, pressing her lips to his jaw. "Not tonight. Stay with me tonight, Ryan. Make love with me."

She couldn't bear to be alone again tonight.

On a romantic whim, Ryan lit the scented candles Taylor kept in her bedroom. Their soft, dancing light deepened the sense of intimacy in the shadowy room, glittered in the gold in Ryan's hair and reflected in his light blue eyes. Standing beside the bed, with her hands pressed to Ryan's strong, bare chest, Taylor gazed at him, thinking that he was the most beautiful man she'd ever known.

He skimmed his hands across her shoulders, displacing the tiny straps of her cream silk teddy. The teddy slipped downward, the flimsy, lace-trimmed fabric clinging to the tips of her breasts. Ryan held his breath as he skimmed one work-roughened fingertip across her cleavage. Taylor trembled, and her eyelids grew heavier, her breathing ragged.

"You are so beautiful," he murmured, his gaze focused on her rising and falling breasts. "You make me ache, Taylor."

She dragged her hands slowly, lingeringly down his chest, savoring the slight tickle of his sparse chest hair, the pulsing warmth of his tanned skin, gently passing over the ridges of his scars. She paused at the waistband of the low-slung jeans that were all he wore, her fingertips toying with the metal snap. "I'm aching, too," she admitted.

"Good. I'd hate to think I felt like this alone." He bent his head to press a kiss to her shoulder.

She buried the fingers of one hand in his thick, soft hair, her head tilting to give him better access to her throat and shoulder. He took full advantage of her cooperation, his lips skimming, tasting, nipping. Silk shifted seductively beneath his palms as his hands moved over her back and hips, the front of the teddy slipping an inch lower. As though beckoned by that movement, Ryan lowered his mouth to the tops of her breasts.

Taylor gasped when his warm lips closed around one straining nipple. Her fingers tightened in his hair. She rose involuntarily on her toes in response to the electrifying sensations he evoked. She shifted her weight toward the bed beside them, suddenly impatient to carry their lovemaking further.

But Ryan wouldn't be rushed. Murmuring endearments and reassurances, he continued his painstaking exploration of her willing body. At a touch of his fingers, her teddy tumbled to her waist, baring her full breasts to his mouth and fingers. On his knees now, he stroked one hand up her leg, lingering at her calf, behind her knee, at the inside of her thigh. And then his fingertips disappeared beneath the hem of her teddy, and she shuddered in reaction when he touched her more intimately.

"Ryan," she said, her voice strangled. "Please—"

He tugged the teddy downward, letting it fall to her ankles. And then he began to explore the feminine territory fully revealed to him in the romantic light of the flickering candles.

By the time Ryan finally urged her to the bed, Taylor was trembling helplessly, her breathing labored, nerve endings tingling madly. She was quite sure that she would have gone up in flames had he taken much longer. She gave a sigh of sheer, blissful relief when he tossed his jeans aside and covered her with his hard, perspiration-sheened body. Her eyes closed, she drew him to her with hungry, eager arms.

"Taylor," he rasped, holding himself very still, though she could feel the fine tremors running through his rigid muscles. "Look at me."

She opened her heavy lids with an effort.

His eyes were only inches from hers. Candlelight reflected in their pale blue depths; fire in ice, she thought dreamily. His face was taut with self-control, his hair tumbled over his damp forehead, dark color burning his cheekbones. She lifted one hand to run her fingers caressingly over his jaw. "Ryan," she murmured, shifting enticingly beneath him.

He groaned. "I can't think when you do that."

She smiled and kissed his throat. "You don't need to think."

"But I wanted to tell you—" He choked when she wrapped her smooth legs around his hair-roughened ones. "I wanted you to know that I—"

Her arms around his neck, she raised herself from the pillow to kiss him, her tongue sliding between his parted lips, her breasts crushed against his heaving chest.

"Oh, hell," Ryan muttered, crushing her down into the mattress. "We'll talk later."

"Yes," she gasped. "Later."

They never got around to talking that night. The candles had burned to puddles of wax and dawn was only a few hours away by the time they finally fell into exhausted, satiated sleep, their nude, damp bodies still locked in a tangled embrace.

Sprawled on his stomach, face buried in the pillows, Ryan was still sleeping heavily when Taylor slipped from the bed Friday morning. She stood by the bed for a moment, smiling affectionately at him. He was exhausted, poor thing, she thought, her smile turning smug. She wouldn't disturb him.

He never stirred when, fully dressed for work, she walked through the bedroom from the connected bathroom. She slipped into the kitchen, where she made coffee and toasted a bagel for her breakfast. Careful to keep the volume down, she turned on the radio she kept on the counter for company and spread the newspaper on the kitchen table, glancing over the headlines during the few minutes she had to spare before leaving for the office. She would leave a note for Ryan if he was still sleeping when it was time for her to go, she decided.

She had just folded the newspaper and rinsed out her coffee cup when the opening piano notes of a familiar song drifted from the radio. She went still, her vision clouding for a moment as Garth Brooks began to sing "The Dance."

She must have listened to that song hundreds of times after Dylan died. She'd found an odd comfort in the lyrics, the story of a heartbroken lover who had reached the conclusion that he would not have sacrificed the pleasure he'd experienced to avoid the pain that had followed. He was glad, he sang, that he hadn't known the way it would end. He could have missed the pain, but then he would have had to miss the dance.

Hundreds of times she'd asked herself if it would have been better if she'd never met Dylan, never loved him, never known the devastating grief of losing him. But each time she'd finally reached the same conclusion—she was glad she'd known him, glad she'd had the chance to be with him, to love him and be loved by him, if only for such a tragically short time.

And now there was Ryan. He'd come into her life at a time when she'd almost given up on finding love again, when she'd almost convinced herself that she'd never again know the sheer joy she'd found in loving Dylan. And she'd discovered that her badly bruised heart was still in working order.

Sometime during the past two weeks, she'd fallen in love with Ryan, despite their rocky, deceptive beginning. She was so much in love with him that she could hardly think straight. And she was utterly terrified.

He could hurt her so badly. Had already hurt her once. She wasn't sure she could bear it if she'd fallen in love again only to discover that there was no happy future for her this time, either.

And then she remembered the way he'd made love to her, the way he'd looked at her in the misty glow of candlelight. Could he have faked those emotions? Why would he? Surely Ryan's feelings were as deeply involved as Taylor's were.

She wished now that she'd given him the opportunity to tell her whatever it was he'd wanted to say in bed last night. Would he have told her he loved her? That he wanted to have a life with her, a future? A family?

She closed her eyes as a wave of emotion crashed through her. It hurt, she discovered, to hope this much. To need this much. To love this much again.

But whatever happened, she wouldn't be sorry she'd known him, she promised herself as she reached for the notepad she kept in a drawer by the kitchen phone. How could she ever regret the sheer pleasure she'd found in his arms last night?

The song ended and Taylor turned off the radio. In a way, she felt as though she was finally telling Dylan goodbye. She stood by the silent radio for a moment longer, then wiped her eyes with her fingertips and propped the note for Ryan by the coffeemaker, where he'd be sure to see it.

As she left the apartment, she found herself thinking that Dylan would have understood—and approved.

It was after ten when the phone rang on Taylor's desk. She lifted it with a hopeful smile. "Taylor Simmons."

"Why didn't you wake me?"

Her smile deepened at the husky sound of his voice. "Did you just get up?"

"Yeah. I guess I was wiped out."

"I guess you were."

His chuckle was a low caress in her ear. "You needn't sound quite so proud of yourself."

"Oh. Sorry."

"I'm not. Last night was spectacular, Taylor. *You* were spectacular."

"Now you're going to make me blush. What will my co-workers think?" she chided him teasingly, glad she was alone in her office at the moment.

"That you're involved in a hot and heavy love affair?" he suggested, his tone as light as hers.

Love affair. Oh, Ryan, I hope so. I love you so much.

But she kept the words to herself, of course. This wasn't the time to say them. "You must be hungry," she said instead. "Help yourself to whatever you find in the kitchen. The coffee should still be good."

"I'm drinking a cup as we speak. Thanks."

"I forgot to tell you I have a professional meeting scheduled after work today. I can always skip it, of course, if you—"

"No, don't miss your meeting. Actually, Tony's asked if I want to work with him on a case this evening. We may get in late."

Taylor blinked in surprise. "You're working with Tony on one of his cases?" she repeated.

"Just a security stakeout. He's got something set up with a local manufacturer who thinks one of his employees is stealing from him at night. Tony and I are going to see if we can catch the guy in the act."

Taylor frowned. "You'll be careful, won't you? Sounds like it could get ugly."

"Don't worry about it, sweetheart. This case is a piece of cake compared to most."

She thought of the scars crisscrossing his chest, back and legs. "Why don't I find that more reassuring?"

"Want me to tell Tony he's on his own?"

"You would do that?" she asked in surprise. She hadn't realized she had quite that much influence with him.

"If it bothers you that badly, I will," he replied without hesitation.

This had to be serious, she told herself with a renewed surge of optimism. She must be important to him if her opinion mattered that much. "Go with Tony, Ryan. Just be careful."

"You're sure?"

"I'm sure." After all, she reasoned, this could work into a full-time partnership between the brothers-in-law. Which meant that Ryan would be staying in Dallas. No way was she going to do anything that could interfere! "Have fun."

He chuckled. "I'll try."

"You'll come to my place afterward?"

"Could be late," he warned.

"I don't care. There's an extra key in my jewelry box. Just let yourself in if I'm already in bed."

"All right. I'll be here."

"Good."

"I'd better let you get back to work."

"I guess so," she agreed without enthusiasm.

"Taylor, I, uh . . ."

"Yes?" she urged when he paused, her fingers tightening around the receiver.

"I'll see you tonight."

She had the distinct impression he'd started to say something else and had changed his mind. She'd have given anything to know what he'd started to say, she thought as she reluctantly disconnected the call.

* * *

It was much later that afternoon when Taylor approached the door to Jay's office, her attention centered on the computer printout in her hand. These expense figures couldn't possibly be right, she thought distractedly, running her free hand through her hair as she tried to make sense of the report. Maybe Jay could explain it to her.

"I wouldn't go in there, if I were you," Erika commented glumly from her desk in the center of the reception area.

Taylor glanced from the report to Jay's door, through which she could hear raised voices. "Don't tell me they're at it again."

"I'm afraid so. Jay called Maxie in half an hour ago to talk to her about office expenses. They started yelling the minute she closed the door." Erika shook her blond head in exasperation. "Don't know what you're going to do with those two."

Taylor sighed, glaring at Jay's door as though she could see her two partners through it. She didn't know what she was going to do with them, either. Maxie and Jay had tended to quarrel from the beginning, but they'd worked well despite their tiffs and had seemed to be genuinely fond of each other underneath it all.

Taylor hadn't really been worried, until lately. Despite her distraction with Ryan, even she had noticed that the quarrels between her partners had grown more frequent and more heated during the past couple of weeks. She hoped it wasn't getting serious. The agency couldn't continue to thrive if two of the partners couldn't manage to get along.

A sudden, suspicious silence came from the other side of the door. It sounded as though Maxie had been abruptly cut off in mid-shout. Frowning, Taylor looked at Erika, who shrugged and held up both hands in a gesture of confusion. "You suppose one of them's strangled the other?" she asked.

"No, of course not," Taylor assured her, then cleared her throat. "But I think I'll go on in—just in case. They may need a referee."

She opened the door without bothering to knock. Then stood frozen in openmouthed shock at the sight that greeted her.

Jay was leaning over the leather chair in which Maxie was sitting, his mouth planted firmly on hers. Maxie was clinging tightly to Jay's lapels, her red head tilted back, her eyes closed, obviously participating fully in the kiss.

Taylor hastily backed out of the office and closed the door. "Well!" she murmured, blinking rapidly in surprise. "Who would ever have suspected that Jay had it in him?"

Erika looked up from the paperback she was reading between phone calls on this slow Friday afternoon. "What's going on? They kick you out?"

"They, uh, didn't want to be disturbed," Taylor answered carefully, hurrying to her own office. "You might want to route any calls to me for the rest of the afternoon."

"Whatever you say," Erika agreed with a shrug, and turned to her book.

"Curiouser and curiouser," Taylor muttered, shaking her head as she walked slowly to her desk.

And then she started to laugh.

It was over half an hour later when Maxie stuck her head into Taylor's office. Erika had already gone home and Taylor had been thinking about leaving. But rampant curiosity had kept her at her desk, one eye on the doorway as she'd steadily cleared away a pile of paperwork. "Come on in, Maxie."

Noisily clearing her throat, Maxie strolled in with exaggerated casualness, her hands in the pockets of her green linen jacket. "You going to that meeting tonight?" she asked as she settled into a chair.

"I was planning on it. Are you?"

"No. I, uh, suddenly have other plans."

"Oh." Taylor eyed Maxie's uncharacteristically crimson cheeks with amusement. "Do those plans have anything to do with Jay, by any chance?"

Maxie's cheeks went even darker. "Yes. He, uh, we're having dinner together."

"I see." Taylor made an effort to keep her voice expressionless.

Maxie groaned and lifted her hands to her burning face. "Oh, God, Taylor, I can't believe this has happened!"

"What, exactly, *has* happened?" Taylor asked curiously, knowing Maxie would tell her to butt out if she wasn't ready to talk about it.

"Jay—and me—and that kiss—and the things he said afterward—"

She stopped in frustration with her stammering incoherence and then spoke again. "I'm five years too old for him and three inches too tall. I'm divorced with two kids and he's never been married. I'm a Catholic, he's a Jew. His mother's going to hate me."

"But you love him."

"I think I have for months, without even knowing it myself," Maxie said, her green eyes huge.

"And Jay?"

"He says he feels the same way. Can you believe this? It's absolutely insane!"

Taylor laughed softly. "I think it's wonderful." And she did, now that she'd had time to get used to the idea. Why hadn't she realized before that Jay and Maxie were perfect for each other?

Maxie drew a deep, unsteady breath. "So do I—I think," she admitted. "Oh, Taylor, I can't believe I'm feeling like this. Giddy and excited and scared and happy. I'm too old for this."

"You're not too old," Taylor chided her firmly. "No more than I am."

Maxie's brows rose. "Does that mean you know how I'm feeling?"

Taylor groaned expressively. "Do I ever!"

"Ryan?"

"Ryan."

"Then you've forgiven him for lying to you about why he was in Dallas?" Maxie, of course, had learned the entire story during the past week.

"I suppose I have," Taylor said slowly. "He's been on his own for so long—except for his brother, of course—and so accustomed to working undercover in his job with the security agency. He's told me that changing identities comes as easily to him as changing his clothes. He's been doing it since he was a defiant, runaway little boy. I've realized, I suppose, that I can't take it personally."

Maxie chewed her lower lip, looking a bit worried. "You have to admit the man you've just described is hardly the stable, dependable sort. Are you sure he's a good risk for a long-term relationship?"

"When it comes to Ryan, I'm not sure of anything," Taylor admitted with a brief, humorless laugh. "Except that I love him."

It was the first time she'd said the words aloud. And even as they left her lips, she knew she meant them completely.

"Well," Maxie said briskly after a moment of thoughtful silence. "Then I suppose you'd better do your best to make it work out. It's not like you have any other choice, is it?"

"No," Taylor admitted ruefully. "I don't seem to have any other choice at all."

"Trust me, I know the feeling. I still have to tell my kids that I've fallen in love with their buddy, Uncle Jay. They're going to think I've lost my mind."

"Maybe you have," Taylor said, her mouth twisting wryly. "Maybe we both have." She moaned and ran her hands through her hair, knowing she'd left it standing wildly on end. "Oh, God, Maxie, what are we doing? Why have we let ourselves get in such potentially disastrous situations?"

"We're women," Maxie replied with a fatalistic sigh, "and women have been taking risks on men since the beginning of time."

They sat in grave silence for several long minutes, reflecting on the truth of Maxie's observation and wondering if they were strong enough to face the challenges their vulnerable hearts had presented them.

Three hours after Taylor had gotten home from her professional meeting, she still hadn't heard a word from Ryan. She paced the apartment restlessly, wondering at how quiet and empty it seemed without him in it. She found herself counting the minutes until he arrived, impatient to see him, touch him, talk to him. She wanted to tell him about her day, about the meeting she'd attended, about the surprising romantic development between Maxie and Jay.

How had he made himself such a big part of her life in such a very short time?

She was just thinking reluctantly of going to bed alone when the phone rang.

Ryan, she immediately thought, snatching up the receiver in the middle of the second ring. "Hello?"

"Taylor, it's Michelle."

Something in her friend's voice brought Taylor's heart to her throat. "What is it? What's wrong? Is it Ryan?"

"He and Tony are at the hospital. It's not serious, but they've both been hurt. Ryan wanted me to call you. I'm on my way over there now."

"I'll meet you," Taylor said, already reaching for her purse. "Which hospital?"

Outwardly, she was calm as she pulled out her keys and hurried to her car. Inside, she was a quivering mess as the old, painful memories battered at her.

Not again, she was thinking as she started the engine and guided the car out of her parking space. *I can't go through this again.*

Oh, please, Ryan, please be all right.

Chapter Thirteen

Taylor found Michelle sitting patiently on a worn plastic bench in the emergency waiting room. "How are they?" she demanded the moment Michelle rose to greet her.

"They're fine. A little battered, but otherwise okay."

"What happened?"

Michelle made a face. "Our heroes caught the bad guys red-handed. Unfortunately, there were four very large bad guys and only two heroes. But you should be proud to know that the thieves are now in jail and I've heard they look every bit as bad as Tony and Ryan."

Taylor wondered how Michelle could look so calm. "You're sure they're all right?"

"Taylor, they're fine. Do I look worried?"

"No."

Michelle's left eyebrow rose in a gesture she'd picked up from her husband. "So you want to tell me why *you* look so frantic?"

Clearing her throat, Taylor looked at her unsteady hands. "I was just worried."

"About Ryan."

"Yes." She knew the stark confirmation revealed more than she'd intended, but her emotions were still a bit too raw to allow dissembling.

Michelle took Taylor's hand and led her to the bench where she'd been sitting, ignoring the people moving around them in the marginally controlled chaos of the emergency room. "It's very serious between the two of you, isn't it?"

"It is for me," Taylor admitted, thinking that nearly everyone knew how she felt about Ryan except Ryan himself.

"I think it is for him, too. He was very insistent that I should call you, so you wouldn't worry. Apparently, you were expecting him this evening."

Taylor cleared her throat again but didn't answer. It really wasn't necessary.

Whatever Michelle might have said was forgotten when Tony and Ryan suddenly appeared. Taylor surged to her feet, her hands clenched in front of her, intently studying Ryan for injuries.

He sported a purpling bruise on his jaw and another below his right eye. The left corner of his mouth had been split, leaving his lower lip puffy and reddened. A white bandage was wrapped around the knuckles of his right hand.

And he was grinning like an idiot, looking for all the world as though he'd just won a ball game or scaled a mountain.

Tony was the same, she noted, looking him over quickly. Bruised, disheveled, wearing two or three stitches at his temple and a bandage over the bridge of his swollen nose. And looking as if he'd had a great time.

Thoroughly disgusted with the both of them, Taylor crossed her arms over her chest and glared at them while Michelle greeted her husband with a kiss and her brother with a fond smile. "Everything check out okay?"

"We're in top shape," Tony assured her, blithely ignoring his wounds. "I kept telling Ryan it wasn't necessary to come to the emergency room, but he was convinced you'd never forgive him if he didn't insist I have someone look at my cracked nose."

"He was right," Michelle assured them gravely. "I'd have been quite annoyed with both of you."

Ryan was eyeing Taylor's expression with a wary look in his eyes. "Um, hi, sweetheart."

"Ryan."

His smile wavered a bit at her tone, but he continued to speak casually as he stepped closer. "I hope we didn't disturb you too late, but I was hoping to talk you into a ride home. My rental car is still parked at Tony's office building."

Home? Taylor replayed the word in her mind, wondering what he considered home. His hotel room? Her apartment? "I'll drive you," she said.

By now even Tony and Michelle were looking at Taylor quizzically. "It's getting late," Michelle said abruptly, making a show of glancing at her watch. "We'd better all go home and get some rest."

Looking like old friends, Tony and Ryan shook hands and agreed to talk the next day. Tony kissed Taylor's cheek before Michelle led him away. "Don't be too hard on the guy," Tony murmured for Taylor's hearing alone. "He was just lending me a hand with a case."

Taylor nodded. "Good night, Tony. Take care of that nose."

"So," Ryan murmured when Tony and Michelle had departed. "Shall we go?"

Taylor nodded, turned and walked toward the exit without waiting to see if he was following.

Made a bit clumsy by the bandage on his right hand, Ryan belted himself into the passenger seat of Taylor's black sports car and waited until she'd started the engine and pulled out of the hospital parking lot before speaking again. "You're very quiet tonight," he observed cautiously, studying her set face in the passing streetlamps.

"I'm tired," she answered shortly without looking at him. "Do you want me to take you by Tony's office so you can pick up your car?"

"Why don't we leave it there tonight? We'll get it tomorrow."

She nodded. "Fine."

"You're mad at me again," he said, turning in the seat to face her, deciding he'd had enough of tiptoeing around her mood. "Why?"

She braked for a red light. "I'm not mad."

He touched her shoulder, finding it tense. "Taylor. Look at me."

"I have to watch the light."

"I'll let you know when the light changes. Look at me, Taylor."

She slanted him a dark, shuttered look. "What?"

He caught her chin with his left hand, holding her in place before she could turn away again. "Why are you angry with me?"

"I'm not—"

"Taylor."

Something in his voice made her frown and say, "I don't know why I'm mad, dammit. I just am."

"Because I went with Tony tonight?"

"No."

"Because you had to come out so late and pick me up?"

"No, of course not."

A horn blew impatiently from behind them. Startled, Taylor pulled her chin out of Ryan's loose clasp and accelerated through the intersection. Since they were so close to her apartment, Ryan let the subject drop for the moment, leaving her to drive the remaining few miles in silence.

"Okay," he said, the moment her front door had closed behind them, leaving them in the privacy of her living room. "Why are you angry, sweetheart?"

"Because " Her breath caught and she wrapped her arms tightly in front of her before speaking again in a rush of anguished words. "Because I was so frightened for you, dammit. Because I rushed to the hospital so afraid you were badly hurt and then I found you looking like you'd had a great time, like it didn't matter at all to you that you could have been killed or badly hurt tonight."

Shaken by the look in her eyes, he reached out to her. "Taylor—"

She flinched from his touch. "You don't understand."

"Help me understand," he murmured, stepping closer to her, careful not to make any sudden moves that would break the spell between them. "Talk to me."

She closed her eyes and drew a shuddering breath. "The last time a man I cared about was taken to a hospital, he never came out again. I don't know if I could ever go through that again, Ryan. I don't think I could take it."

Ryan's pleasure at her admission that she cared about him was dimmed by her reference to the other man she'd loved. The ghost who'd stood so solidly between them from the beginning. Helpless to know how to compete against a painful memory, he groped for words to reassure her. "I can't promise you I won't ever be hurt," he began.

She shuddered. "No."

"But," he continued firmly, "I can promise that I won't take any unnecessary risks. Maybe I've been a daredevil and a risk taker in the past, but it was always because there didn't seem to be any reason to be particularly careful. Now there's a reason. You, Taylor."

Her smoky eyes were huge in her pale face. "I—"

"I've never felt this way about anyone else. I've never let anyone else be this important to me." He thought briefly of the woman in his past, the woman who'd apparently meant more to him than life, since he'd been told he risked his own to save hers. But whatever he'd felt for her was gone now, lost in a past he would probably never remember. All he knew was that, as far as he knew, he'd never felt for anyone the things he felt for Taylor Simmons. He had to make her understand.

"I love you," he said, his voice low. If he'd ever said the words before, he'd forgotten.

Her eyes grew even bigger, in a way that would have been almost comical had he felt like laughing. What little color had been left in her face faded.

"Taylor?" he prodded hesitantly when she remained silent.

"I wasn't expecting that," she whispered.

"You should have been."

Her hands lifted, fluttering nervously. "How could I? We've only known each other a couple of weeks. There are so many things we still don't know about each other, so many things we haven't talked about."

"The only important thing is how we feel about each other," Ryan cut in. "And I know how I feel. I love you. If it's too soon for you, if you need more time, you've got it. I won't rush you. But I just wanted you to know I—"

"I love you, too."

The words were little more than a breath of sound. They cut Ryan off as effectively as a shout. He felt his chest tighten. "You do?"

"Yes." Her color was returning in becoming waves of pink. "I think I have from the first."

"Taylor. Oh, God." He was strangely torn between swinging her into his arms—and bolting for the door. A line had been crossed, he realized dazedly. A bridge burned. And, dammit, he was starting to think in clichés again!

Her mouth tilted into an unsteady smile. "You look as terrified as I feel," she said.

He made a rueful face. "Neither of us seems to be very cool about this."

"I haven't had a great deal of experience with it," she admitted.

"Neither have I."

She ran her hands up and down her forearms, as though warding off a chill. "So—what do we do next?"

He started to smile, the momentary panic easing into a deep-seated pleasure. "I suppose we could kiss or something."

"Or something," she agreed, her smile growing stronger.

He reached for her and she went into his arms in a rush, her own closing tightly around his neck. "Oh, Ryan," she murmured, her lips moving against his. "I'm so glad you weren't badly hurt. I couldn't have—"

He kissed her deeply, reassuring her that he was perfectly healthy. He ignored the twinge of protest from his split lip. "Tell me again," he demanded, releasing her mouth for a moment, greedy to hear the words.

"I love you."

He groaned and kissed her, knowing he would never hear the words enough. He wanted to hear them for the rest of his life.

Taylor smiled at him and took his hand, taking a step backward toward her bedroom. Ryan followed eagerly.

Taylor lay with her head cradled on Ryan's bare shoulder, her left hand lying over his heart, his left arm beneath her, holding her close to his side. She couldn't see the clock, but she knew it was very late. "Are you getting sleepy?" she asked, keeping her voice soft in the quiet room.

"No. Are you?"

"No. Good thing tomorrow's Saturday, so we can sleep in. You don't have any plans, do you?"

"Only to be with you."

She smiled and kissed his shoulder. "I think we can work something out."

He chuckled and settled her more comfortably against him.

"Are you feeling okay? You didn't hurt your back tonight, I hope," she fretted.

"My back is fine," he answered a little too quickly, a bit too defensively.

That pesky male ego again, she thought ruefully.

"I just have a few bruises." He added firmly, "It wasn't a big deal. If I hadn't been so sure Tony's nose was broken, I wouldn't have insisted he drive to the hospital. Once we got there, everyone decided I needed to be checked out, too."

"Was Tony expecting trouble when he asked you to go along with him tonight?"

"He knew there was a possibility, though he wasn't really looking for trouble."

"What would he have done if you hadn't been available?"

Ryan shrugged. "He'd have managed. Apparently, he's been having trouble keeping qualified operatives during the past year. He had to fire one for disloyalty and another because of a drinking problem the guy refused to work on. Then Cassie quit to start her family, so Tony's left with one full-time investigator and one part-time. He wants to expand his business enough to afford more payroll, but he can't expand until he gets more help to take on more cases. It's been a rough year for him professionally."

"Sounds like he could use a partner," Taylor commented. She'd known, of course, that Tony had been having personnel problems, but hadn't realized the extent.

"That's what he says."

"So, are you going to do it?" she asked bluntly.

"I'm thinking about it. We thought we'd talk to Joe when he gets here. Joe wants to get into a line of work that doesn't require as much travel as the one we've been in, so he can spend more time with Lauren. Tony's got the idea that the three of us can turn the agency into a big-league security company."

"Do you agree?"

"I certainly see the potential."

Taylor had to bite her tongue to keep from begging Ryan to give Tony an answer quickly. Just the possibility that he'd be settling down in Dallas, committing to a long-term business partnership and establishing a connection with his family, made a ripple of hopeful excitement race down her spine.

It had bothered her that he'd seemed so rootless, so likely to pick up and leave at any time. She wondered if she would have been willing to leave everything she'd established here—her friends, her third of the advertising agency, her life—to go with him if he asked.

Though the idea scared her silly, she suspected that she would walk away with hardly a glance back. Now it sounded as though it wouldn't really be necessary to face that decision. She mentally crossed her fingers.

"You and Tony seem to get along very well" was all she allowed herself to say.

"Yeah, he's okay. Reminds me a little of Miller, my boss in Denver."

Taylor propped her chin on her hand so she could look at him in the shadowy light coming from outside. "I'm looking forward to meeting Joe. Are you really identical in appearance?"

"Except for the scar at my left eyebrow, we're exact duplicates," he confirmed. "Even people who have known us for years tend to get us confused."

"Does Lauren?"

"No. She claims she'd know the difference even without the scar. I tend to believe her. She sensed a difference from the minute she met me."

"Are you and Joe as alike in personality as you are in appearance?"

Ryan laughed softly. "Hardly. There are similarities, of course, after so many years of being together, but on the whole we're different in temperament. He's more serious, more conservative than I am. He's always been the careful one, while I've tended to rush in without always considering the consequences. Drove him crazy when we were younger, I can tell you. He always said that life was a chess game to me, and I was always one move away from checkmate."

Taylor found little reassurance in Ryan's airy self-analysis. "Is that right?"

He laughed again and gave her a quick hug. "That used to be right. I've settled down considerably during the past couple of years, since my, um, car accident. And now that I've met you, I'm thinking of settling down even more."

She smiled. "That's nice to hear. I think it would be difficult to be in love with someone who was always risking everything for a challenge."

His smile faded. "Yes. I can see that it would. I promise you, Taylor, I won't give you any reason to regret falling in love with me. I plan to spend the rest of my life with you, and I want as much time with you as I can get."

A strange little chill coursed through her. She shivered.

"Are you cold?" Ryan reached for the comforter and tucked it carefully around her bare shoulders. "Is that better?"

"Yes, thanks," she said gratefully, though she suspected the temperature in the room had had little to do with her sudden chill. She hoped she was just being fanciful, but it had felt very much like an ominous premonition. To distract herself from such uncomfortable thinking, she said, "What made you settle down after your car accident?"

He shrugged again, the movement shifting her against his shoulder. "Partly necessity. I was so physically messed up afterward that it took me a long time to recover—nearly a year. Joe stayed with me during that year, taking care of me at first, then nagging me to stay with my physical therapy and get back in shape. I don't know what I would have done without him."

Again, Taylor sensed the bond between the twins and realized that the connection was strong, deep and lifelong. She accepted then that she could not allow herself to be intimidated or threatened by that bond she could never quite share or understand. It was part of Ryan, part of what made him who he was. It had nothing at all to do with his feelings for her, which she hoped were equally strong, though obviously different. "He must have been very worried about you after your accident."

"Yes." The simplicity of the answer spoke volumes. "He says I've changed a bit since. I guess he's right. It was the first time in my life I really had to face my own mortality. That's enough to make any man sober up and take a long, hard look at himself and his philosophies."

"How did the accident happen?"

He cleared his throat and shifted beneath her as though suddenly uncomfortable. "That's a long story," he said.

"Why don't we save it for later this weekend. I want you to know all about it, of course, but it's kind of late to go into it tonight."

Obviously there was more to his story than a simple car accident, Taylor realized with a curious lift of her eyebrows. She wondered if the accident had occurred during an assignment for the security agency, which might explain his reticence to talk about it.

The thought that he could have died before she'd even met him made her hold him more closely. "All right," she murmured, her cheek pressed tightly to his chest, which let her hear his strong, steady heartbeat. "We'll talk about it later."

"Thanks." He seemed relieved. Was the story that difficult to tell? "So," he said, abruptly changing the subject, "you don't have to go to the office at all tomorrow?"

"No." She smiled. "I think Jay and Maxie will have other plans for the entire weekend."

Ryan seemed to sense something in her voice. "What do you mean?"

Still smiling, Taylor told him of the new development between her business partners, chuckling as she described Maxie's nervous reaction.

Ryan seemed somewhat less amused by the budding romance than Taylor was. "Aren't you worried about this?"

"Why should I be? I think it's wonderful for them."

He shook his head against the pillow. "I don't know. Seems like it happened awfully suddenly."

"Ryan," she said dryly, "you and I have known each other two weeks and one day. Maxie and Jay have known each other for over a year. How can you say *their* relationship has developed too suddenly?"

He made a rueful sound. "You're right, of course. I guess I'm just worried about your company. If anything goes wrong between Maxie and Jay, your agency will suffer. There are no worse business partners than ex-lovers."

"I hadn't thought of it that way," Taylor admitted with a slight frown. "But," she said, pushing the doubts away, "I'm sure everything will work out. Despite their differences, they make a great couple. Jay is exactly what Maxie needs, and vice versa. I'm very happy for them."

"Then so am I."

"Good." She sighed and rubbed her eyes, which were starting to feel a bit grainy as the night wore on, the adrenaline rush of the evening's events finally fading into weariness. "I'm really glad Maxie has finally allowed herself to love someone again," she murmured. "After her fiasco of a marriage, I wasn't sure she'd ever trust anyone that much again."

"It must have been difficult for her."

"Mmm. I know how she felt. I wasn't sure I'd ever risk loving and losing anyone again," Taylor admitted. "It hurt so much when Dylan died that sometimes I thought it would be easier never to care that much about anyone for the rest of my life. I'm glad you convinced me otherwise," she added, pressing a quick kiss to his jaw.

He lowered his head so that their mouths brushed lightly. "So am I." He settled her into his shoulder and stroked her short hair with his bandaged right hand. "We'll have to talk about him soon, you know," he said after a moment, his reluctance evident in his deep voice.

She sighed again. "I know. We can't keep avoiding it. Dylan was very important to me, even though I knew him only a few weeks before he was killed by a hit-and-run driver. The experience made an enormous difference in my life and in my personality. Michelle says I came back from the Caribbean a different person than when I left. It's definitely something you and I should talk about.''

Growing silent, she realized that Ryan had suddenly gone rigid beneath her, his firm muscles knotted beneath her cheek and hand. Frowning, she lifted her head to look at him. "Ryan? Is something wrong?''

"What did you say his name was?'' Even his voice sounded tense.

"Dylan. Dylan Clark. I met him on an island in the Caribbean two years ago. Do you want to talk about it now?''

He seemed to force himself to relax. He shook his head. "No, you're right. It's getting late. Let's get some sleep. We'll talk tomorrow.''

She nodded. "That seems best. I really am getting tired.''

He pulled her down. "Then go to sleep, sweetheart. Don't think about anything tonight, except that I love you.''

"I love you, too,'' she murmured, her eyes closing. All the volatile emotions of the day were catching up with her, leaving her feeling drained and detached. She needed a few hours' rest before she was up to dealing with anything more, she decided, letting sleep overtake her.

They'd talk tomorrow. About a lot of things. For tonight, she would sleep, content with the knowledge that Ryan Walker loved her, and the future was suddenly looking very promising.

Chapter Fourteen

Rubbing his pounding head with his right hand, Ryan clutched a half-finished can of beer in his left as he sat on the edge of the motel bed, staring at the telephone on the nightstand.

He'd slipped out of Taylor's bed over an hour ago, leaving her sleeping soundly, unaware of his departure. He'd scribbled a note and left it in her kitchen. He couldn't remember what it said. He hoped it made sense.

Dylan Clark. Oh, hell.

He closed his eyes and shuddered, then took another long swallow of the beer, wishing the tablets he'd taken would hurry and go to work on his headache. It hurt like hell.

He'd spent the past hour sitting in this room, staring at nothing and straining with every ounce of energy he had to remember something—anything—from those missing weeks in his past. The headache had been the only result of his efforts. There was still a dark, gaping void prior to his waking up in that hospital bed, a void he now knew held some life-altering events.

How could he have forgotten her? How could he have loved her before and not remember? What weird twist of fate had taken her away from him once, only to let him find her again without even knowing who she was?

Muttering a curse, he reached for the telephone, tired of waiting for a more considerate hour to make a call. With the time difference, it was still practically the middle of the night in Denver, but Ryan couldn't wait any longer. He had to have some answers.

Miller didn't sound happy about answering the phone. "What is it?" he barked, his voice gruff.

"Miller. It's Ryan."

"You seem to be making a habit of dragging me out of bed before dawn," Miller growled, reminding Ryan of a call he'd made a couple of months earlier, after Ryan had successfully completed an assignment. "What is it this time?"

"I need you to tell me exactly what happened in the Caribbean two years ago. Everything you know, no matter how trivial it may seem."

There was a lengthy pause while Miller apparently assimilated the unexpected request. And then, "Why?"

"Something's come up that might be connected. Tell me what happened, Miller."

"Are you getting your memory back? Is that what this is about?"

"No," Ryan answered with some regret. "I don't remember anything for a good four weeks prior to being hurt. But I need to know everything you found out during your investigation afterward. I know there were some things we never talked about."

"Only because you didn't seem interested in hearing them," Miller pointed out.

"Right." Ryan conceded the truth with a wry nod. For the past two years he'd been oddly reluctant to discuss the assignment that had ended so tragically. He'd been aware without remembering the details that he'd screwed up royally. Blown a case for the first time in his career. His supervisors had been supportive and forgiving, but Ryan had still blamed himself for everything that went wrong. After the first few months of recuperation, the details had no longer seemed to matter. Now he needed to know. "That has changed. Start from the beginning, please."

Miller exhaled gustily, apparently resigned to the loss of the remainder of his night's sleep, and began to talk.

"Ryan?" Dragging her fingers through her hair in a careless attempt to straighten it, Taylor padded out of her bedroom, noting how empty the apartment seemed. She hadn't been concerned when she'd woken alone in the bed, assuming Ryan was in the bathroom or making coffee, but everything was so quiet. Where could he be?

Tightening the sash of her short terry-cloth robe, she walked hopefully into the kitchen, only to find it empty. She was just turning to leave the room when she spotted the scrap of paper on the kitchen table.

A note. She snatched it up. She was still frowning when she finished reading it. Ryan had left to make some calls? *What* calls? Why couldn't he have made them from her apartment? And when the hell had he left? It was only eight now!

It didn't make sense. Chewing her lower lip, she tried to tell herself not to overreact, tried to believe there was no reason to be concerned. Ryan loved her. He wanted a life with her. He would be back.

But where had he gone? And why had he left without saying anything?

Why was she suddenly so very much afraid?

It was just after nine when Ryan was awakened by a knocking on the motel room door. He'd fallen asleep fully dressed, without even bothering to climb under the bedsheets. Scrubbing his hands over his bleary eyes, he stumbled off the bed, grateful that the vicious, pounding headache had receded to a dull pain he could pretty much ignore.

He didn't have to ask who stood on the other side of the door. He recognized the knock. He tugged it open. "Hi, Joe. Good to see you again."

"Wish I could say the same about you," his brother growled, his pale blue eyes searching Ryan's face as he entered the room. "You look like hell."

The pretty auburn-haired woman at Joe's side gave her husband a look of reproval and reached out to Ryan. "Ryan, what's wrong? Are you ill? Oh, my goodness, look at those bruises! Were you in an accident?"

Ryan ran a hand through his hair and shook his head. He'd forgotten about the bruises. "No, Lauren, I'm not ill, and I haven't been in an accident. I had a whopper of a headache earlier, but it's better now."

"Another one of your migraines?" Joe asked matter-of-factly, his casual tone belied by the visible concern in his eyes.

Ryan nodded. "Yeah. But don't worry about it. It's almost gone."

"So who gave you the shiner?"

"D'Alessandro and I got into a minor altercation last night with some guys who were stealing from one of his clients. One of them jumped me before I had a chance to get ready, but he turned out to be more show than action. I took care of him."

Joe nodded. "So you've been working on your vacation, have you? Why doesn't that surprise me?"

Smiling wryly, Ryan shrugged. "Just habit, I guess."

Lauren went up on tiptoes to kiss his cheek. "It really is good to see you, Ryan. Bruises and all."

He smiled and gave her a hug. "Good to see you, too, sweetheart. How was Mexico?"

Her emerald eyes glowed. "Fabulous," she breathed. "Oh, Ryan, we had the most wonderful honeymoon."

His smile deepened. "Good for you." He turned to Joe. "You just flew in this morning?"

"Yeah. We took an early flight. Lauren was impatient to meet the family," he added with a wry twist to his rather hard mouth.

"They're looking forward to meeting both of you, too." Ryan and Joe had talked once since the past Sunday, and Ryan had described his involuntary reunion with his siblings.

"Have you spent much time with them?" Lauren asked eagerly, obviously bursting with curiosity about the in-laws she'd be meeting soon. "What are they like? Do you like them?"

"I've spent some time with all of them during the past week," Ryan replied. "Except Lindsay, of course. She lives in Little Rock and I haven't seen her yet, though she's planning to visit soon to meet us. And yes, Lauren, I like them. They all seem to be very nice people. I think you'll enjoy visiting with them."

"Now tell us about Taylor," Lauren demanded, the officious tone softened by the sparkle in her eyes. "Joe tells me you're thoroughly hooked."

Ryan sent his brother a chiding frown, which was returned with a bland smile. The sound of Taylor's name had Ryan's stomach knotting at the reminder of the long, serious discussion he was going to have to have with her very soon. "I'm sure you'll be meeting her soon. I'll let you form your own opinions about her."

"How's the courtship going?" Joe asked. He was smiling, but his tone was serious as he continued to search Ryan's haggard face.

Ryan managed a shrug. "It's...hit a snag," he admitted.

Joe frowned. "A serious one?"

"I don't know yet."

"She'd be an idiot not to fall in love with you!" Lauren insisted loyally. "And I can't believe you'd be interested in an idiot."

"She cares," Ryan assured her. "But there are some problems we still have to discuss."

"She hasn't forgiven you for deceiving her about your identity?" Joe asked.

"I think she's gotten past that."

"Then she's bothered by your resemblance to her late boyfriend?"

Ryan ran his hand through his hair again.

"That's it, isn't it?" Lauren said sympathetically. "What a shame. I can understand how unsettling that must be for her, but she'll have to learn to love you for yourself and put the old memories behind her. You can't help it that you resemble someone she loved before, nor should that make any difference in her feelings for you."

Ryan shook his head. "You don't understand," he said, looking from Lauren to Joe. "I think I *am* the dead boyfriend."

His brother and sister-in-law looked at him blankly. Joe was the one who seemed to catch on first. "You don't mean she—"

"Her lover's name was Dylan Clark. He died in the Caribbean two years ago."

"Oh, hell."

Joe's heartfelt curse mirrored Ryan's stunned reaction to the staggering probabilities.

Bewildered, Lauren looked from one brother to the other. "I don't understand. What on earth are you talking about?"

"It's a very long story," Ryan answered with a sigh. "One I don't even know in its entirety. I have to talk to Taylor and try to figure out the rest of it. And then I have to try to convince her she's fallen in love with a damned ghost."

Trying to remain calm about Ryan's mysterious disappearance, Taylor took a leisurely shower, blew her short hair into its usual tousled style and donned a bright yellow T-shirt and matching loose knit slacks, tying a yellow, orange and green patterned scarf around her waist in lieu of a belt. She completed the outfit with colorful dangling earrings and orange ballerina flats, needing the bright colors to bolster her mood.

Where was he? Why hadn't he called her?

Pushing the questions to the back of her mind—or at least trying to do so—she spent the next couple of hours doing some housework and laundry. Chores she normally hated, but welcomed today as a distraction from her worries.

Had it been something she'd said? Was there still something he hadn't told her?

She hadn't been interested in breakfast, but as noon approached, she started to get hungry. She'd just opened the refrigerator and was reaching for a package of cold cuts when the doorbell rang. She jumped and slammed the refrigerator door closed, just missing her fingers. Her heart leapt into her throat.

It must be Ryan, she thought, nervously smoothing her palms over her slacks as she headed toward the door.

Oh, please, let it be Ryan.

It was. She stepped quickly out of the way to allow him to enter the apartment, noting that his smile of greeting looked rather forced. His crystal blue eyes seemed more intent, more serious than usual. He'd apparently showered recently; his hair was still a bit damp. He wore jeans and a navy knit shirt that stretched enticingly across his broad chest. "Did you sleep well?" he asked.

"Yes. Did you?"

"Not very."

"So I see," she replied, eyeing his bruised, weary face. "Come on in the kitchen and I'll pour you some coffee. Or would you rather have something stronger?"

"Coffee sounds good. I skipped breakfast."

"So did I. Want a turkey sandwich?"

"Yeah, that sounds good."

The conversation was ridiculously stilted and Taylor suspected Ryan was as aware of it as she. Something was hovering between them, something obviously very much on Ryan's mind. Last night they'd agreed there were several serious discussions they needed to have soon, probably this weekend. His career, the mysterious accident that was still affecting his life, her tragic love affair with Dylan. Was that what was bothering him now?

They said little while Taylor made sandwiches and coffee, and their conversation during the light meal was casual and impersonal. At one point, they actually discussed politics. Taylor made a face into her coffee cup, thinking that if they weren't careful they would find themselves talking about the weather.

Ryan led Taylor into the living room after lunch, and she could tell he'd reached a decision that it was time to talk. She settled onto the couch beside him and turned to face him, drawing a deep breath to prepare herself for whatever was to come.

"We need to talk," he began.

"I know." Where did he want to begin? His past? Hers?

"Tell me about Dylan," he said in answer to her mental question.

She'd known it was coming, of course. She just wished she knew exactly what to say. "What do you want to know?"

"Everything," he replied. "I need to know what I'm competing against."

"A dead man is hardly competition," Taylor pointed out quietly.

He gave her a brooding look. "I've been competing against this dead man since you and I met."

She knew he was right. From the beginning it had been his resemblance to Dylan that had bothered her more than anything, that had stood between them before she'd even known of the other obstacles to be overcome.

She sighed. "I was on a photo assignment in the Caribbean. I'd been working very hard for a couple of years, so I arranged for some free time, vacation time, after the assignment ended. I met Dylan a couple of days before the shoot wrapped up. We collided in an outdoor market. I dropped my purchases and he picked them up for me."

Ryan looked a bit startled.

Taylor nodded wryly. "That's one reason it shook me up so much when you retrieved my purse and its contents in that discount store the day we met. Not only did you look enough like Dylan to be his twin, but I had an eerie sense of déjà vu when you knelt to gather my things."

"I'm identical in appearance to him?" Ryan asked carefully.

She moistened her lips. "It's been two years, of course, and I haven't had a photograph of him to keep his image fresh in my mind—but yes, you look amazingly like him. Except that his eyes were green, not blue, and his hair was almost as dark as mine. And of course, he didn't have a scar on his forehead."

"What happened after you met in the marketplace?"

"We had drinks. And dinner that evening. And then spent most of every day of the next three weeks together. It happened very fast, very intensely, but it was very real," she murmured, trying to explain.

"I loved him, Ryan," she said, willing him to understand. "I really did. But it was a long time ago, and I've put that love behind me. It's you I love now, with all my heart. I don't want you to think I'm still grieving for him or that I love you any less than I did him. Please believe that you have all my loyalty now. I have no regrets, except that a very good man died much too young."

Ryan returned the pressure of her fingers and she thought she saw a glimmer of emotion in his eyes, but then he blanked his expression again and asked, "What did he tell you about himself? Where was he from? What did he do?"

She couldn't help wondering why he wanted all these details, but she answered cooperatively, "He said he was a stockbroker from the Midwest. He said he'd started to burn out, that he needed some time away from the stress and pressure of his job while he considered his options. We didn't have time to talk about either of our home lives much. We were so absorbed in getting to know each other and coping with our developing feelings. We talked about our likes and dislikes and our joy in finding each other, but we didn't really discuss our pasts or our future. We made plans, but vague ones. Dylan—''

She had to stop to clear her throat at the onslaught of memories. ''Dylan said he loved me and he wanted to marry me. And he was going to tell me everything about himself. In fact, I think he was going to tell me over dinner the day he was killed.''

Ryan flinched when she mentioned Dylan's love for her, and his talk of marriage. She hoped she wasn't telling more than he really wanted to know—but he *had* asked to hear everything.

''How did he die?'' he asked, and his voice was a bit gruff.

She tried to keep her own steady. ''A hit-and-run driver. The car came out of nowhere, bearing down on us before we even knew it was there. Dylan shoved me out of the way. He saved my life, but he lost his own.''

''He, um . . .'' Ryan paused as though trying to decide how to phrase the next question. ''He didn't die instantly?''

''There was still a pulse when he was loaded into the ambulance. A very faint one,'' she explained, remembering how she'd clung to his hand, how his blood had covered her skin, her clothing. How someone had torn her away from him and insisted that she be taken in a separate vehicle to the island's only hospital.

"He died on the operating table. I'd been alone in the waiting room for hours before someone came to tell me." She swallowed hard, remembering how lonely and horrifying those hours had seemed, how devastated she'd been when an unemotional, weary-looking doctor had bluntly broken the news to her.

"*Who* told you?"

"A doctor. I never caught his name. I think he tried to get me to stay, maybe to ask more questions, but I had to get away. I think I went into shock or something after he told me that Dylan had died. Almost before I knew how I'd arranged it, I found myself on a plane headed home. I needed to get home," she added in a whisper. "There was no reason for me to stay there."

"So you didn't talk to Dylan's family? Didn't try to attend a funeral or memorial service?"

"His family never even knew I existed. I was told that his . . . his body would be returned to the States to be claimed by his relatives. Dylan and I had known each other such a short time. I knew it was possible no one would even believe he'd loved me and had wanted to marry me. I thought it was better, for me and for those strangers, for me to just quietly disappear."

Ryan made an odd, harsh sound and shook his head, his fingers tightening almost painfully around hers. "That's everything? You've told me all you know about him, and about the, uh, accident?"

"Yes, everything." She searched his face, wondering at the deep lines around his mouth, the stark look in his eyes. "Ryan, what is it? Why are you asking me all these questions? What is it you're trying to learn?"

"There's something I have to tell you now, Taylor. It's not going to be easy. In fact," he added with a snort of laughter that held no amusement, "you're probably not even going to believe it."

"Ryan—"

He gave her a reassuring smile, though it didn't quite reach his eyes. "Just hear me out, okay?"

She nodded warily.

He cleared his throat. "Two years ago I woke up in a hospital bed in Miami with no memory of who I was or how I'd gotten there. I was bandaged like a mummy and strapped to what seemed like dozens of tubes and monitors. I could tell I was in bad shape, and I hurt like hell, but I couldn't for the life of me remember what had happened to me."

Taylor's chest tightened painfully. Forcing in a breath, she asked, "This is about your accident, right? The one that left all the scars."

He nodded. "Only it wasn't an accident. Someone had targeted me for murder."

"Oh, Ryan—"

He silenced her with a look. "I was on an assignment for the security agency. Sometimes I worked with a partner, but Joe was involved with another case and this one seemed easy enough. A dentist from Colorado Springs, a guy named Hardison, had apparently faked his own death, and his 'widow' was trying to collect on a sizable insurance policy. The insurance company hired me to find out the truth. They had a lead that Hardison might be hiding out in the Caribbean."

"Oh, God."

"Because it amused me to change appearance and identity when working undercover, I dyed my hair—not for the first time, by any means—chose a pair of the colored contacts I kept on hand, packed a wallet full of fake ID and headed for the tropics, utterly, smugly confident that I could wrap the case up in a few days and be off on some more exciting adventure. The last thing I remember before waking up in that hospital bed is packing my bag and leaving for the airport.''

She jerked her hands out of his, a rush of adrenaline bringing her to her feet, her arms locked tightly, defensively around her. ''You're trying to tell me—''

''Taylor, the name I used for that assignment—one I'd used a couple of times before—was Dylan Clark. I'm the man you knew two years ago.''

Chapter Fifteen

"No." Taylor shook her head, her denial hardly more than a hoarse whisper. "I don't—you couldn't—"

He rose and reached out to her, but she flinched away from his touch, her head spinning, her heart racing. "I don't believe you."

"I hardly believe it myself," he admitted, shoving a hand through his gold-streaked hair. "I didn't put it together until last night, when you said the name for the first time."

She lifted both hands to her temples, pressing against the pounding there, trying to make sense of this bizarre, surreal conversation. "Dylan died," she said flatly, certainly. "I *saw* him die. The blood—and the injuries—and the doctor—"

"I was hurt very badly, Taylor. I was in a coma for almost a week, then in recuperation and therapy for nearly a year afterward. At first they didn't think I was going to live, and then there were some doubts that I'd ever fully regain the use of my arms and legs. If it hadn't been for some excellent physical therapists and for Joe's insistence that I stick with the exercises, no matter how hard or painful they were, I probably wouldn't have recovered.''

"But the doctor told me he—you—Dylan had died," Taylor stammered insistently. "Why would he have said that if it wasn't true? Why would he have been so cruel?"

"I was undercover. My identity was protected by some pretty heavy security. Hospital personnel contacted my supervisor—the emergency number listed in my wallet—and explained what had happened. Miller, my supervisor, had already been frustrated with that case. I'd taken longer than usual to get my information—our lines of communication met interference from a tropical storm between the island and the States, but he'd gotten word that Hardison had no intention of being captured and prosecuted, no matter what he had to do to avoid apprehension.

"And then there was you," he said, still watching her closely. "All I'd told Miller was that I'd met a woman and had fallen hard. I told him I didn't want you involved with the case, didn't want anyone snooping into your background, so I refused to give a name, promising I'd tell him everything as soon as the assignment ended. Miller had no way of knowing who you were and what your connection might be to the guy we were after. For all he knew, you could have set me up for the hit-and-run—he couldn't figure out how else Hardison would have known where we'd be at that particular time."

Looking horrified, Taylor covered her mouth with her hands. "But I had nothing to do with that! I had no idea who you were or what you did! Ryan, I wouldn't have..."

"I know that," he said gently. "Miller would have known, too, had he ever met you. But when he was told that there was someone hanging around the hospital, someone who seemed very concerned with whether I was still alive, he automatically gave instructions that anyone who asked was to be told that I had died. It was standard procedure, designed to protect me from a second attempt."

Her eyes grew even larger. "*Was* there a second attempt?"

"No. I was heavily guarded by the island police, at Miller's orders, of course. Hardison was cornered by authorities within hours after the attack. He shot himself rather than surrendering into custody."

"The man who tried to kill you is dead?" she asked slowly, still struggling to put everything together.

Ryan nodded grimly. "Joe said it saved him the trouble."

"I wouldn't blame him for feeling that way," Taylor whispered. "To run you down that way, without warning, without caring who else would be hurt...."

Ryan fought down a wave of impotent fury at Hardison for risking Taylor's life along with his. According to eyewitness accounts Miller had gathered during the investigation, Ryan had managed to shove her out of danger at the last possible moment. Had his reflexes been even fractionally slower, she would have been injured with him. Perhaps killed.

And would she have died, leaving Ryan with no memory of having ever known her? The very thought made him shudder. He pushed the grim speculation aside, knowing he still had explanations to make to Taylor about what had happened next.

"Miller headed for the island himself, with the intention of finding out exactly who you were and whether you were involved. By the time he arrived, you'd disappeared from the hospital, and you never made an effort to follow up. For all he knew, you *had* been working for Hardison."

Taylor was suddenly cold—ice-cold. She shivered and tightened her arms around her waist. "You're telling the truth, aren't you?"

"Yes."

"You're—oh, God—you're Dylan."

Ryan nodded, his mouth set in a grim, humorless line. "Yes. You were right that first day, Taylor. You *had* seen a ghost."

She shuddered and closed her eyes, wondering almost absently if she was going to faint for the first time in her entire life.

Taylor went so pale that Ryan reacted instinctively, catching her shoulders and urging her into a chair. He knelt in front of her, warming her icy hands in his own, searching her face for signs of color—or some other reaction to what he'd told her. "Taylor? Sweetheart, are you okay?"

"Dylan called me 'sugar,'" she said, seemingly inconsequentially, her gray eyes oddly blank. "I told him it sounded silly, but he thought it was funny. I'd just started to like it when—"

She fell silent, her long lashes damp with unshed tears.

"God, Taylor, I'm so sorry. When I think what you must have gone through... If only I'd told Miller your name or taken Hardison more seriously. If I'd had any idea..."

She blinked and seemed to focus on him. "You really don't remember me at all?"

"No," he answered regretfully. "As far as I can remember, I saw you for the first time when you were standing with Michelle outside her house. I thought you looked a bit familiar, and I wondered why I reacted to you so strongly, but I can't recall anything that happened between us two years ago. It's called retrograde amnesia. Apparently, it's not all that rare after a head injury. The doctors told me I was lucky not to have any more severe neurological damage."

"You remember everything else?"

"It took me several hours after I came out of the coma to even remember my name. Took several months for me to regain everything. Now I remember almost everything except those weeks in the Caribbean."

"Everything except me."

"Yes," he said in answer to her stark whisper. "Chances are I'll never get those weeks back. I'd give anything if I could remember them, if I could remember our time together then, but it's gone."

"Gone," Taylor repeated, her voice hollow.

His hands tightened convulsively around hers. He couldn't seem to stop holding her hands, couldn't bring himself to break that tenuous connection between them. "Taylor? Can you talk to me now? Can you tell me how you feel about this?"

"I don't *know* how I feel. I don't know what to think or how to react. I don't even know who you are now."

"I'm Ryan," he insisted, frowning. "Ryan Walker. The man you met just over two weeks ago in a discount store. The man you fell in love with during the past two weeks."

"And Dylan? Am I supposed to pretend now that he never existed? That I never loved him—you?" She stopped with a frustrated shake of her head. "How do I know I can believe anything you told me then, anything you tell me now?"

"I *was* Dylan," he said flatly. "Everything you've told me about what happened between us makes me believe I was honest with you in everything but my name and my job—"

"That seems to be a habit with you."

He ignored her interruption. "I must have loved you then, Taylor, just as I love you now. I couldn't have known you under any name, under any circumstances, without loving you. We were meant to be together. Fate brought us together then and has brought us together now. Maybe I'm different now, in some ways. I'm sure you are, too. But I love you. I can't lose you again."

She caught her breath on a choked sob. "I—"

"Taylor." He drew a deep breath, his next question the hardest he'd ever asked. "Do you love me?"

"Yes," she said after only a momentary hesitation, one tear escaping to trail down her still pale cheek. "I loved you as Dylan, and I grew to love you all over again as Ryan, even when I thought I was losing my mind for doing so. But—"

He briefly closed his eyes on a near-shattering wave of sheer, glorious relief. And then he opened them again and spoke sincerely. "I can't give you back those three weeks, sweetheart, or the two years since. I wish I could, but I can't. All I can tell you is that I love you with all my heart, all my soul. And if you'll have me, I will give you the rest of my life—however long that might be."

She drew in a deep, tremulous breath. "There are so many things I still don't understand. So many questions that don't seem to have answers. All I know for sure is that I love you, and I can't—I won't lose you again. Not if there's anything I can do to prevent it.''

''Just say you'll marry me. Say you'll be my wife—until death truly parts us,'' he murmured, tugging her to her feet.

She slipped her arms around his neck. ''Death couldn't part us before. I love you, Ryan. I'll love you for eternity.''

''Is that a yes?'' he asked unsteadily, his mouth hovering inches above hers.

''Yes.'' She rose to close the distance, her kiss eagerly welcoming him back to her.

Ryan left Taylor's apartment Sunday morning to pick Joe and Lauren up at the hotel and take them to Michelle's for lunch. Taylor, not quite ready when he left—she'd been detained when he'd joined her in the shower and again when she was putting on her stockings afterward—promised to meet them there.

She was anxious to meet Joe and Lauren, but nervous about it, too. How would she feel meeting Ryan's twin? And how would they ever explain to the others that Ryan and Dylan had turned out to be the same man?

Even after having twenty-four hours or so to think about it, she was still having a little trouble accepting that Dylan had come back into her life—and that he had no memory of the time they'd spent together. The first time they'd fallen in love.

It would have been easy to resent the twist of fate that had taken that time away from him—from them—but she was too grateful that they'd found each other again to waste her energies on useless regrets.

Ryan loved her. He wanted to marry her. They would never be separated again. That was all that mattered to her.

It was starting to rain as she turned into the artfully winding driveway that led into Michelle's spacious estate. The first few drops were just splattering against the windshield as she parked at the foot of the stairs. Climbing out from behind the steering wheel, she spotted Ryan's beige rental car—the only other one there as of yet—then smiled broadly when she saw him bent into it, hurriedly rolling up windows.

"Hey," she called out, ignoring a fat raindrop that landed on the end of her nose. "I finally made it, completely dressed. No thanks to you."

He turned with a faint smile, opening an umbrella he'd pulled out of the car. "Hurry, you'll get wet."

She ducked under the shelter of the oversize umbrella and looped her arms around his lean waist. "Sharing an umbrella in the rain. How roman—"

She stopped abruptly when she looked into his face. "Oh."

His slight smile deepened. "Something wrong?"

He was looking at her with obvious interest, as though she was a stranger he was delighted to be meeting. Not at all the way he'd look at the woman he loved. Either he'd bumped his head and lost his memory again or—

She hastily dropped her arms. "You must be Joe."

He chuckled. "Right. And you're Taylor."

"Yes." She shook her head, blushing a bit at the way she'd greeted him. "Sorry about that. I thought you were Ryan for a moment."

"I know. I'd have corrected you sooner, but I owed Ryan one. He let my wife throw herself into his arms and kiss him before he got around to telling her she had the wrong twin."

"Well, at least I didn't go that far."

"No. But there's no need for Ryan to know that, is there?"

Taylor laughed and linked her arm with Joe's, certain she was going to like Ryan's twin a great deal. She knew they were different—already she sensed some of those differences—but in other ways she suspected Ryan and Joe were very much alike. As for the eerie physical resemblance—well, she must be getting used to that sort of thing.

"Ryan and Lauren have already gone in," Joe explained unnecessarily as they climbed the stairs. "I was just about to go in myself when it started to rain and I remembered that I'd left my window down."

"So you haven't spoken with Michelle yet?" Taylor asked, sensing his slight nervousness.

"No."

"It'll be okay, Joe. They're very nice people. I think you'll like them."

"They're strangers," he said, as they stepped under the covered archway at the top of the stairs. Joe lowered the umbrella, his face, so incredibly like Ryan's, set in taut lines.

"They're your family," Taylor said gently, reaching out to pat his arm. "And they aren't expecting anything more from you than you're willing to give."

He gave her a thoughtful look. "Thanks."

She smiled. "You're welcome."

Ryan was waiting in the entryway with Michelle, Tony and an attractive auburn-haired woman. He frowned when Joe and Taylor came in arm in arm, shaking off raindrops and still smiling at each other. "Joe, you didn't—"

"Taylor, I'd like you to meet my wife, Lauren," Joe said, ignoring his brother as he held out his hand to the auburn-haired woman. "Lauren, this is Taylor."

"I can't tell you how delighted I am to meet you," Lauren said, taking Taylor's extended hand. "Ryan was telling us about you this morning on the way over here. I hope we'll all be good friends."

"So do I," Taylor replied, approving of what she saw of Joe's bride.

And then she stepped back to let Joe meet his sister and brother-in-law. Ryan made the introductions.

Wide-eyed, Michelle looked from Ryan to Joe. "I can't get over how much identical you are. It's incredible."

"It's good to see you again, Michelle," Joe said, having already been briefed on the names his siblings were using now.

"And it's nice to see you, too, Joe. I wish I could say I remember you from when we were children, but I don't. I'll have to get to know you all over again."

Taylor swallowed hard and avoided Ryan's eyes.

"I can't say I remember you all that well, either," Joe was saying to his sister. "We were all very young."

"Yes. But I'm glad we have another chance to know each other," she murmured, giving him a somewhat misty smile. "And Jared and Layla will be so glad to see you again. Oh, I haven't even introduced you to my husband yet! Tony, this is Joe."

Tony chuckled as he extended his right hand. "Yeah, I'd sort of figured that out. Nice to meet you, Joe. Ryan already introduced us to Lauren."

Michelle looked happily around her. "I'm sure the others will be here soon. Jared and Cassie and Shane were going to pick Lindsay and Nick up at the airport, and Layla and Kevin and their children are on the way. Please, come on into the den and let's get comfortable.''

Ryan slipped an arm around Taylor's shoulders as they moved en masse toward the den. ''You knew Joe wasn't me, didn't you?''

She gave him a vague smile. ''The resemblance is absolutely amazing. It would be very easy to get the two of you confused.''

''Taylor, you didn't—''

She laughed softly and led him into the room behind the others.

''When are we going to tell them?'' Taylor murmured to Ryan while the others were engaged in conversation.

''Maybe we'd better wait until later. This isn't a story I want to tell more than once today,'' he answered soberly.

She shook her head. ''They're never going to believe it.''

He gave her an understanding smile and touched his lips to her cheek. ''We'll get through it, sweetheart.''

''I know,'' she murmured, touching his arm. They would handle the explanations together.

Epilogue

Taylor and Ryan were married late in October. Michelle served as matron of honor and Joe as best man in the simple ceremony held in a small, lovely chapel near Taylor's apartment.

Shane took great pleasure in pointing out that both Michelle and Cassie were round as pumpkins, which he thought appropriate to the season. Nearing the end of her pregnancy, Cassie didn't find his teasing particularly amusing—or at least, she pretended she didn't, though Taylor saw the smile Cassie tried to hide.

The entire family was there. Layla spent most of the day dabbing at her overflowing eyes with an ever-present handkerchief, and took great pride in her children's participation in the ceremony—Keith as ring bearer, Dawne and tiny Brittany serving as flower girls. Kevin hovered on the sidelines, keeping a close, monitoring eye on the children, looking every bit as proud as Layla.

Lindsay and Nick, who'd accepted the twins into the family with the same pleasure as the others, had flown in from Little Rock and had brought with them a painfully shy, hearing-impaired teenage girl who was their first foster child. Shane had already gone out of his way to make Dixie feel welcome at the family event, serving as a volunteer interpreter when the girl's hearing aids weren't quite adequate. Taylor beamed at him in approval, hoping her own children would turn out as nicely as Shane—who, she reminded herself happily, was now officially her nephew.

Tony looked smugly pleased with himself for reuniting all the living Walker siblings, as though he'd been personally responsible for finding the twins—now his business partners, an association they all believed would be a profitable move. No one, least of all Taylor, had the heart to remind him that Ryan and Joe had been the ones to bring themselves into the fold. It was, after all, Tony's search for them that had first tipped them off that the others wanted to see them.

Taylor's family attended the ceremony, of course—her parents, her grandmother and her younger brother, all delighted that Taylor was finally getting married at twenty-seven. And, of course, Jay, Maxie and Erika from the advertising agency had been invited. Maxie and Jay, whose love affair was still going strong, despite their inevitable clashes, held hands during the ceremony and gazed at each other with amusingly limpid eyes.

Dressed in a simple white Empire-styled wedding gown and a short veil attached to a ring of fresh flowers, Taylor walked down the aisle alone, having declared that she wasn't being given to Ryan. This was a choice she had made on her own, and one in which she found incredible joy.

Ryan's gaze held hers as she made that short walk to the altar, and she saw her own profound emotions reflected in his beautiful crystal-blue eyes.

His hand was warm and strong when it closed around hers, no unsteadiness or hesitance in his voice when he repeated his vows. And when he turned to kiss her, the happiness shining in his smile brought a lump to her throat.

Taylor wondered what she'd done to deserve such happiness, to be given this second chance at finding her one true mate. The only man she had ever loved.

Michelle had insisted on having a reception at her home after the wedding. Ryan grinned as he received the congratulations of his family, cheerfully accepting the inevitable teasing that followed.

"I don't know about you," Jared complained at one point, tugging at his tie, "but I'm about ready to get out of this monkey suit and into some flannel and denim."

Ryan chuckled, thinking how much more suited jeans and boots were to his older brother than formal wear. "It won't be much longer. Taylor and I have a plane to catch in a few hours."

"Where'd you say you were going on your honeymoon?"

"Bimini. I'm leaving a phone number with Joe. He has instructions to call me if your baby comes before we get back."

"The doctor said it could be any day," Jared admitted, looking just a bit dazed at the prospect of becoming a father again after fifteen years.

"The family's getting awfully large," Joe commented, joining his brothers and handing Ryan a flute of champagne. "Good thing Michelle's got such a big place if we're going to keep getting together like this."

Ryan smiled. "I have a feeling that we will, don't you?"

Joe returned the smile with one of his rare, more serious ones. "Yeah. Looks like it's getting to be a habit."

"Either of you sorry?" Jared asked, looking from Ryan to Joe.

After another quick exchange of glances with his twin, Ryan answered for them both. "No. We're not sorry."

Jared was watching his wife, who was standing across the room, carrying on a laughing conversation with his son. "Neither am I," he admitted.

Ryan couldn't help thinking back to the terrible day when the siblings had been separated. So long ago. And their lives had taken such diverse paths since. How strange that those paths had led them all to this place now.

He thought wistfully for a moment of his mother and Miles, who would have been as pleased by the belated reunion as the others were. And then his gaze found Taylor across the room, talking to Michelle and Layla, and he pushed any sad thoughts to the back of his mind. He was feeling much too content today to dwell on old regrets.

And he was eager to start doing his part to further enlarge the family.

Swallowing the last of his champagne, he shoved the empty glass at his twin and murmured an excuse, focusing on Taylor as he worked his way across the crowded room, leaving his brothers grinning at his sudden impatience.

"Don't you think it's about time for us to leave?" he murmured into her ear as soon as he'd gotten within range.

Taylor turned to him with a loving smile. "Whenever you're ready," she said obligingly.

He drew her close, all too conscious of the many watching eyes. "I'm ready right now. It's been too long since I had you alone."

"Five hours. No more."

"Too long," he insisted. "I'm ready to start the honeymoon."

Her glowing eyes reflected the memories of the previous night. "I thought we'd already done that."

"Oh." He grinned and mentally replayed a few of his own choice memories. "Then I'm ready to continue it."

"We will, Ryan," she whispered, her hand clasped tightly in his. "We're going to make this honeymoon last for a lifetime."

The entire extended family watched in approval as Robert Ryan Walker thoroughly kissed his bride to seal the vow.

* * * * *

JUST HOLD ON TIGHT!
Andrea Edwards
(SE #883, May)

Being a single, adoptive mom was tough, yet
Gabbi Monroe insisted on independence. But she
secretly dreamed of a loving partnership with the
gentle, reserved Luke Bennett. Behind Luke's laid-back
visage lay a passionate, although wounded, man—
who needed Gabbi's help to heal before he could
pledge his love to her....

She's friend, wife, mother—she's you! And beside
each Special Woman stands a wonderfully *special*
man. It's a celebration of our heroines—and the men
who become part of their lives.

Don't miss **THAT SPECIAL WOMAN!** each month—
from some of your special authors!

Only from Silhouette Special Edition!

TSW594

MILLION DOLLAR SWEEPSTAKES (III)
AND
EXTRA BONUS PRIZE DRAWING

No purchase necessary. To enter both prize offers and receive the Free Books and Surprise Gift, follow the directions published and complete and mail your "Match 3" Game Card. If not taking advantage of the book and gift offer or if the "Match 3" Game Card is missing, you may enter by hand-printing your name and address on a 3" X 5" card and mailing it (limit: one entry per envelope) via First Class Mail to: Million Dollar Sweepstakes (III) "Match 3" Game, P.O. Box 1867, Buffalo, NY 14269-1867, or Million Dollar Sweepstakes (III) "Match 3" Game, P.O. Box 609, Fort Erie, Ontario L2A 5X3. When your entry is received, you will be assigned Million Dollar Sweepstakes (III) numbers and be entered in the Extra Bonus Prize Drawing. To be eligible entries must be received no later than March 31, 1996. No liability is assumed for printing errors or lost, late or misdirected entries. Odds of winning are determined by the number of eligible entries distributed and received.

Sweepstakes open to residents of the U.S. (except Puerto Rico) Canada, Europe and Taiwan who are 18 years of age or older. All applicable laws and regulations apply. Sweepstakes offers void wherever prohibited by law. Values of all prizes are in U.S. currency. This sweepstakes is presented by Torstar Corp, its subsidiaries and affiliates, in conjunction with book, merchandise and/or product offerings. For a copy of the official rules of the Million Dollar Sweepstakes (III), send a self-addressed, stamped envelope (WA residents need not affix return postage) to: MILLION DOLLAR SWEEPSTAKES (III) Rules, P.O. Box 4573, Blair, NE 68009, USA; for a copy of the Extra Bonus Prize Drawing rules, send a self-addressed, stamped envelope (WA residents need not affix return postage) to: Extra Bonus Prize Drawing Rules, P.O. Box 4590, Blair, NE 68009, USA.

SWP-S494

IT'S OUR 1000TH SILHOUETTE ROMANCE, AND WE'RE CELEBRATING!

JOIN US FOR A SPECIAL COLLECTION OF LOVE STORIES BY AUTHORS YOU'VE LOVED FOR YEARS, AND NEW FAVORITES YOU'VE JUST DISCOVERED. JOIN THE CELEBRATION...

April
REGAN'S PRIDE by **Diana Palmer**
MARRY ME AGAIN by **Suzanne Carey**

May
THE BEST IS YET TO BE by **Tracy Sinclair**
CAUTION: BABY AHEAD by **Marie Ferrarella**

June
THE BACHELOR PRINCE by **Debbie Macomber**
A ROGUE'S HEART by **Laurie Paige**

July
IMPROMPTU BRIDE by **Annette Broadrick**
THE FORGOTTEN HUSBAND by **Elizabeth August**

SILHOUETTE ROMANCE...VIBRANT, FUN AND EMOTIONALLY RICH! TAKE ANOTHER LOOK AT US! AND AS PART OF THE CELEBRATION, READERS CAN RECEIVE A FREE GIFT!

YOU'LL FALL IN LOVE ALL OVER AGAIN WITH SILHOUETTE ROMANCE!

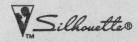

CEL1000

DANGEROUS ALLIANCE
Lindsay McKenna
(SE #884, May)

Vulnerable Libby Tyler intrigued Captain Dan Ramsey.
He was willing to take a chance at love, but Libby had
promised she'd never fall for a marine again. Drawn
together in the face of a perilous situation, could they
deny their dangerous attraction?

MEN OF COURAGE

It's a special breed of men who defy death and fight
for right! Salute their bravery while sharing their lives
and loves!

MENC2